Thin Places

THIN PLACES

For Bonnie,
May you find all the
Thin Places in your life.
Elie Axelroth

ELIE AXELROTH

Thin Places
Copyright © 2015 by Elie Axelroth
Published by Scatterbrain Press

All rights reserved. No part of this book may be used or reproduced in any manner whatsoever including Internet usage, without written permission of the author.

This is a work of fiction. The names, characters, places, or events used in this book are the product of the author's imagination or used fictitiously. Any resemblance to actual people, alive or deceased, events or locales is completely coincidental.

Cover photograph © Blair Turrell
Author photograph by Colleen Rosenthal

Book design by Maureen Cutajar
www.gopublished.com

ISBN(Print): 978-0-9962847-0-7
ISBN(Kindle): 978-0-9962847-1-4
ISBN(ePub): 978-0-9962847-2-1

Your task is not to seek for love, but merely to seek and find all the barriers within yourself that you have built against it.

—RUMI

Chapter One

SKYE HAD BEEN PREOCCUPIED, thinking about the accident again. And her mother. It was inevitable that leaving Oakdale would stir up all the old doubts about what had happened on that snowy morning eight years ago. Nothing about being dropped off in Oakdale had been Skye's choice. No one had asked what *she* wanted. All along, the arrangement was supposed to have been temporary—even though she'd been pretty sure the social worker, and Grace and Jackson, and Sheriff Wilding had stretched the truth about the chances of her mother ever coming back to get her.

What she remembered from the accident: The images were hazy, lodged behind her eyes and deep in her chest, along with the fear and disbelief. She and her mother were driving back home to San Francisco. They'd spent the weekend skiing and sledding with her mother's old college friends. Her mother was edgy, and she was driving fast around the hairpin turns, and they skidded a couple of times. Skye, ten years old, was sitting in the backseat, and she remembered leaning over to peer out the window, trying to convince herself they'd be safe, but the shoulder dropped steeply into a wide canyon, and any car jettisoned from the road was almost certain to be torn to shreds by the tall stands of pines and thick brush.

At the moment the car left the road, it felt like flying—at first, then she heard the scouring of metal, fractured branches, and paint scraping. There wasn't any time to think about what was happening, except she remembered her head jolting back and then forward, her chest abruptly restrained by the seat belt. The car, when they landed, must have been cushioned by the ten-foot drifts of snow. She heard her mother groaning, and tires skidding on the road above, sudden braking. Worried voices shouted at them. A dog yelped in the distance.

It seemed like a long time before she heard sirens, and then Sheriff Wilding grasped her hand, shepherding her up the snowy embankment. The ambulance and EMTs and Jaws of Life fished her mother out of the car and strapped her twisted body to a stretcher. It took three emergency responders to haul her up the steep slope. Sheriff Wilding shielded Skye's eyes, but through the cracks in his fingers, she caught a glimpse of her mother's face, crusted with blood. She could still smell his leather gloves.

"Are you okay?" her mother asked. She spoke slowly, deliberately, her jaw clenched between long, lingering moans. The paramedics were giving her an injection and swabbing her face, putting a splint on one arm. Her neck and head were clamped taut in a brace.

Skye nodded, too stunned to say anything out loud, her throat choked with fear.

"What will happen to her?" her mother asked. She'd somehow managed to dislodge the oxygen mask from her face. Her voice was thick and gooey, long blonde hair matted to the side of her face as they loaded her into the ambulance.

Sheriff Wilding was a tall, sturdy man, intimidating with his badge and bulky winter jacket. His thick black mustache was coated with ice crystals. "We'll take good care of her, ma'am. Until you're better." Skye remembered his voice was even-tempered, but there was a hint of threat. Not the kind of man she'd imagined might be her father.

"Why can't I go with you?" Skye reached out her hand, only barely managing to graze her mother's chilly fingertips before Sheriff Wilding pulled her back. Moments later, the ambulance and one of the police cars sped off down the mountain, with hardly enough time to hear the sirens dying in the distance.

OUTSIDE HER BEDROOM WINDOW, Skye could see the pond in Grace and Jackson's backyard, where she and her friends had ice-skated in the winter, and the vegetable garden that was neatly contained in long furrows. There were clusters of red tomatoes, tendrils of spaghetti and acorn squash; pumpkin vines were tied back to prevent them from spilling out of the garden beds. Jackson was shoveling compost while Grace picked berries for canning. Chester, their oversized bulldog mix, was gnawing on a rawhide doggie treat and periodically barking and rummaging with his nose in the gopher holes. Through the open window, Skye could smell sage and basil and an earthy, hot smell from the chicken manure.

It should have been enough—more than enough. But the bucolic routine of a small mountain community in the Sierras had never been like her life in San Francisco with her mother. She missed the colorful neighborhood fairs with jugglers and street musicians and Italian ices. Squealing brakes and trucks shifting gears on the downhill side of cascading streets. The bellowing of the foghorn underneath the Golden Gate Bridge, lolling her to sleep. She and her mother had read Harry Potter together at the neighborhood Laundromat on Sundays while waiting for the rinse cycle to run its course. One July 4th, they'd climbed the fire escape up to the roof to watch fireworks. It was a rare fogless summer night, and they sat on lawn chairs and drank fresh-squeezed lemonade. Skye remembered seeing the sparks of color before hearing the pop of the fireworks.

But now, after eight years of living with Grace and Jackson, she was setting off to college, not sure when she might be coming back again—at least she might not be coming back if everything turned out the way she planned. Back to her old life in San Francisco. Skye thought about her time living in Oakdale with Grace and Jackson as if it were a placeholder or a narrow space between her old life in San Francisco with her mother and the life she was going to have once she moved back. She wasn't naive; she knew it wouldn't be easy to start all over again, but she was determined not to let the past get in her way.

Skye's new life was spread out in piles on the bed: jeans and T-shirts, underwear, a high school sweatshirt, socks, shoes. A faded photograph of Skye and her mother at the top of the Santa Cruz roller coaster, their hands up, screaming. And another, less dramatic photo of Skye with Grace and Jackson and Chester, standing in front of the garden one late-summer afternoon. The photo had been Jackson's idea: he was wearing a cowboy hat and overalls and held a pitchfork. Chester's tongue hung out, obviously panting. Grace and Skye were standing on either side of Jackson, alongside bushel baskets filled with produce—zucchini, yellow crookneck squash, green beans, tomatoes, peppers—like a send-up of the painting *American Gothic.* Jackson and Grace were somewhat taller than Skye, but with their dark hair and brown eyes and stocky builds, they were often mistaken for her real parents. Her mother, on the other hand, had looked more like a friend or maybe an aunt or older cousin: tall and thin and blonde.

Skye pulled her cleats and a soccer ball out of the closet and gathered up her phone and charger and a poster of Van Halen from her best friend, Jasmine. And the new laptop the church had given her with their best wishes. Everything she wanted to take with her fit into two cardboard boxes and a large duffel bag.

Skye looked up. Standing in the doorway of her bedroom, Grace was offering her two sets of mismatched sheets, clean and neatly folded, a bath towel and washcloth. With her stiff smile and forward-leaning posture, it seemed to Skye that Grace was always trying too hard to be liked. It made her appear needy and permanently worn-out. And, ironically, unlikable. Grace had wrinkles around her eyes and neck, but she wore makeup only on special occasions and to church. Over the time Skye had lived with them, her wispy brown hair had turned a dull, self-conscious gray.

"I remember the day you came to our front door," Grace said, leaning against the doorjamb, "with that old battered green suitcase. You know, the one with the leather handle and broken clasp. I think it weighed more than you. But you were always stronger than you looked. And more determined. You insisted on carrying it all the way to your bedroom; even Jackson couldn't wrestle it away." She sounded wistful, and Skye wondered if she thought the two of them were actually embracing the same memory.

Skye appreciated all Grace had done for her, but she recalled the day differently. It had been icy cold, the kind of cold she wasn't accustomed to, coming from San Francisco, where it rarely froze. After the accident, she was taken to a children's shelter, a long concrete building that also housed a juvenile detention center and what she found out later was the county jail. There were lots of men in uniforms like Sheriff Wilding's, and busy-looking women running back and forth between workstations, and an aide in blue scrubs, her hair tied back in a ponytail. When the aide bent over, Skye could see an eagle, its head and wings tattooed across her lower back. They were serving chicken, her name was Patty, and she asked if Skye wanted dark meat or breast.

"I'm vegetarian," she said. A dented metal tray appeared sometime later with a thigh and limp broccoli smothered in orange cheese sauce. Skye scraped off the cheese sauce, eating it with her spoon, and pushed the broccoli to the side. She wasn't really hungry, and she wondered guiltily what her mother would say about the meat, trying hard not to picture her mother's face just before they'd lifted her into the ambulance. Skye had cringed when she'd seen the broken front teeth, a bone hanging loose from one arm, her mother's legs twisted, not to mention all the blood.

The dorm room had a dozen or so other beds—some empty, some filled with girls even younger than she. The pajamas they'd given her were stained and had holes where the buttons should have been, so she went to bed in her street clothes. The overhead fluorescent lights were kept on all night long. It was hard not to feel she'd done something terribly wrong. The girl in the bed next to Skye tried to comfort her when she woke up in the middle of the night crying. She'd dreamed her mother had been thrown from the car and killed. Skye wasn't sure if the nightmare meant her mother really was dead.

"You'll get used to it here," the girl said, patting her on the back as if she were a much older friend or an adult.

"My mother's coming to pick me up really soon," Skye said, hoping it could be true. But then the girl told her how all the kids thought that at first.

"You wouldn't be here if your mother wasn't in trouble," the girl said. "My parents got arrested for selling drugs. I'm hoping my grandmother will let me live with her. Maybe your father can come get you."

Skye was pretty sure that wasn't an option.

The next morning, the social worker, Mrs. McNulty, came to see her. Mrs. McNulty had long, red, wiry hair and blotchy freckles all over her face and arms. She was probably Skye's mother's age but older-looking, with a raspy voice that made Skye wonder at first if she was a man.

Mrs. McNulty said her mother was going to have to stay in the hospital for a couple of weeks.

So at least she was alive, Skye understood with relief. Her mother was going to get better, and then she would come to get Skye.

"I want to visit her," Skye told the social worker.

"Not quite yet," Mrs. McNulty said, "but soon. There's a very nice couple who want you to stay with them for the holidays. Just for now." She added, "They live on a farm with animals and a vegetable garden and a small pond for ice-skating. I bet you'd like to learn how to ice-skate."

Skye wasn't interested in living with the very nice couple. And apparently Mrs. McNulty didn't understand how important it was for Skye to see her mother, to make sure she was going to be okay. So Skye could stop picturing the worst.

"I already know how to ice-skate," she said. This was true: at Christmastime, her mother, who'd grown up in Boston and was a really good skater and even knew how to skate backward, used to take her to the rink at Union Square in front of Macy's. Afterward, they would drink hot chocolate with whipped cream.

"Good. Then you're ahead of the game." Mrs. McNulty smiled, turning up the corners of her mouth without parting her lips, making her seem less than forthright. It was obvious she wasn't interested in discussing the issue further. She signed Skye out of the shelter. One of the men who looked like a prison guard unlocked the double doors for them, and they walked out the front of the building, where they got into the official state car. Mrs. McNulty checked to make sure Skye had fastened her seat belt. Then they snaked through the mountains. There was a thin fog and light snow falling; they stopped for fries and a vanilla shake at a local food shack. As the afternoon darkened, the snow fell in thick clumps that stuck to the road.

Skye stared at the side of the road, where the shoulder tumbled over the edge. The slapping of the windshield wipers was loud. Pasty flakes of snow melted down the glass, and her body tightened whenever the car swung around a curve. She glanced over at Mrs. McNulty, who was clutching the steering wheel, her tense, blotchy face leaning toward the windshield.

"It's okay, honey, I'm driving very carefully," she said, taking one hand off the wheel very briefly to reach over and pat Skye's hand.

Up ahead, the road was closed except for cars with chains or snow tires. Mrs. McNulty pulled over and got out of the car while two chain monkeys installed snow chains, and the rest of the way they clattered and pinged up the mountain.

"We're pretty close now," she said after they'd driven for what seemed to Skye like a long time.

When they finally arrived, Mrs. McNulty pulled into the long driveway. She got out of the car and rang the doorbell.

Skye hung back by the car, eyeing the small ranch house painted brown with yellow trim, with long icicles hanging from the eaves and snow plowed up against the porch and along the driveway. Snowflakes dampened her hair and shoulders; her breath was vapory. She had on jeans and sneakers, no gloves, and the bottoms of her feet were cold. Mrs. McNulty was waiting by the front door, running her fingers through the mass of wild red hair, attempting to rein in the loose strands. What kind of people would want to take in a total stranger, Skye wondered, even if it was just for the holidays? Maybe she should get back in the car, but that meant driving down the mountain on the slippery roads, back to the shelter. She figured it was better to go along with the plan, at least for now.

It was Mrs. McNulty who got the green suitcase out of the trunk and brought it to "her" bedroom in the strange house, opened it on the bed and showed her the clothes and toiletries she'd managed to scrounge up for Skye. Skye didn't understand: there were perfectly good clothes and shoes and a toothbrush and soap and books and toys back at her real house in San Francisco. And what about her boots and gloves and hat that had been in her mother's car?

Grace smiled and knelt down to say hello, treating Skye like a little girl. She wore a denim skirt and white cardigan sweater. Her bone-straight bangs were cut midway between her eyebrows and the top of her forehead, and she flitted around the house, desperate to be helpful. It was obvious she wanted to make a good impression for the social worker, wanted Skye to like her as she offered cookies and a peanut-butter-and-jelly sandwich, a glass of milk. Skye was hungry but said, "No, thank you." Later Grace gave her fluffy slippers and flannel pajamas that came up to her calves, a towel and washcloth, an extra pillow, and a tattered handmade quilt for her bed.

That night, Grace tucked her in, something her mother—with everything that had been going on—hadn't done in a long time. She leaned over as if she were about to kiss Skye on the cheek, but Skye turned away, and then Grace seemed to reconsider, busying herself with smoothing the covers and pulling down the shades instead. Skye wasn't sure how to tell Grace, *You're not my real mother*, but even so, she was glad not to be sleeping at the shelter.

From the start, Skye liked Jackson better. He was a man of few words and didn't ask her a lot of questions. He showed her around the house, the garage that was his workshop where he built cabinets and furniture, the backyard. He took Skye to meet Greta, their goat, and the dozen Rhode Island Red chickens. He pointed out back to the vegetable garden, blanketed with snow.

"That's where we grow tomatoes and broccoli and cabbage and squash, and Grace likes to grow flowers. She's even won a couple of blue ribbons at the county fair."

They tossed a stick to Chester, Grace and Jackson's new puppy.

Mrs. McNulty left soon afterward. "I'll stop by in a week or so," she said, "to see how you're doing."

There was no way a week or so was *just-for-now*, Skye thought. She wanted to tell them, *A week isn't temporary. A week isn't just for the holidays.* She didn't understand why she couldn't go home and why the green suitcase was filled with other kids' clothes. She wanted her mother to get better so she could go back to her real life.

But living with Grace and Jackson became her real life. She started in fourth grade at Oakdale Elementary, where she got good grades in school, and she made friends, played soccer, won a statewide essay contest in junior high. For a year or so, Mrs. McNulty would call or stop by and give her updates about her mother. After a while, Skye stopped worrying about her mother, but she never stopped wondering what had happened. How had their life together gone so far astray?

WITH HIS FOOT FIRMLY on the brake, Jackson shifted into low gear. He was a cautious driver, and he took his time driving down the mountain. Skye wondered if he ever thought about the accident and how she might be uneasy driving past the place where they'd crashed all those years ago. In reality, she didn't know exactly where the accident had happened. Sometimes she scanned the roadside for clues—broken branches, skid marks, twisted car parts. But, of course, everything had long since been swept away.

In Merced, they pulled off the highway to fill up the gas tank. Across the street was a run-down motel and a large billboard advertising AAA Bail Bonds. The pickup, Jackson's work truck, smelled of sawdust and motor oil. There were rips in the seats, half the knobs were loose or missing, the blue paint was scratched and dinged, and there were mottled patches of rust around the wheel bases. But still, it kept running. Skye turned around and looked through the rear window at the bed of the truck, where a heavy tarp was strapped over her meager belongings. Just before they'd left Oakdale, Grace had come out front to say good-bye. She was wearing her garden apron, and she nervously wiped her hands on the bottom of the apron; then she gave Skye a hug and kissed her on the forehead. Grace didn't say anything, but Skye figured it was because her lips were trembling and she was afraid she might cry. Skye was relieved that Grace didn't cry in front of her. As they drove away, Skye glanced out the back window. Grace was standing at the end of the driveway, waving good-bye.

Skye got out of the truck and washed the windshield, leaving a streak down the middle where she couldn't reach. Jackson wasn't that tall, but he was tall enough that he could squeegee the whole windshield without even walking around to the other side. But Skye, who was only five foot three, must have gotten her father's genes. At least, that was what she remembered her mother saying once. It was a dim memory—and strange; Skye had thought her mother sounded angry about it.

It was only 10 a.m. but stifling hot in the Valley; the asphalt was soft enough that the bottom of her sneakers stuck to the pavement, as if she'd stepped on a wad of gum. They made a spongy sound when she walked into the convenience store to get a soda. Jackson called out to her: he wanted a large iced coffee, extra ice. When they got back into the truck, the seats and the door handle were too hot to touch. The air conditioning didn't work very well, so they rolled the windows down and let the wind blast through. Jackson had long, dark hair that he tied back with a thin cord of leather, and he was always untying the cord and gathering up the wispy, loose strands.

With the windows open, it was too noisy to have much of a conversation—not that she and Jackson were big talkers. Occasionally, he would look over at her and smile. They were driving along the aqueduct, next to huge expanses of evenly furrowed fields, mostly plowed under with fall coming. And there were orchards, oranges and walnuts, and rows of grapevines, mostly for raisins. Despite all the agriculture, the Central Valley was flat and unattractive. Rusted-out cars and abandoned tractors and irrigation equipment sidled up next to gray, weathered barns leaning away from the wind.

"Thanksgiving," Jackson said, almost shouting because of the wind through the truck cab. "You'll be home then?"

Most parents wouldn't be asking their kids that question, but it was as if Grace and Jackson's contract as backup guardians expired once she went off to college. In June, Mrs. McNulty had called to say happy birthday. "You're eighteen now," she said. "On your own." At the time, Skye hadn't really thought about it, given that she'd felt on her own since the freezing day Mrs. McNulty had left her with Grace and Jackson. But now she suddenly wondered what Mrs. McNulty had meant. That she wouldn't be calling again, checking up on her?

Skye looked at her reflection in the side-view mirror and tried to imagine Thanksgiving somewhere else. But where?

"Sure," she shouted to Jackson. "Why wouldn't I come back?"

MORGAN COLLEGE WAS A small liberal arts school located on 175 acres in a largely wooded area east of Oakland. Skye had chosen the school because she wasn't sure yet what she wanted to study—maybe architecture or philosophy or prelaw—and they'd offered her a generous scholarship package with a combination of grants and work-study. The college prided itself on small classes and lots of interaction with the faculty. It was located across the bay from her old life, making it possible for Skye to imagine casually running into her mother in a bookstore or on a bus and finally finding out what had happened all those years ago.

The residence halls were terraced against a hillside: Mediterranean-style stucco-and-wood buildings with red tile roofs, surrounded by pine and elm and maple trees, chaparral, wild sage, and succulents—some flowering in massive stalks dotting the hillside. Jackson parked the truck while Skye checked in and got her keys. She was in Mary Warren Hall, a two-story mission-style building with large, wood-framed windows facing the street. They only needed two trips to haul everything upstairs to her room.

Her dorm room had a lived-in, musty smell, or maybe it was the smell of having been unoccupied since May. Sharing a dorm room suddenly reminded her of the shelter, and she hoped her roommate wasn't someone who wanted to talk all the time. Skye picked out the bed farthest from the door for more privacy. The bed was narrow with a thin mattress and plastic cover. There were two closets, each with a dresser. Skye chose the desk facing the window.

They stood in the center of the room, looking around, contemplating what to do next. Jackson stacked the two boxes and the duffel bag at the foot of her bed. Out the window was a view of the college, a mixture of one-story red-brick and taller concrete-and-glass structures, presumably classroom buildings, and a walkway leading around the perimeter of the campus.

Skye had visited the campus early in her senior year and gone on a tour. "Maybe you could show me around," Jackson said. They walked across the street toward the main part of campus, wandering past buildings with names like the Brady Center for Science and Math and Paula Cameron Institute for the Study of Economics. The buildings were locked. Skye stood back while Jackson peered into one of the classrooms, his face against the glass, but there wasn't much to see with all the lights off except rows of desks and chairs and a white-board at the front of each classroom.

Around the corner was a three-story building with ramps and tall glass windows through which they could see bookcases lining the walls and jackets and sweaters hanging on the backs of the doors. Faculty offices? Farther on, beyond a curve in the path, was a small stone amphitheater with auditions posted for a fall production of *Much Ado about Nothing* and a sign for the arboretum. "I remember this," Skye said. "The tour guide was a student, and she walked us through the garden." There was a waterfall, and the trees and plants were labeled with black plastic tags: *Lavandula stoechas* Winter Lace, *Ceanothus* Dark Star, *Arctostaphylos densiflora* Vine Hill Manzanita. Jackson bent down to look at the plants; he pointed out the gnarly bark on the manzanita and remarked on how it sloughed off, revealing shiny red branches. "The Indians used the leaves as toothbrushes, and they say you can boil the bark to help soothe a poison-oak rash. Never tried it, but seems like something good to know." Over the years, Skye had discovered that Jackson knew a lot about plants and trees—which made sense; he was a carpenter, after all. And he read a lot—science fiction, physics, philosophy. When he did have something to say, it was often smart.

Now he looked at Skye, and she wondered what he was thinking. Was he itching to leave? No, she thought. He didn't want to go. Didn't want to leave her.

They were delaying the inevitable, wandering around campus, as if a little more time could make any difference. Skye wanted the good-bye to be over with. She was afraid she might say something edgy or rude that she'd later regret. Or maybe she'd cry. In high school, when all she could imagine was moving back to San Francisco to track down her mother, she'd pictured this moment, but it had only been from *her* point of view. She hadn't counted on how Jackson would feel. She'd figured saying good-bye would be easy. There'd be nothing to lose, she'd thought, no sad feelings. Everyone would understand that it was time for Skye to move on.

"I guess I gotta go," Jackson said. "I promised Grace I'd be home for supper." It almost sounded like he was choosing Grace over Skye. Then he added, "And that job off Cedar

Creek, installing cabinets. There's work left on the doors and hardware." He was looking off in the distance, in the direction of highway.

Suddenly, Skye felt queasy in the pit of her stomach. She wanted the good-bye part to be over, but she didn't want Jackson to leave.

They walked back to the parking lot. Jackson had his arm around her shoulders, and with the difference in height, she kept bumping into him.

"It might take a little time. To make new friends," he said. "You know, like in fourth grade." He untied the leather cord around his ponytail and swept the stray hairs behind his ears, and the familiar movement surprised her, even though she'd seen it a million times. Then he bent down and kissed the top of her head and tousled her hair.

Just as he pulled out of the parking space, he waved good-bye. Skye watched the car drive away. It was a warm day, warmer than she was used to, but a breeze was blowing through the tall trees. And the rustling reminded her of living on a farm in the mountains.

THAT WAS WHEN SHE saw her mother—or thought she saw her—wearing a flowing, off-white dress, a matching blouse, sandals, and a straw hat, just like an outfit her mother had worn one summer when they'd rented a cabin at Stinson Beach with her mother's friends. Skye could barely remember the cabin, but she remembered the dress.

Standing frozen behind a row of cars, Skye hid from the woman in the straw hat and her son, hoping they wouldn't notice her staring. Clearly, the woman was dropping her son off at school, probably just like Skye, for the first time. The woman was tossing the contents of the car trunk—a pillow, a basketball, a duffel, a large plastic garbage bag—in her son's direction, fast enough that he had to scramble to catch everything and put it on a dolly. They were laughing, especially the woman, who wouldn't let up, despite her son's pleas to slow down. The woman closed the trunk and locked the car while her son pulled the dolly past her, onto the sidewalk and then across the street. Skye trailed them, hoping to get a better look at the woman.

The path between the parking lot and the dorms was swarming with parents carrying boxes and bags, TVs, computers and printers, cases of ramen noodles, blankets and sheets and wicker trash baskets. The son was pushing the dolly up the ramp one building over from Skye's dorm; it was where the freshman guys lived. She thought the woman was saying something about giving him quarters for the laundry. "I hope you'll acquaint yourself with a washing machine and dryer," she said. Skye squinted into the sun, staring, trying not to be obvious. Her breathing slowly settled; her hands stopped shaking. No, she reassured herself. This woman wasn't her mother; she wasn't tall enough, and though her hair was blonde, it was wavy.

Of course, Skye had no idea what her mother would look like now and what kind of toll the years since the accident would have taken on her body. Watching this woman and her son, their playful intimacy, felt eerie to her. Skye remembered times she and her mother had been close, when she'd spent evenings helping Skye with homework and on the weekends they would go to the movies or out to eat. It seemed to Skye that this woman could be her mother. Under other circumstances, she might have been.

TEN MINUTES LATER, AS she stood outside the open door of her dorm room, Skye was still thinking about the woman—not the woman, really, but her mother. The dorm room had looked so empty when she and Jackson had left, but now it was full of things she didn't recognize. Her new roommate and her parents had practically taken over.

"Hi," Evelyn said. She was tall, African American; her long fingernails were painted with bright red polish and small flower decals. She was leaning against the closet door, watching her parents busily organizing her side of the room. Evelyn rolled her eyes in Skye's direction as if to say, *I know it's ridiculous. They insisted on helping.*

They'd friended each other on Facebook the week before. Skye knew Evelyn liked rhythm and blues,'70s music, and swing dancing, wanted to major in cultural anthropology, had a boyfriend back home in Monterey and a younger sister and brother, and went to church on Sundays.

"These are my parents," Evelyn said. Her father reached out and shook Skye's hand. Her mother smiled in Skye's direction and said, "Nice to meet you."

Evelyn's bed was already well dressed with brightly colored yellow-and-orange sheets, a matching polka-dot comforter, and two decorative pillows. Her mother was organizing Evelyn's clothes in the closet (she'd bought a new twelve-pack of hangers for the occasion) while her father began to set up her computer. A stapler and tape dispenser were lined up in the top desk drawer; paper clips, pencils, and pens were stowed neatly in containers on the shelf above her desk. A framed print—a watercolor of shops along Cannery Row—had already been hung on the wall. Evelyn had a microwave, small refrigerator, TV/DVD player, PC, and laptop.

Skye unzipped her duffel bag and pulled out the mismatched sheets and towels from Grace and the striped comforter from Jasmine's mother. She made her bed and stashed her clothes in the dresser—the one on her side of the closet—set up her CD player, put the laptop on her desk.

She'd forgotten to bring thumbtacks for the Van Halen poster and stared at the poster and then the wall, trying to figure out how to hang it.

Evelyn must have noticed. "Here," she said, handing her a handful of thumbtacks. "You can use these."

Her parents were talking about how much allowance Evelyn might need.

"You'll want to go out to eat occasionally and go into the City," her mother said. "Museums and concerts, and what about buying books and school supplies?"

Her father had stopped working on the computer. He had his wallet out, and he was dispensing a wad of crisp notes.

Skye started to put the two photographs on her desk—the one of her mother and Skye and her mother's college friend Melanie in Santa Cruz and the other of her and Jackson and Grace in front of their vegetable garden. In the past, Skye hadn't had to explain about Jackson and Grace—only the one time when she'd started fourth grade at Oakdale Elementary. She'd stretched the truth, telling the other kids her mother was looking for work out of state and would be coming to pick her up any day. They all knew differently: Oakdale was a small town, and a photograph of her mother's car, squeezed between two trees at the bottom of a ditch, had made the front page of the local *Oakdale Mountain News*. For months, they'd teased her, asking about her mother, and had she found a job yet? But they liked Skye, and at some point people stopped asking, or maybe they even forgot. Except for her friend Jasmine, who knew more about what had really happened.

Before she'd left for college, Jasmine had told her, "You have this great chance to make yourself over. Any way you want." Jasmine had a reputation at school for being easy with guys, and Skye suspected it was a wish she had for herself. At the time, Skye hadn't wanted to think about her mother and Jackson and Grace and what she'd tell new friends who'd never met her before. They would make assumptions—that she had a father and a mother, maybe not married to each other, but certainly that she'd known both of them. Skye wasn't ready to explain her awkward past to anyone, especially not to Evelyn, so she left the photo of herself with Jackson and Grace on the desk. And she hid the photo of her mother on the top shelf of the closet, underneath the duffel bag. She still didn't know what she was going to say when the first person asked her about the people in the photo.

Evelyn and her parents were talking about getting a bite to eat. "I saw a cute little bistro just off campus," her mother said, "in that area of Oakland that's being revitalized."

She turned to Skye: "Come with us."

"Oh, no, thank you," Skye said.

But Evelyn's parents insisted. "We couldn't leave you here to get lonely."

Skye wasn't worried about being lonely. It was people she worried about. But Evelyn's mother put her arm around her, and they were asking if she liked cold gazpacho and Italian soda, and did she have any siblings, and what did she think about living near the City.

Chapter Two

SKYE'S TWELFTH BIRTHDAY FELL a few days into summer vacation. Grace and Jackson took her whitewater rafting down the Stanislaus River, along with Jasmine and her brother, Jake, and Sally and Jerry Miller, Jasmine's parents. It was steamy hot, and they loaded up the Millers' station wagon with towels, a picnic lunch, and life jackets and strapped inner tubes to the roof. At the river, they parked by a patch of sandy beach and barbecued hamburgers and sang "Happy Birthday." It made Skye think of her mother. Last year, she'd received a postcard in the mail, a glossy photo of Caesar's Palace, postmarked Las Vegas, Nevada, and her mother had even called. She'd needed to catch a bus, so the phone call had been rushed and she hadn't told Skye where she was going, only "Happy Birthday, baby. I love you." But this year, Skye kept checking the mailbox. Nothing had arrived. It made her worry about her mother. Something must have happened.

When they got home, she asked Grace to please call Mrs. McNulty.

"Give it a few days," Grace said. "I bet a card'll arrive in the mail as soon as you stop thinking about it."

The next afternoon, Grace was out delivering Meals on Wheels. Jackson was in the garage, sawing and hammering, assembling cabinets for one of the vacation homes in the overpriced development on the north side of town. Skye and Jasmine were sitting on frayed lawn chairs in the backyard, tossing a stick to Chester. They'd spent the morning riding their bikes around town. Skye told Jasmine about asking Grace to call Mrs. McNulty and Grace's admonition to wait.

"Call her yourself," Jasmine said with an air of defiance. She was tugging on the stick, trying to extricate it from Chester's mouth, unfazed by the slobber dripping down her hand. Jasmine was always getting in trouble at school for ignoring the rules.

Skye opened her hand and offered Chester a strip of fake bacon in exchange for the stick. He looked torn, trying to figure out how to keep hold of the stick and eat the treat at the same time.

"Drop it," she said. Chester shook the stick loose and scarfed up the bacon treat. Jasmine grabbed the stick and tossed it out into the yard again.

Skye knew she'd never get up the courage to call Mrs. McNulty on her own, but she figured Grace must have papers somewhere, probably in the back room where they stored odds and ends like remnants of fabric and yarn and holiday decorations.

It was Jasmine who slid open the closet door. There, next to the winter coats and vacuum cleaner and extra leaves for the dining room table, was a tall, beat-up metal filing cabinet. Skye opened the top drawer. She had to stand on her tiptoes to see inside. It was stuffed with maps and a couple of files labeled "Travel Ideas." The next drawer down was where Grace stashed bills: credit-card statements, utilities, mortgage payments, health insurance, and folders for "New Life Church" and "1998 Dodge Ram." The third drawer, in the back, was a thick folder with her name on it. Skye pulled it out, and they took it into her room and laid it out on the bed.

At first Skye thought maybe she'd just get Mrs. McNulty's phone number and put the folder back, but once she opened it up, Jasmine grabbed the stack of papers and started flipping through everything. There was an information sheet about Skye with her birth date and physical description: brown eyes, brown hair, stocky build, athletic. Born June 15th. Fourth grade, good student. A color photo was stapled to the corner, something like a mug shot with her hair uncombed, one side of her shirt collar turned under, her mouth crooked as if she'd been too angry to smile.

"OMG," Jasmine said, staring at the photo. "I'm surprised *anyone* took you in."

Skye acted as if she was too absorbed by the report written by Mrs. McNulty to hear what Jasmine was saying. The report was detailed, with an extensive history of her mother's drug abuse, concluding with "There's likely to be a long period of detoxification." Skye didn't understand a lot of the words, like *addictive personality* and *poor boundaries* and *complicated reunification*, but she knew enough to understand that it painted a pretty bad picture of her mother. At the end of the report, just above where Mrs. McNulty had signed her name, under "Conclusions," she'd written, "Child endangerment and abuse due to neglect," and strongly recommended that Skye be placed in foster care.

Skye closed the file and arranged the papers so they looked untouched. Then she snuck into the den and crammed the file back into the cabinet.

"At least get her phone number," Jasmine said.

"What good will that do?"

FOR A WHILE, THE words *child endangerment* and *neglect* remained lodged in her brain, and she thought about pulling out the file folder again. Maybe if she read it over a second time, she'd understand what Mrs. McNulty meant. But then she decided it didn't matter. She just wanted to find her mother.

It was a couple of weeks later when she got up the courage to ask Grace again. Would she call Mrs. McNulty? They were out in the garden pulling weeds, digging in compost, harvesting carrots and radishes, the last of the lettuce. Summer was receding, and Jasmine's family had driven off to Yellowstone in their motor home. Her friend Amanda was still away at summer camp. Skye had ample time on her hands to contemplate the twist of fate that led to her spending the summer watching thick bloodworms root around in the soil instead of hanging out in Golden Gate Park or riding BART across the bay or driving up the coast to the beach with Melanie.

Grace sighed in a way that suggested Skye's request was either a heavy burden or raised precarious issues that would have to be handled delicately. "If Mrs. McNulty knew anything about your mother, I'm sure she'd contact us," she said.

But Skye wanted to hear it from Mrs. McNulty herself. "Maybe she's really busy," Skye said, "and forgot to call." She was grabbing at the weeds, pulling off the tops, not reaching down to get the roots like Grace had shown her.

Grace frowned, took a red bandanna out of her skirt pocket, and wiped her face. "It's more complicated than that," she said in a tone that suggested finality.

Jackson, who was repairing a hole in the chicken coop, had been quietly listening in on their conversation. He often played peacemaker, trying to head off any arguments. "Hey, Skye, grab the staple gun for me, will ya?" He'd cut the chicken wire with metal shears and was holding it up against the coop. "Squeeze it like this," he said, "with your hands around the grip. You don't want to staple a finger." She put on a pair of thick garden gloves and held the staple gun against the side of the chicken coop, squeezing the trigger. It made a louder noise than she expected, and it startled her. The first couple of staples were uneven, sticking out on one end, but then she got the hang of it. Jackson was always showing her how to do things around the house, like how to drive the snowplow and the riding mower and how to make miter joints and glue and clamp pieces of wood together.

At first Grace and Jackson both acted as if Skye hadn't asked anything of consequence. Jackson unrolled more chicken wire, pointing out the places where Skye should shoot a staple. Then there'd be a loud *snap*, sometimes two or three snaps when she missed the edge of the chicken wire. Grace had collected the wheelbarrow from the shed and was loading up more compost from the bin.

"What's so complicated about me talking to my mother?" Skye finally asked. It came out sounding angrier than she'd intended, though the fact was that she did feel angry at Grace for trying to avoid the subject.

Jackson looked over at Grace as if they had some tacit understanding.

"What Grace is trying to say is that she's been hearing from Mrs. McNulty. All along."

Grace pursed her lips and threw down the shovel. "Then you deal with it," she said, starting back to the house. Grace and Jackson hardly ever argued, but when they did, it was usually Jackson who apologized after a couple days of stony silence, like the time Grace took something from the drugstore by mistake and they hauled her down to the police station. "Just drop it," she'd said when she got home later that afternoon. "It was a misunderstanding, that's all, just an ugly misunderstanding."

"But why would you take kids' crew socks and a crib blanket? We don't even need that stuff." They both got quiet because it was obvious why Grace might want kids' socks and a crib blanket.

Jackson put more staples in the gun and handed it back to Skye. "We should have been telling you all along, but we knew how much you wanted her to come back. I think the last time Mrs. McNulty heard from your mother, she was in Arizona somewhere, working at a drive-through burger joint."

Skye stiffened her jaw and shot out another staple. It missed, and she shot three more, all more unevenly than the first.

Jackson took the staple gun from her. "I'll finish up," he said. "Go see if there's any of that strawberry pie left. And bring me a piece, too."

Later that afternoon, she pressed them again, and Grace got Mrs. McNulty on the phone. The social worker confirmed that her mother had called from Reno a couple of months before, and then Arizona.

Then Grace handed the receiver to Skye.

"The last time your mother called, she asked how you were doing," Mrs. McNulty said.

Skye didn't understand. Was that supposed to make her feel better? And if her mother was doing all this traveling, then why wasn't she visiting her?

"What'd you say?" she asked.

"That you were doing well in school, you'd made friends, that you seemed happy."

Skye wasn't sure if she was happy or not; it was obviously something Mrs. McNulty thought was important to tell her mother. But it made her mad, Mrs. McNulty letting her off the hook for doing such a lousy job as a mother.

"When's she coming for me?" Skye asked insistently.

There was a long pause on the other end of the phone and a clipped response: "Not yet."

Chapter Three

OVER DINNER AT THE fancy bistro with Evelyn's parents, it was obvious to Skye that she and Evelyn didn't have much in common. Evelyn seemed preoccupied, wrapped up in herself and her boyfriend still in high school back home. She'd spent most of the meal texting her boyfriend while Evelyn's parents asked Skye all the usual questions: Where had she grown up? Oh, really, you must be a good skier. Had she thought about what to major in at college?

On Sunday, after all the parents had left, Skye ended up wandering around campus by herself, trying to figure out which direction to hold the campus map and how to find her classes. On the way back to her dorm room, she walked through the arboretum again, staring at the waterfall, picturing Jackson leaning over the plants, caressing the leaves. She missed him, more than she'd expected. With dinnertime approaching, she was relieved that a group of girls from her dorm had invited her to eat with them. They all seemed equally excited about the prospect of college, and equally anxious and disoriented. It was a relief going to sleep that night, knowing classes would be starting the following morning and her time would be taken up with studying and finding a job and becoming a college student.

When she got to class the next day, her philosophy professor, Dr. Morris, was handing out the syllabus, expounding on what seemed to be all the reasons to drop the class: two midterms and a final, a twenty-page paper, no credit for late work. "I have an attendance roster with your pictures, and I'll be calling on you—at random," he said, waving portrait thumbnails. "So if you haven't done the reading, don't bother coming to class." His hair was strewn about as if he'd driven to class in a convertible with the top down, and he was slightly pudgy. There was a half-eaten blueberry scone on the desk. Skye was staring at him, trying to figure out if he was serious or just giving the students a hard time. Given his disheveled appearance, he didn't seem the demanding type.

The only open seat was toward the front of the room. Skye's alarm hadn't gone off, and then, on her way to class, she'd gotten turned around and had to search for her map to figure out how to get to the Social Sciences building.

"No cell phones, no gum-chewing, two excused absences—provided you supply me with a note from your doctor." He pointed out the books on the syllabus that were required and the supplemental reading on reserve at the library. Skye scanned the page of bulleted rules: no makeup exams; errors in spelling and grammar would result in point deductions; plagiarism and other forms of cheating were grounds for automatic failure; inappropriate or offensive language and/or uncivil behavior would not be tolerated.

Dr. Morris's office hours were listed at the top of the syllabus along with his grading policy.

"Contrary to what you might expect, philosophy isn't for BS artists, at least not my class. If you want an easy A, try organic chemistry or quantum mechanics." Morris squeezed out a snicker. Two students closed their notebooks and exited through the back door.

It was Jackson who had encouraged her to take a philosophy class. "It'll help you think about life in a big way." Studying the course catalog, she'd been skeptical: *Introduction to Philosophy 110. A survey course on Western philosophical thought from Plato through postmodern deconstruction. Will explore fundamental methods of inquiry including logic, epistemology, inductive and deductive reasoning, and metaphysics. No prerequisites. 3 credit hours.* She knew what induction and deduction were, and they'd read Plato in high school humanities. But she was fuzzier about some of the other terms. She thought about what Jasmine had said about reinventing herself. Why shouldn't she be more adventurous and take courses she knew little about? And she liked what Jackson had said about a big-picture view of things.

Dr. Morris took off his glasses; he looked through them at a distance and blew on the lenses, then took out his handkerchief, steamed the lenses with his breath, and wiped them clean. "We have a lot to cover," he said. And with that, he folded the handkerchief, put his glasses back on, and opened a black loose-leaf binder with bright yellow and orange tabs. With an array of dry-erase markers, blue and green and black, he proceeded to write a series of words on the board: *Epistemology. Ethics. Philosophy.*

He looked out at the classroom, then down at his roster. "You there, Jonathan, is it? Why did you decide to take this class?"

Jonathan was slightly overweight, with a scruffy beard. He pursed his lips in a way that suggested answering Morris's question was beneath him and likely to take more energy than was worth his while. "It's required," he said.

Morris frowned. "That's the best you can come up with?"

Morris pointed to a young woman in the back row. "Monica? Why study philosophy?" he asked.

"It helps you think critically."

Glancing around the classroom, Skye could see there was a lot of squirming. Morris had a glass beaker, or maybe it was a small wine decanter, filled with water that he poured into a glass, pausing long enough to take a few sips. He seemed misplaced, like he'd grown up in an earlier time, or maybe he'd been born into a family with unconventional ideas. It was easy to imagine he'd been teased as a child.

Over the course of his lecture, Morris managed to kick-start a discussion about politics and history and current events, and how philosophy might help people formulate ethical, thoughtful decisions in their lives. Was violence ever justified? Should the death penalty be repealed? On what grounds should abortion be legal?

That summer on a drive to the lake, she and Grace and Jackson had had a heated discussion about abortion. Grace couldn't imagine any time abortion was justified. "If it's killing, then it's killing even if the mother's life is in jeopardy." She turned to Skye. "What if your mother—"

Jackson interrupted before she finished her question. "It depends," he said, "on whether you believe a woman has the right to determine what happens to her own body. Or whether you believe the fetus has some absolute right to be protected."

Skye raised her hand, offering Jackson's reasoning as her own.

"Yes," Morris said. "That's just the kind of complex thinking we're encouraging here." He finished off the scone and brushed the crumbs from his shirt. "It would be easy enough for us to dissolve into polemics," he said. "But that wouldn't be philosophy." He wrote the word *polemics* on the board with a green marker. "Look it up," he said, "if you don't know what it means."

Then Morris glanced at his watch and closed his notebook. "You will be required to use your minds in this course. I assure you that laziness and Thursday-night carousing will not be rewarded. Philosophy isn't sloppy like a lot of your lives. It's a rigorous discipline, and that's what I expect in here. When we study the empiricists, you will see there is room for our emotional lives, but this is not meant as some uninformed, willy-nilly foray into …"

He clasped his hands together and looked around the room. "All right, then," he said. "I hope to see at least some of you back here on Wednesday." He cast a weak smile in their direction, waited to see if any students had questions, then picked up his belongings and walked purposefully out the door of the classroom.

The student sitting next to Skye closed his laptop. He'd been making periodic eye contact, occasionally rolling his eyes. "Jeez," he said, looking toward the classroom door to make sure Morris had gone. "Pretty full of himself. I'd drop the class, but it's required."

Philosophy wasn't required for Skye, and for sure, Morris was a piece of work. But she thought the class would be challenging. Not like in high school, where everyone's opinion was taken seriously, no matter how absurd. When Morris asked a question, it was clear he wasn't seeking an easy answer.

"I think it sounds interesting," Skye hazarded.

"Really? You're not worried about all that reading and

how hard it's gonna be?" he said, shifting his backpack higher on his shoulder. "Hey, I'm Matt,"

"Skye."

Matt had chin-length, curly brown hair. He was tall, but his shoulders slumped, suggesting he was uncomfortable towering over everyone else. "Haven't I seen you? Out in front of Mary Warren?" he said.

"Maybe. That's where I live."

Matt asked if she wanted to get something to eat. They walked over to the cafeteria, a compact redbrick building set up as a food court with a salad bar and sandwiches and chicken strips and stir-fry. Skye ordered a sandwich, Matt a burger, and they took their food outside and sat down on a grassy slope near the university plaza. It was sunny, and a local band was playing in the small amphitheater, loud enough that they had to strain to talk. Girls were in cutoffs and tank tops and short skirts and sandals. A guy sitting next to them was talking sharply into his cell phone; it sounded like he was having an argument with his girlfriend. "Where were you? I waited an hour."

Matt took a bite of his burger. "So, where you from?"

Skye hesitated. The best answer was Oakdale, near Yosemite. If he asked her anything about high school, she could tell him about her friends and hiking in Yosemite and what it was like to grow up riding horses and shoveling snow. But instead, she said, "San Francisco." It wasn't really a lie, given that she was born there. And she figured on moving back after college—even if it was too early to make any plans.

"Really? So you basically moved across the bay. Cool. I grew up in the Central Valley, in Visalia. It has a bad rep, maybe not like Bakersfield, but we have a pretty good baseball team, and it's close to the mountains. My sister was a ski bum after high school, and we'd get free passes."

Matt kept talking, but Skye didn't mind. It was easier than talking about herself. He seemed easygoing and friendly, and she thought he was cute with his sunglasses perched on top of his head and his curly hair and the one little beauty mark on his upper lip. He was in the middle; he had an older sister and a younger brother who'd just started high school. His father was in sales and traveled a lot; his mother was an elementary school teacher.

Of course, Skye had heard of Visalia. In fact, they often drove into the Valley to do shopping there, and one Fourth of July, Jackson and Grace had even taken her to a baseball game, and they'd watched fireworks there.

Matt asked about her major, what classes she was taking. "I'm leaning toward history."

"I'm undecided," Skye said.

It turned out Matt lived in Fielding Hall, the next building over from hers.

"How's your roommate?" he asked.

So far, Skye didn't know much about Evelyn except that she was always rushing out of the room to talk to her boyfriend back home. After the phone call, she'd throw herself on the bed and turn on the TV.

"She's taken over with her microwave and refrigerator, puff pillows on the bed," said Skye. "Made her side of our room into a fashion statement." After she said this, she wondered if it sounded mean. Evelyn was okay. It was just pretty obvious already that they weren't going to be best friends.

THAT AFTERNOON, BACK AT Mary Warren, Skye tossed her backpack on the bed and opened the window. Their room smelled of vanilla beans and fruity-scented candles. It wasn't that she minded the smell, but it was overpowering in the small room yet still didn't manage to quite mask the lingering musty odor she'd hoped would dissipate.

She left the door propped open to air out the room, and in case anyone wanted to stop by to say hello. Over the weekend, she'd met a couple of the other girls in the dorm. They seemed nice, but there wasn't anyone she thought would turn out to be a best friend, not like Jasmine. Down the hallway, she could hear the muffled undertone of talking and music and what sounded like someone throwing a tennis ball against the wall. *Thunk, thunk.* And then the crash of a metal wastebasket. *Thunk.* She opened her laptop and checked her e mail. There was a message from her math professor with a link to the class web page and how to log on, something from Campus Dining about her meal card, and a welcome from the president of the college with a link to the college's honor code. Jasmine had posted a picture on Facebook, of her running the sack race at the Oakdale Labor Day picnic, only this time it was with Heather Parker, who until now they'd been in agreement was too full of herself to fit into the burlap sack. But there they were, screaming and falling over each other.

Skye's fingers lingered over the keyboard, and then she typed her mother's name into the browser—something she'd found herself doing pretty often lately. She hadn't been able to find an address or a phone number, no employment, no mention in the white pages or yellow pages. There were lots of sites claiming to have information on her mother's whereabouts, but she'd have to pay a fee, and Skye figured it wouldn't be all that helpful given how often her mother moved around. Clicking on pages one and two and three led to nothing. On page four, there was a reference she'd seen before; her mother must have worked for an architectural landscape firm in San Francisco. Skye wasn't sure if she'd been hired as an architect or a receptionist, although she distinctly remembered her mother working late into the night, with coffee cups and art supplies strewn across the table. She clicked on the firm's website. Based in San Francisco, they specialized in community and civic parks and green roof design. Her mother's name wasn't listed under current staff contacts. Skye had looked before, but even the first time, she'd known it wouldn't be.

Skye closed her laptop and picked up her philosophy textbook. She flipped to the Allegory of the Cave, their first assignment, and lay down on the bed, her head propped up on her elbow. Prisoners are shackled in a cave, facing forward so that all they can see are shadows of objects, people, animals. Morris had said all people were prisoners, unable to perceive what's real. "That's why you're here," he said. "To escape from your own cave, see your past and the world the way it is, stripped of illusion." Her new life, it wouldn't be easy, just erase everything and start again. Jackson and Grace—they rarely mentioned her mother, acting as if she'd never existed, as if none of them thought about her. But of course, her mother had been living with them in every room of the house, every birthday, every school play, every time Skye asked Grace to sign her report card, high school graduation, the time she fell on the ice and had to get seven stitches, every stubbed toe, passing her driving test, that road trip they took to the Grand Canyon, the morning she discovered bloodstains on her underpants, Career Day in junior high, the drive to college.

Especially on the drive to college, her mother had been there.

ON FRIDAY AFTERNOON, THE RAs from Fielding Hall and Mary Warren organized a volleyball tournament on the sand court behind the gym. They'd survived the first week of classes, and everyone was ready to celebrate. The RAs fired up the barbecue and carted over a couple of coolers with ice and cans of soda. Matt was there, along with his roommate, Casey, who was in Skye's math class. Casey was slim but athletic; he had dark brown eyes and a buzz cut and an unassuming manner. Evelyn had gone home for the weekend to see her boyfriend, who was on the fence about their relationship, but most of the other girls from her dorm were there, wearing skimpy bikinis, whether it was a good idea or not. Skye had on cutoff jeans shorts and a tank top and flip-flops. She'd walked over with Sylvia, who lived at the other end of the hall. Sylvia had been avoiding her own room most of the week; she and her roommate were already not getting along.

Before the game, the two RAs had everyone get into a circle and go around and say their name, where they were from, and a fun fact about themselves. Skye hated those games. There were so few facts about herself she wanted to share with a group of mostly strangers, and none of them were *fun.*

One guy said he had eight brothers and sisters.

"My family's from Tibet," Casey said.

"Both my parents came to college here," Matt said. "That's how they met."

Jenny from across the hall had a pilot's license.

One girl had worked on a housing build with Habitat for Humanity in New Orleans that summer.

Rachel had been hospitalized for an eating disorder in high school, "but I'm *totally* fine now," she said. Apparently, she didn't have a clue all the girls on the hall had been talking about how bony-thin she was and how they'd heard her throwing up in the bathroom.

They were all considering what to say, wanting to seem

open and friendly but not revealing too much. It was a delicate balance.

Skye said, "This summer, my dad and I built a greenhouse."

They played volleyball and then ate hot dogs and potato chips and bland coleslaw. After the game, Matt and Casey and Sylvia and Jonathan from their philosophy class and Sylvia's friend Alison walked back together, and they all ended up in Skye's room. Matt and Casey were sitting on Evelyn's bed, leaning against the puffy pillows. Flip-flops and sand were strewn across the floor; Skye and Sylvia and Alison were sitting on Skye's bed.

Jonathan, who looked more mature than the others with his stubbly dark beard, was flipping through the CDs on Evelyn's shelf. "Who listens to Jennifer Hudson and Beyoncé ?"

"They're my roommate's."

He pulled a CD out of the case and held it up to the light, rubbed it on his sweaty T-shirt.

Skye wasn't sure how Evelyn would feel about their listening to her CDs. Hopefully, nothing would happen. Jonathan must have seen the wary look on her face.

"Hey, lighten up." He slipped the CD into the player. Jay Z with Kanye West and Rihanna, *Run This Town.* He turned the volume up.

"I need to find a new roommate," Sylvia said. "Know anyone who's looking?"

Jonathan was leaning over, inspecting his right foot. He'd bashed his toe against the concrete walkway next to the volleyball court; it was swollen and turning black and blue. "Already?"

Sylvia looked over at Skye, as if she were privy to some secret.

A couple of days earlier, Evelyn had told her that Chelsea needed a new roommate, that she didn't feel comfortable with Sylvia. She'd said it with a knowing roll of the eyes, as if it were obvious, but Skye didn't know what she meant.

"I might as well say it now. Get it over with," Sylvia said. "I'm gay."

The music suddenly seemed louder while they all looked at each other.

Casey said, "So?" And they all laughed.

"Shit, I'm glad it's not a big deal. I mean, in high school I was out and everyone knew—even my parents, who aren't all that cool with it. But now, I can't believe it. Chelsea's got some Christian moral compass stuck up her ass. We have to meet with someone from the Housing office. I thought we graduated high school, but I guess only some of us did."

"That sucks," Skye said. She hoped Sylvia wasn't thinking they could be roommates. She liked Sylvia, but she was pretty intense, and Skye thought Evelyn was going to be easier to live with in a confined space; already she felt lucky she'd gotten a roommate who didn't feel the need to share every detail of her day or pry too much into Skye's. Of course, she didn't want Sylvia to think it had to do with her being gay because it didn't.

WHEN EVELYN CAME BACK on Sunday night, she threw her suitcase on the bed and turned on the CD player. Skye hoped she wouldn't notice that the CD cases had been rearranged. But Evelyn seemed wrapped up in downloading photographs onto her laptop—photos of her boyfriend that she was eager to share with Skye. Eating pizza on Cannery Row. Tossing a Frisbee on the beach. Evelyn was happier than when she'd left for home on Friday afternoon, now that she'd been able to convince him they shouldn't break up. Nelson was white—something Skye wished she hadn't noticed.

She wondered what it was like for them—other people noticing. He was tall and had his shirt off in a lot of the photographs; his chest muscles and arms were sculpted. His father hung drywall for a living, and Nelson, who was still a senior in high school, helped out in the summer—probably why he was so buff. There was a certain irony in the assumptions people made—that Evelyn's family, being African American, were probably poor and uneducated and that she probably had a brother in prison and was likely on a full scholarship. In reality, her father was a corporate attorney, her mother a physician. They vacationed in Hawaii and Cabo San Lucas, skied in Aspen.

"Nelson's going to apply here for next year," Evelyn said, "so I told him it's just the rest of this year that we have to deal with the distance. And next weekend he's coming here. I hope you don't mind."

Skye almost asked, *Why should I mind?* but then realized what Evelyn was saying—that she and her boyfriend would be sleeping together in their dorm room. Skye could either put up with the slippery noise or find somewhere else to spend the weekend. She'd ask Sylvia. Or maybe she could camp out in the lounge. There were official dorm rules about having guests in your room, but, like alcohol and pot, the written rules were pretty much irrelevant.

IT HAPPENED AGAIN, THE second week of school. On the way to calculus, walking across a pedestrian bridge between the Social Science and English buildings, holding her notebook in one hand, a cup of coffee in the other, Skye heard the crisp tapping of high heels on the bridge's wooden slats. Coming toward her on the bridge was a woman in tan slacks and a blazer. She was tall and thin, with shoulder-length blonde hair, and she walked cautiously, making sure her high heels didn't catch in one of the grooves on the bridge. Skye shut her eyes tight and then opened them, squinting as the woman approached her and the clicking of her high heels on the concrete became ever more distinct. A wave of nausea ran through her. Her arms and neck tightened, and she spilled her coffee across the front of her sweatshirt and jeans. The woman, probably on the faculty, with her brown leather satchel and stack of papers, was walking in the direction of the Student Services building. Skye put the coffee and her notebook down on the pavement. As the woman passed her on the walkway, she smiled at Skye, who was staring at the brown streaks of coffee down the front of her jeans and sweatshirt.

Skye hurried the rest of the way to her calculus class. It was unnerving, imagining that any thirty- or forty-something woman, slim, with blonde hair was her mother. She hadn't been sleeping well, had been waking at odd hours of the night after dreaming of showing up to class late and finding all the seats empty. Skye had confided in Sylvia.

"You should go to counseling," Sylvia said.

"How's that going to help?"

"I don't know, but you could talk about what happened. Maybe they could help you find your mother."

When Skye got to class, her calculus professor, Dr. Levy—who insisted they call her Erica—was writing formulas on the board that were barely legible. She had on worn jeans and a crumpled button-down shirt and earthy-looking leather sandals; she seemed way too young to be teaching in a university. Skye tossed the empty coffee cup into the garbage and sat down next to Casey, who was reviewing his notes from last week. Differential equations. *What's the velocity of a moving object falling in space?* Skye couldn't help but imagine her mother being suddenly air-dropped onto the bridge that morning. It made concentrating in class a challenge; she was relieved when Dr. Levy finally dismissed them.

After class, Skye and Casey met up with Matt, and they walked over to the library together. It was the tallest building on campus, four stories of massive block concrete with an inner courtyard that looked out over a simulated Japanese rock garden. On the second and third floors were small group-study rooms where they were allowed to talk, so Skye and Casey could work on calculus problems while Matt griped about Morris. He was already struggling with understanding the reading, not to mention the lectures.

"It's supposed to make you think," Skye said. It was actually a bit of advice from Jackson when he'd given her Bertrand Russell's hefty volume, *A History of Western Philosophy*, to read over the summer. "I only understood about half of it," he'd said, "but still, it makes you think about life." Skye had only gotten through the first chapter over the summer, but she'd taken the book to school with her, and now it was sitting on the shelf above her desk. She'd promised herself she would finish it—by when she wasn't sure.

"Is that something your mother told you?" Matt's tone was sarcastic. He was leaning his chair away from the table, balancing on the back legs.

Skye frowned. "What?"

"Forget it," Matt said.

Matt glanced over at Casey, who was working on a homework problem, and then he opened his philosophy textbook, got out a yellow highlighter, and slouched intently over his book, shrinking his six-foot frame.

His bratty attitude surprised her, and she pressed him again, jostling his book with the end of her highlighter.

Matt pulled the book toward him and turned the page, as

if he'd been paying attention to what he was reading. Without looking up, he said, "Sylvia spilled the beans."

Casey got up to sharpen his pencil.

"Told you what? About my mother?"

"I'm not sure how it's my fault—just for listening to Sylvia spout off. Casey, help me out here."

But Casey, with his two number 2 pencils in hand, was standing by the mechanical sharpener attached to the wall. He put one of the pencils in, rotated the handle, and blew off the sawdust. He barely looked up.

"Oh, I forgot," Matt said. "That's the beauty of being Buddhist. Above all that drama. Anyway, what's the big deal? It's not like it's your fault about your mother being an addict."

"Is that what Sylvia said? That she's an addict?"

Mat set the chair legs back down on the floor and backed away from the table, as if getting further away from Skye would keep him out of trouble. "So ... is it true?"

Skye had to admit it was probably an accurate summary. Of course, it was more complicated than that.

"And she said you were kind of adopted."

"It's a long story," Skye said.

He closed his book and leaned his elbows on the table. "I'm guessing the basics wouldn't take more than about ten minutes."

"Less," she said.

Skye thought about the shortest distance from point A to point B. "My mother was pretty messed up," she said, "and the sheriff in Oakdale knew Jackson and Grace wanted to have children but couldn't. So he thought maybe they'd let me live with them for a while, and it lasted. Well, till now."

"Do you think you'll ever try to find her?"

Skye told him about surfing the Internet and how the social worker called every once in a while to give her an update, although she couldn't remember the last time she'd heard from her.

"Everybody knows, huh?" Skye said.

Casey glanced up long enough to exchange looks with Matt.

"That's what I thought."

Chapter Four

THE COUNSELING CENTER WAS located at the south end of campus in a nineteenth-century redbrick, originally built as a men's dormitory, replete with sconces and built-in dressers, showers in the bathroom. (Women hadn't been admitted to the college until 1956.) The building had been recently earthquake-retrofitted with structural supports, a clean sand-blasted facing, and a new roof. Unfortunately, halfway through the project, the college had run out of funds, and the inside decor remained much the same, with its cracked linoleum, leaky windows, and antiquated radiators.

Alix scanned the paperwork. There was nothing out of the ordinary—not much drinking or drugs, no thoughts of suicide or hospitalizations, good grades. The handwriting was immature, with large, angular letters, and the answers were clipped, as if the girl weren't ready to reveal herself. (*I want to talk about some personal issues.*) Some students were like that—they wouldn't write much about what brought them to counseling, but once she provided the opportunity to talk, it was tricky getting them out the door at the end of the session. The space listing family members had been left blank.

She put the clipboard on the floor by her chair and looked up. "Tell me what brings you to counseling."

Alix's office was on the second floor. One window was slightly ajar and she could hear a bus pull away and a lawn mower and someone talking too loudly on a cell phone. The student was looking around the office at the row of bookcases, Alix's desk with files neatly stacked, a box of tissues on the table next to the student. Lots of clients started out that way, unsure where to begin. Unsure what to expect from coming in to talk with a total stranger.

"You keep notes on what I say?" the student asked. "I mean, I guess it's okay because how else would you remember?"

The student rubbed her hands along the tops of her pants. She was wearing sneakers, a hooded sweatshirt, and jeans. Her hair looked as though she'd cut it herself with one hand on the scissors and the other holding a mirror. Running her hand along the ragged edges, she pushed a strand to the side once and then twice, but still, it fell back over her eyes. An overlapping front tooth was quite noticeable —the kind of thing most parents would have insisted on having straightened.

"Yes," Alix said, "I keep notes on our sessions. You can see them anytime you'd like, but I can tell you, it's just pretty much what we talk about; you won't find any secrets." She paused to see if the student had any other questions.

"My friend Sylvia sees you. She thought it would be good for me, you know, to come in and talk."

Alix remembered Sylvia well. She'd been in the first week of school to talk about coming out to her friends and an awkward roommate situation. She was thin and edgy, and the whole session she'd barely paused to let Alix get a word in edgewise. But Alix had to respond to this student's comment; fortunately, she was well practiced in not reacting one way or the other, not giving away any clues about whether she was indeed seeing her friend. "I'd want to be sure you know that whatever we talk about is confidential, so I can't share—even your name—with anyone else."

"Sure," she said. "I mean, I was just trying to ... You asked why I'm here."

"Yes, of course."

The student took off her sweatshirt and slid the loose strands of hair around her ears. She ran her tongue over the overlapping tooth, making it obvious to Alix that it was something she felt self-conscious about. "What do you want to know?" she asked.

"Just tell me about yourself," Alix said, "whatever seems important."

"I grew up in San Francisco, just across the bay from here," the student said, lifting her chin toward the window as if she were pointing toward the City. "My mother ... well, we'd go to the park on the weekends and have friends over and watch movies and make brownies."

Alix glanced down at the paperwork. *Skye,* she reminded herself. The student's name was Skye. She motioned for her to continue.

The mother, Eva, was an architect, although Skye seemed uncertain whether that was how she made a living. Maybe sometimes she was a receptionist or a waitress, she told Alix, and Alix understood that even though this student was an adult—not a fully formed adult but an adult nonetheless—

her memory of her mother was from a child's perspective. Her mother was funny and smart, the kind of person everyone wanted to be around. "I remember hearing something about my mother taking me to work with her when I was a baby—at least that's what I think she told me—and she'd plop me down in the corner of the studio in a playpen. She might have shown me how to read architectural plans because I can picture the blue writing. And I remember making tiny people and animals and trees out of Popsicle sticks and Elmer's glue and colored thread."

It was obvious to Alix that the mother was no longer a part of Skye's life. "Then things changed?" Alix asked.

"Like overnight, she started acting ... I don't know, really weird. And everything fell apart. She lost her job and pretty much lay on the couch all day. We'd have fish sticks and tater tots for dinner, and half the time I had to make them myself," she told Alix.

"What do you think happened?"

Skye hesitated. "Prescription pills. For pain. At least that's how it got started. Something about a shoulder injury from a skiing accident in college." She bit the bottom of her lip and looked away. "The worst was when I was about eight or nine and she slept all day and paced the apartment at night, talking to herself, with the TV on loud enough to keep me awake. Her friends stopped calling. And it was just the two of us in the apartment all weekend long watching old movies and playing gin rummy. She wouldn't go shopping, and then she'd send me out to the Japanese restaurant for takeout or the grocery store around the corner."

"What else do you remember?"

"I used to ask her about my father, and she'd say, 'You don't have a father.' But you know how little kids are. In school, we'd learned that everyone had a father and a mother. And then she'd say, 'It's not important. Lots of kids don't have a father.' I remember walking down the street with her and asking her about the mail carrier, the man living downstairs from us, the principal at my school, a man in line ahead of us at the library. 'Is that him? Does my daddy look like that? Where did you meet him?' Sometimes she'd get really mad about it, and I never got an answer anyway. So I stopped asking."

Alix nodded and waited for the student to continue.

"Then one weekend when I was ten years old, we drove up into the mountains with my mother's old college roommate, Melissa, and some other friends. We stayed in a cabin. It was fun playing in the snow and building a fire in the fireplace—more fun than we'd had in a long time. My mother promised she'd stop taking the pills, and she seemed pretty happy for the first time in a while. I figured everything would finally go back to normal. Then, driving home, I was in the backseat, and I could see in the rearview mirror that she was upset, not crying exactly, but she looked pale and she was jumpy and driving too fast. I wanted to tell her to slow down, but I was afraid to say anything, afraid I'd make her mad, but then we skidded off the road and crashed into a gully." She paused before adding, "I guess it could've been way worse."

It seemed to Alix that the student was trying her best to tell the story as if it were someone else's story. Her face was flat, devoid of emotion, and her words ran together in a monotone. The neglect and then the car accident and having been abandoned obviously had had serious consequences for this student. Alix wondered what else had happened to the girl.

Skye took a pack of gum out of her backpack and offered a piece to Alix. Alix never gave her patients gifts, and she'd learned not to accept anything from them, either. She held up her hand to say no. Years earlier, when she'd been naive, thinking there had to be good in all people, one of her clients, who had terminated abruptly, had brought a collage that Alix had hung in her office—until one day she'd looked up at it and seen her own nude body, camouflaged in a cascading array of wildflowers. She didn't want to think about how he'd gotten a photograph of her without clothes. For days after that, she'd take the collage out of the closet and stare at it, inspecting the details of the print, wondering if it really was her body or some cut-and-paste digital job. If it was a fake, then he had an uncannily accurate imagination. After that, she'd decided it was best not to take anything at all from her clients.

"It's sugar-free," Skye said, still holding the package out to her.

"No, thanks."

Skye unwrapped a piece and put it in her mouth. She had dark brown eyes, almost black, long eyelashes, and a pronounced cleft in her chin. She was obviously strong and athletic; with a little grooming and better-coordinated clothes, Alix thought she could be quite attractive. Some of the students worked hard to get that sort of carefree, disheveled look, but obviously not Skye.

"I keep seeing my mother," the girl said. "All over campus. I'm not even sure what she looks like—at least not now—but I turn around and she's there and my brain goes numb and it feels like this weird energy screeching in my body like I'm watching a slasher movie and I have to talk myself down because I really think it's her. Just for that split second.

"Of course, it's not her," she said. Skye's voice was tense, her words strung together in a pressured knot. "And I don't understand, but all of a sudden I'm remembering things that happened a long time ago. Except I'm not sure they really happened."

Alix was beginning to realize the depth of this young woman's pain. It was true that children raised in chaotic homes often had scant, fragmented memories of the past, sometimes remembering not much of anything before age five.

"Tell me more about the accident," Alix said. "What happened to your mother?"

"We were trapped in the car. My mother was groaning at first, but then I think she went unconscious, except I could hear this watery kind of breathing. It was cold and pretty soon I was shivering and I wasn't sure if I should climb out the window and leave my mother in the car. I'd seen stories, you know, on TV about how you should stay with the car and let the rescue people find you. But then I heard sirens, and the ambulance and police showed up and fished me out of the car. I should have stayed with my mother. Maybe then ... I don't know. But they wouldn't let me go with her. Sometimes I think I could have helped her; then maybe she wouldn't have gotten lost." Skye was holding her hand up to her mouth, so some of the words were muffled, and it seemed to Alix that sometimes she stopped breathing, especially when she talked about her mother.

"I stayed in a shelter for a couple of days, and then Grace and Jackson took me in. I remember Grace was chatty, and she told me how she delivered Meals on Wheels and knitted hats for the soldiers and organized spaying and neutering for stray animals—only she didn't say it that way. She said they helped stray pets get an operation so they wouldn't have any more puppies. I thought it was cruel, and I wondered if doctors did that sometimes to children who'd lost their parents."

Skye smiled, and her face flushed. "I know, it was silly, but back then ..."

"Of course," Alix said, "I can see how you would be terrified about everything that was happening."

Skye took the gum out of her mouth, folded it up into the wrapper, and stuck it in her sweatshirt pocket.

"You can put that in the wastebasket," Alix said, but Skye seemed to be looking at the four or five books standing on end along the back of her desk, each marked with yellow tabs and multicolored index cards.

"You writing something?"

"Yes," Alix said, glancing behind her at the desk.

Skye opened her water bottle and took a swig. "What about?"

Alix had been intrigued for many years by the trajectory of individuals who'd suffered multiple, often horrendous traumas and losses in their lives. Some few evidenced enormous resilience, while the vast majority watched their lives disintegrate beyond repair. Earlier in her career, she'd conducted interviews. Her research had been published in professional journals, documenting horrific accounts—like the young girl kidnapped and confined for years who had raised her kidnappers' children. The girl had even protected her kidnapper from apprehension. More recently, Alix had been writing a mainstream book geared to the general public. But ever since Richard's death, she'd stared at the manuscript, unable to squeeze out anything more than a couple of haphazard paragraphs.

"It's about loss and how people recover," she said.

"Like me," Skye said, "only without the recovery part."

Alix smiled. "Yes, I guess so. For now." Alix reached down to retrieve the paperwork from the floor, checking to make sure she hadn't missed anything—unanswered questions relevant to her initial assessment, signs of risk she might have overlooked.

"I want to find her," the girl said.

Alix glanced up, and it was suddenly clear to her that this student had come in for that very reason. Skye was leaning forward in her chair as if she were waiting for Alix's answer—yes or no. But it wasn't that simple. The chaotic childhood, early parentification, traumatic flashbacks involving the image of her mother all over campus, Skye's disorganized appearance. Alix didn't want to commit to seeing her for more than a handful of sessions. It promised to be messy and uncertain. There'd surely be no happy ending. "That's something we can talk about, what it would mean to find her."

"So you think it's a bad idea."

"It's not good or bad," Alix said, putting off the inevitable. "But it's complicated, and I'd want you to be prepared—whatever happens." Prior to Richard's death, she'd have been challenged by a client with this degree of trauma and distress, but not now. Maybe not ever again.

Alix stood up and opened the door for Skye. "Downstairs, at the front desk, tell Candy to schedule you for next week."

ALIX HAD JUST FINISHED writing up her notes when Betsy stuck her head in. "Want to get some lunch?" Alix dug out her wallet and sunglasses from the bottom drawer of her desk; she closed her office door on the way out. They descended the back steps of the clinic, crossed the street, and headed up the steep hill toward the center of campus. The faculty dining hall was located across from the university plaza.

Alix and Betsy had both started working at the clinic about five years before and had lunch together a couple times a week. Since Richard's death, Alix's friendship with Betsy had been one of the few steady relationships in her life. Unlike Alix, Betsy had three grown kids. She was married and had—at least superficially—a happy relationship. Right now she was chattering about Stan wanting to buy a new car. He favored a hybrid, something ecologically responsible.

All day Sunday, they'd test-driven practical cars with good gas mileage.

"He'll beat this thing into the ground," she said, rolling her eyes, "and then I'll get my sporty roadster. I just don't know why we have to go through this lengthy *pas de deux.*"

Betsy was known for her unconventional style—the other therapists in the clinic often heard her laughing with her clients. For Betsy, therapy was a game of chess, and the laughter was how she got away with being brutally honest. Instead of defending kings and queens, the client was merely trying to save face. "You can't be too greedy," she was fond of saying. It was far better to just patiently watch them fidget and squirm and twist their rationalizations into something less than coherent, waiting for the right moment to intervene. In the end, checkmate was always hers.

At the dining hall, the hostess seated them at a small table against the window, close enough to the kitchen that they could hear barking orders and dishes and utensils clattering. Alix ordered a Caesar salad and a Diet Coke, Betsy the mushroom burger. The dean of math and science, a surprisingly scruffy man in his forties, sat down at a table on the other side of the room, and they half smiled in recognition. Alix didn't noticed when Betsy changed the subject: something about the annual conference on trauma Alix had attended last week in New York.

"And how's Sam?" Betsy took a bite of her burger.

Sam was Alix's brother, who lived in New York. They'd been close growing up and had kept in touch even when Alix had moved to California. But lately, whenever he called, she let it go to voice mail.

"Fine," she said.

"You didn't see him, did you?"

"There wasn't time."

"Honey, it's been six months since Richard died," Betsy said, wiping her mouth with the napkin.

Alix slid her fingers along the outside of her water glass. The icy condensation dripped down the tumbler onto the tablecloth. "It's complicated," she said, stabbing at the lettuce in her salad.

"It's not complicated at all. You're leading a double life: doctor in control during the day, morose shut-in on the weekends."

"That's hardly ..."

Betsy took the last bite of her burger. "I just hate to see you so miserable."

"I'm not miserable."

Betsy turned her head. A gaggle of administrators sat down at the large table in the center of the room. "No, of course not. How's the book coming? Still marinating?"

"It's a work in progress," Alix said.

HER NEXT CLIENT, JEREMY, was a young man with sparse stubble. He was wearing torn jeans that hung below his waist, a dingy white T-shirt, and a wool beanie covering what looked like a ratty mass of unwashed hair. He seemed indignant from the moment he walked in the door, as if he had far more important business to transact than sitting through a counseling session. When Alix asked what brought him in, he launched into a nonstop diatribe, swearing there'd been no warning, and how could "she" do this to him? It didn't take long for Alix to figure out that "she" was his girlfriend. Or ex-girlfriend. Out of the blue, the young woman had broken up with him. In an e-mail.

"She called the police on me," he said, incredulous. He'd been driving by her apartment at odd hours of the night, leaving sticky notes on her windshield demanding answers, texting her.

"I mean, can't we just talk?" he asked Alix defensively.

Apparently not, Alix thought. "Let's figure out how you're going to move beyond this," she tried.

"I can't," he insisted. "I'll never get over her."

Alix sat back, adjusted the knot in her scarf. She already knew how this would play out. He'd continue to stalk the ex-girlfriend, and the texting would intensify. She'd spot him standing outside her classroom or unexpectedly peering over her study carrel in the library. He'd profess his love to her, and she'd feel sorry for him, and then she'd give him another chance.

How was he going to stay out of trouble? she wondered out loud. "You've already had a visit from the police, and I'd hate to see you dismissed from the college."

He reached under his wool beanie and scratched at his hair, then forced the knotted strands back under the beanie. "I don't know," he said. "I really love her, and I've acted like an idiot. I just want another chance."

Alix was irritated with his misdirected sense of entitlement. In reality, the likelihood of Jeremy convincing his ex-girlfriend to give him another chance was better than fifty-fifty. Over the last ten years, Alix had worked with more than her share of couples. It was always the most dysfunctional who broke up and got back together, then broke up again, swinging with great certainty between jealous rage and undying love until one of them was finally able to disengage and move on. Sometimes it took parents intervening, or the college judicial affairs office, or the police. Or a new girlfriend. Helping Jeremy through it was more a matter of waiting out the inevitable than anything therapeutic.

The clinic was empty by the time Alix locked her office door and walked to the parking lot. It had taken her well over an hour to return phone calls and slog through the stack of notes on her desk. After her session with Jeremy, she'd seen two more students: an ongoing client who'd been abused as a child and a student wanting to transfer to his community college back home. His parents had insisted he come in for counseling before making a decision. Unfortunately, the student wasn't terribly interested in participating in the counseling process; it was more a question of placating his parents. In the end, she'd gotten him to commit to checking out the rec center facilities and going to at least one club meeting before their next session. For the moment, it felt like a success.

THE HOUR-LONG COMMUTE from campus to her home on the peninsula was like driving through a long, narrow tunnel loosely connecting one part of her life to another, letting her mind siphon off the day like water trickling down the side of a mountain. Alix found herself mulling over the session with Skye and the chances she'd even be able to function at college. The girl seemed smart enough, but what resources did she have to count on? And what about her mother? Was she even alive? It had been too soon to broach that question with her.

The sky was milky gray by the time she stopped at the grocery store for a frozen Lean Cuisine and a half gallon of rocky road ice cream and picked up her mail at the post office, clothes at the dry cleaner. She pulled into the gravel driveway, turned off the engine, and sat in the car while she scanned the mail. There was a letter addressed to her deceased husband offering a low-interest credit card and a donation request from his alumni association (actually, Richard had never finished graduate school, discovering midstream that philosophy wasn't his thing). Alix unlocked the front door, laid the keys on the table, and locked and dead-bolted the door behind her. The house still smelled of Richard, a smell that assaulted her every time she walked in the front door. It was an earthy scent, mixed with the smell of well-tended wood—a maple rocking chair in the living room, wood floors he'd polished with linseed oil, the air a lingering mixture of rich soil and pine bark.

Except for a narrow swatch of light from a table lamp, she left all the lights off. The frozen dinner went in the microwave, the ice cream in the freezer. She uncorked a bottle of wine and set the glass on the coffee table. Still standing, she opened the newspaper, scanned the headlines, then turned to the back section, studying the obituaries. Three deaths—one heart attack. A valiant battle with cancer. Weren't they all courageous or valiant? Alix had never once seen what she thought was a more accurate description—long-suffering. Or torturous. Another obituary looked like an inadvertent overdose. She scrunched up six newspaper sheets into a ball and laid them under the fireplace grate, two pine logs and four pieces of kindling on top, lit a wooden match, and stood watching as the flames took hold. Then she slid off her high heels and sat on the couch to eat her low-fat lasagna. The bottle of red wine next to her full glass slowly emptied while she stared at the flames and the shadows until she couldn't see the space between them.

If she thought there was reason to reconsider her life, Alix might have been moved to get up and call Betsy or her brother, Sam, or read a book, or take Richard's clothes to Goodwill, clean out the junk drawer in the kitchen, or rake leaves—or sit in the living room with the lights on. Lately she hadn't even needed the sleep medication her doctor prescribed; there was nothing in her mind to keep her awake at night. By the end of the day, she'd let everything drain out.

IT WAS TEN IN the morning when she woke up and rolled over to look at the clock. At first she thought she'd only been asleep a short while, but it was light in the room, even with the curtains closed.

Shit, she thought, or more likely said aloud. She'd already missed a clinic meeting and an intake appointment with a new client. Why hadn't they called her from work?

She phoned the office and got Candy, the receptionist. "I've overslept."

"I tried to call you," Candy said.

Alix vaguely remembered hearing the distant ringing of the phone. She must have incorporated it into a dream—something about the dentist's office needing to drill a well in her front yard.

"I'll be there in an hour," she told Candy apologetically.

She glanced in the mirror; it would take more than the usual dab of foundation to cover up the dark circles under her blood-shot eyes. She turned on the shower and got in before the water warmed up, rousing herself under the cold stream. She'd never overslept, never been so out of control that she missed work. And the funny thing about it: she didn't really care.

It was a little after 11 o'clock when she got to the office. Candy had already canceled the rest of her morning appointments. There was a note from Nora, the clinic director, to please see her when she had a chance. Alix crumpled up the note and tossed it into the recycling bin. Still standing next to Candy, she asked, "How did Rachel react?"

"Relieved, I think."

During their last session, Alix had gently confronted Rachel about her eating disorder—something the girl ardently denied. "How can I work on my self-esteem if I'm so fat? Just help me lose a couple more pounds," Rachel had said defiantly. It didn't bode well for her progress.

"And what about the new client?" Alix asked.

"He stayed about fifteen minutes and left in a huff. I tried to get him to reschedule, I'm sorry, but he was too upset. I even asked if he wanted to speak to one of the other counselors."

"That's okay." She found herself trying to justify her lateness. "I must have turned off the alarm without realizing it."

Candy went back to filing charts; Alix thought she detected a roll of the eyes.

Alix poured a cup of coffee, stirred in a spoonful of lumpy powdered creamer, and went upstairs to her office. She turned on the computer and waited for it to boot up, then sorted through yesterday's e mail, deleting all but a message from a former client wanting to reschedule. She called Rachel and the new intake, left messages apologizing and offering another appointment time later in the week.

When she found out Alix had overslept—which she inevitably would—Betsy was going to have a field day. "You can't act as if nothing happened," she'd say. "You of all people—the queen of trauma. What good is all that research doing you?"

Chapter Five

THE FIRST TIME THEY'D met, Alix had thought of Richard more as data for her research than as a prospective mate. It was about the time she started working at the clinic. She was writing an article on risk-taking behavior for the North Atlantic Psychoanalytic Society and read a story in the *Los Angeles Times* about a man who was able to fly, or nearly fly (more like a slow fall), in a hand-tooled aluminum contraption fashioned with fabric wings. He was offering trips along the Pacific Coast Highway near Santa Cruz, and she thought it would be worthwhile to meet this man who'd managed to successfully complete over 1,300 flights. Between 1930 and the early 1960s, seventy-two out of seventy-five people had died trying.

"Tell me about flying," she said.

They were standing on hard-packed sand near the water's edge, south of Santa Cruz on the Pacific Coast Highway, watching surfers and hang gliders navigate the waves. Bright orange and red and yellow and green, slick nylon sails flying through the air above the foamy crests. Alix held her notebook and pen in one hand, her sunglasses in the other. It was foggy, what California coasters called "June gloom"—a misnomer given that the coast was socked in with a thick marine layer more months than not.

"Well, technically, it's not flying. More like extended gliding."

Richard brushed his hair back from his face with the top of his forearm, his eyes fixed on the ocean, staring beyond the horizon, his thick eyebrows creasing slightly. He looked up at a flock of pelicans flying by in formation.

"I've been watching birds all my life. My father was a birder, and his father. It has to do with the surface area–to–weight ratio. How a feather drifts, but a person falls like a cannonball. It's pretty much the same idea."

Alix pictured a cannonball plunging into the ocean. "And how do you deal with the danger?"

Richard shrugged. "Let me ask you," he said, "if you had the choice of living a really long, uneventful, tedious life or an expansive, death-defying, tragically short life, which would you choose?"

Alix's father had died when she was only fourteen years old. Perhaps selfishly, she wished he'd lived a really long life, however boring and uneventful.

"We don't have those choices," she said.

Richard shifted his gaze from the ocean to Alix. "You're avoiding the question."

"I suppose," she said. "As much as I hate to admit it, I'd choose the long, boring life. Not tedious but predictable."

They walked across the street to a fish-and-chips dive, ordered fried calamari and popcorn shrimp, and sat on a picnic table along with the bikers and the kids with sand falling out of the bottoms of their bathing suits.

"You can't prepare for a crisis," he said. "By definition, then, it's no longer a crisis, and you couldn't say it's even unexpected if you've thought about it enough to make plans—even if they're just preliminary plans. If we weren't so afraid to die, then nothing would be a crisis."

Alix listened, a list of objections bubbling up that she didn't voice. She never left home without her cell phone and a full tank of gas. The riskiest decision she'd ever made was to take a job in California—three thousand miles away from her friends and the little family she had left in New York. At the time this had seemed a bold, independent move, but in retrospect, it was equivalent to deciding to vacation in Spain rather than San Diego. Richard, however, seemed fearless. She had to admire him for it.

"You're not afraid to die?" she asked.

"I'm not ready to die," he said, "but afraid? No, I'm not afraid."

"You're just in denial."

Richard smirked. "If you really want to understand why I fly, you have to come with me. We'll go tandem; you won't be alone."

As if that mattered, Alix thought. She was reminded of a recent trip to Montreal to present a paper. "Have you ever seen the traffic lights in Canada?" she asked. "They're red and yellow at the same time. Are you supposed to get ready to go or stop?"

"Don't worry," he said, "there aren't any brakes when you're flying; it's either glide or plunge."

She waited for him to say something like "Just kidding," but instead he simply drenched the last piece of calamari in hot sauce and finished it off.

THE NEXT WEEKEND THEY hiked up into the Santa Cruz mountains, winding their way through the evergreens to a view of the ocean. He pointed out red-tailed hawks, the California towhee, tree swallows. A condor, with its nine-foot wingspan, soared along the rocks, eclipsing the side of the cliff. "Did you know," he said, handing her a pair of binoculars, "condors don't have feathers on their head or neck, and the skin flushes, showing emotion? It's one way they communicate with each other."

"Makes it easy," she said.

It seemed neither of them was ready for their time together to end, so he invited her to dinner. "I'll cook," he said, and what woman in her right mind would turn down an offer like that, she thought.

They drove back to his house, a two-story, wood-framed home with a wide porch, set back in the trees, bordering on national forest land. The living room was an open hexagon with large windows, white stucco walls, and exposed wooden beams. He'd largely built the house himself with a couple of friends, the year after he'd dropped out of graduate school. The front window overlooked a wide swath of untamed lawn and the narrow mountain road. A seasonal stream ran along the back edge of the property. Upstairs were two bedrooms. There were photographs of Richard flying—off the coasts of California and Brazil and the Gaspé Peninsula; there were inky woodblock prints of birds, too, and weavings from all over the world. He poured her a glass of wine. Alix sat on a high stool leaning over the counter, looking out a span of windows onto a stand of Douglas fir and cedar and ponderosa pines, watching him snap the ends off the asparagus, chop up yellow bell pepper and broccoli, and sauté fresh ginger and garlic. She wanted to know why he wasn't teaching philosophy or writing but instead taking tourists hang gliding.

"Mostly it's because I'm doing what I love. Besides, the last thing the world needs is another philosophy professor."

He served up the ginger stir-fry with basmati rice, told her about the time he'd eaten guinea pig in Ecuador, and then listened to her drone on (her word, "drone," not his) about her morbid fascination with how people coped with trauma, like firemen rushing into a burning building or the paramedic who'd rescued Baby Jessica from a well and eight years later committed suicide. Some individuals flourished in the face of adversity, and others caved in.

"You'd flourish," he said.

She knew better. "I hope I'm never tested."

A FEW MONTHS LATER, it was a Saturday in April. She'd woken up with his arms around her, resigned to the fact that he was right: she could hardly expect to understand his passion for hang gliding if she didn't experience it at least once. He'd been telling her about the coastal winds that are most predictable and steady in the spring. "Unlike winter, when the wind is almost always accompanied by rain," he'd said. "Fall winds gust and then falter. And in summer, the air currents are slack with indolence, waiting for the most inopportune moment to fade away."

"It's today or never," she told him. And if this was her fate, to go with the wind—literally—then she would surrender. Her greatest fear was not that she'd be killed in a fall but seriously injured, most likely paralyzed, and then spend the rest of her life in a wheelchair deriding herself for being so stupid, for agreeing to something not in her nature.

Instead of reassuring her (which of course would have been somewhat empty), Richard simply said, "Yes, that would be horrible. I wouldn't want that to happen, either. I've only lost one person." And then he smiled, and it was fortunate she looked up at him just then, before she revealed her shock. It was the kind of remark her father would have made—clever but bordering on insensitive.

They drove to a steep cliff overlooking the beach, some twelve hundred feet above the ocean. It was sunny, with a cool breeze, scattered cumulus clouds just offshore, which Richard said was good for flying since the air is denser when it's cold and they could fly farther, maybe even catch a couple of thermals. Alix wasn't sure she wanted to fly farther; up and down would be fine as long as they didn't descend too quickly: glide without the plunge.

They dressed in a tight synthetic fabric that looked fine on Richard, but Alix was self-conscious, especially about her small breasts, which generally did not seem proportionally small because she wore loose clothing as a rule. Richard had a tan-and-black Galileo-like design on his suit, but Alix's was bright yellow. "It's easier to spot," Richard said. "Plus, the sharks are less likely to think a creature in a yellow suit is edible. Black looks like a seal to them." Alix realized there were all sorts of dangers she hadn't accounted for.

Richard pulled up a couple of handfuls of grass and threw them into the air, looked up at the gulls and cormorants, and then pulled binoculars out of his jacket pocket and looked out to sea. At what, Alix wasn't sure.

"Want to help with the equipment?" he asked.

"Just like that," Alix said, walking back to the car with him.

"What do you mean?"

"Just like that you've decided it's safe?"

"Didn't you say something about surrendering?" he said. "And yes, it's a good day for flying."

He set up the glider, piecing together lengths of aluminum tubing, like oversized tent poles, and webbed cloth cinched together with thin bungee cords. It didn't look high-tech enough; Alix wasn't sure if this was a good thing or not. Sometimes simplicity was better. She tried to imagine the ocean as one big safety net—without the sharks.

They put on helmets and stood side by side on the edge of the cliff.

"We'll practice a couple of times, first running toward the cliff, and then I'll show you how to jump off—without actually jumping off—at least not yet."

The only thing keeping her moving in the direction of the cliff was Richard's exuding confidence. And the fact that she couldn't run off in a bright yellow suit that made her look like an irradiated porpoise. Speechless, she managed a nod.

They backed up in measured steps from the edge of the cliff and then ran forward. She could feel his warm shoulder against hers, his voice that was patient but stern, unyielding. She hoped he couldn't feel her body trembling in small spasms.

"One," he called out. He moved her forward one gaping step; she felt out of balance, the straps cutting into her inner thigh. "Two." She had to take one additional step to catch up. "Three." Alix nearly fell over, but he caught her arm just in time. "Jump," he said. They both jumped straight up in the air, but Alix landed first with a jolt.

They backed up again to get the right distance and repeated the running forward. Richard took smaller steps, what looked like tiny, child-like movements for his six-foot frame, but this time Alix could keep up with him and they traveled together more evenly. They practiced half-a-dozen times until it seemed they were running and jumping in sync.

Richard put his arm around her. "Ready?"

Alix nodded.

"On the count of three, we'll run forward and jump—just as we did—and I want you to simply lean forward and let the wind lift your legs behind you. I'll do everything else. Got it?"

Alix nodded.

Out of the corner of her eye, she saw him look at her and smile. Alix wanted to smile back at him, but she felt frozen, stuck to the ground, wondering how she was going to run and then jump, but they'd practiced and … *Is this going to be the last thing I remember,* she thought, *before slamming into the side of a cliff? I suppose there are worse ways to die.* The house was clean, but what else would someone find scavenging through her belongings—jewelry, her manuscript, those pathetic love letters from her old boyfriend Dante. *Okay, just breathe, we're moving, one, two, three, we're jumping.*

They were in the air, and she could feel the wind underneath her chest, and the muscles in her belly were stretched and taut. Their flying contraption tilted spasmodically in jerky movements. She felt cold air against her cheeks, and her hands tightened around the crossbar. The jerky movements began to subside. The tension of their wings wasn't flapping like a bird but steady, filled with the wind. Alix couldn't see anything, and she realized her eyes were closed, but she didn't want to look down, didn't want to see just how far from land they had strayed, separated from the ground, her legs stranded behind her. Straining, as if she were underwater without goggles, she finally opened her eyes. They were out over the ocean; she couldn't tell how far because their backs were to the land. Seagulls flew out in the distance, squawking; there was a sailboat crisscrossing below them. It was cold, but Richard had been right about the wind being steady and strong. She could feel his body alongside hers, and she was glad he was controlling the glider and all she had to do was keep her hands around the bar since she was strapped in. She smelled the sun and the air, which smelled crisp without intrusion from the land, and there wasn't anything else to compare it to, as if it wasn't a smell of something but the smell of nothing. A full moon was setting, and she glanced over at Richard. She couldn't see his face with the goggles and the crash helmet. Crash helmet. *Don't think about landing. He got us up here, he'll get us down. Hold onto the bar. Feel the wind. Breathe.* Birds drifted on the currents, gulls and cormorants, close enough that Alix could see the black and white lines on their bodies, long orange beaks and finger-like feathers on their wings. Richard seemed to be following a hawk, mimicking the circles and dips and twists, lifting in the thermals and then gliding along the air currents.

They meandered downward in serpentine turns, and Alix had to concentrate on keeping her eyes open as they approached the beach. Richard had given her specific instructions for how to land, but she'd completely forgotten, and she imagined her ankles being forced into her thighs, snapping off like tiny wooden matchsticks. She could see the strands of seaweed and driftwood and sea foam coming into sharp focus and a single-minded breeze pushing them downward. And then they were on the ground, Richard having taken the brunt of the landing, and she ran alongside him in the soft sand along with the gulls and snowy plovers and oystercatchers.

Alix's teeth were gritty with sand, her fingers ached from clenching too tightly on the crossbar, her legs were wobbly. But she'd survived. Richard got them unhooked and began taking the glider apart, laying each piece carefully in the sand. Alix didn't say anything, and Richard seemed to know better than to ask; she thought he'd probably witnessed dozens of others, reluctant passengers strapped to his side, landing in a different place from where they'd taken off.

Back in the car, he asked, "Are you going to say anything?"

She wanted to go again, this time without the fear, focusing on the sensation of freedom and weightlessness. "I'm thinking about it."

"Don't think too long," he said. "It messes up the experience."

THE DAY RICHARD DIED, they'd argued about the redwood-burl coffee table. He'd bought it one afternoon on the way home from hang gliding. Alix insisted that the coffee table didn't match anything else in their home. It was gaudy, she told him, and they should get rid of it in a yard sale; she'd never liked it anyway.

Richard disagreed. "It's not *gaudy,*" he said. "Perhaps *kitsch.*"

"Now you're playing with semantics," Alix said.

Richard didn't care what anyone else thought; he loved the burgundy tones and the imperfections. The knots and darkened areas epitomized how complicated and how elegant life could be all at the same time, he said. And how the natural world seemed utterly unconcerned with perfection—yet wasn't this table an exquisite example of perfection?

"Still," Alix said, "it was never meant to be stained and lacquered and set in our living room."

Richard was standing on the uppermost rung of a twelve-foot ladder, installing the last of the smoke alarms, humoring her. She'd insisted on an alarm in every room, but the cathedral ceilings were an added complication.

He'd just started to tell her a joke: "How many philosophers does it take to install a smoke alarm?"

"I don't know," Alix said. He kept looking down at her, and she wanted him to concentrate on the task without distraction.

"Two," he said, "one to—"

Alix felt a wave of nausea, an imminent sense of doom, and then the rumble, like a train or a subway running along the rooftop. Books were tossed from the shelves; china rattled and crashed, wineglasses teetered off the edge of the kitchen counter. A picture of the two of them that Richard had given her on one or another birthday flipped facedown onto the wood floor and shattered.

At that very moment, Richard's arm extended—he was reaching for the cordless drill. A 5.9 earthquake rattled the valley, the epicenter just twenty-five miles from their home. In a string of unlikely coincidences, the ladder teetered, and Richard grabbed the exposed cedar beam to which he was securing the smoke alarm, lost his grip, and fell. It wasn't the fall—exactly—that was fatal but the redwood-burl coffee table Alix had moved, not two minutes before, safely out of the way. In losing his grip, Richard was thrown to the side; he hit his head on the corner of the table and was instantly knocked unconscious. A subdural hematoma was listed as the cause of death. Alix, of course, had been wearing shoes at the time and suffered not so much as a splinter.

Chapter Six

Skye hadn't wanted to go back to see the therapist, but Sylvia convinced her it wouldn't hurt to give her a second chance. "It's hard to get any advice out of her," Sylvia admitted. "She just keeps asking me what I think. Why would I be seeing her if I had any idea what to do?" It didn't help Skye feel any better about making another appointment.

A couple of minutes past one o'clock, the receptionist, Candy, told her to go upstairs.

The door was ajar, and when Skye peeked in, she could see that Alix was finishing up her lunch. Seeing Skye, she shoved what looked like a half-eaten salad into a paper bag and tossed it into the trash. There were papers on her desk, as if she were preparing for some kind of presentation. Or maybe she was working on that book she was writing. Alix motioned for her to come in.

Skye tossed her backpack onto the floor and sank into the chair. She could feel Alix staring at her, waiting for her to say something. It made it even harder to make eye contact. Skye could feel her body tighten up, and her shoulders were slumped over her chest. She had made the appointment herself; still, it felt as if she'd been dragged in against her will.

"So, can you help me?" she asked. Skye didn't want to have an attitude about being there, but that was what came out anyway. It was something that got her into trouble with Grace. Jackson was always cautioning her to take it easy on Grace.

"Help you with what?" Alix asked.

"You know, finding my mother."

Skye looked up in time to see Alix's eyes narrow; a thin smile appeared ever so briefly. Skye figured students asked her for all sorts of advice: help with scoring a date, how to ace a test, or whether or not they should have sex with their boyfriend. Probably she thought Skye was asking her to be a private investigator. She couldn't really fault Alix for being less than enthusiastic.

"What do you imagine it would be like, seeing her again?" Alix asked.

Skye got a pack of gum from her pants pocket. She reached out to offer Alix a piece but then pulled back, remembering Alix's polite but unambiguous refusal the previous session. There was another awkward silence but for the crinkly noise as she slowly opened the wrapper and put the gum in her mouth. Skye rearranged herself in the chair, positioning one leg underneath her body.

"How should I know?" she said.

Alix didn't seem to react to Skye's attitude, continuing with her line of questioning. "When was the last time you saw her? Or had any contact with her?"

Skye found herself staring up at the ceiling, trying to

remember. "When I was eleven, I got a birthday card from her, postmarked Las Vegas," she said after a minute. "And maybe there was a Christmas card after that, I'm not sure. The social worker, Mrs. McNulty, calls me a couple times a year—whenever she hears from her. For all I know, she could be dead."

Skye could feel her stomach tighten. Didn't Alix realize she just wanted an answer? Could she help or not? "So what if I find her, and let's say, just for argument's sake, she's some down-and-out drug addict living in a halfway house?"

"And?"

"Maybe she needs me."

"Needs you how?"

"I don't know ... she's strung out on drugs and homeless and dying of AIDS. Or she needs a kidney transplant, and I'm the only match. Or she has another kid and could use a babysitter." Skye didn't really think any of that was true, except maybe that her mother was strung out on drugs, or dead.

Alix sat back in her chair, took a sip of coffee. "You chose a college pretty close to San Francisco."

"It's a good school. And the scholarship money."

"Any other reasons?"

Skye wondered why Alix would even need to ask why she'd chosen Morgan College. "Well, it's obvious. Don't you think? I came back to find her."

Saying it aloud was embarrassing, and Skye could feel her jaw tighten. If Alix wasn't going to help her, what was the point of spilling her guts? She picked up her backpack, at first reaching for her water bottle. But instead, Skye pulled on the zipper and stared at Alix for a moment, then looked up at the clock. It was only half past the hour, which meant another thirty minutes of getting nowhere. Suddenly she was standing up, her hand on the doorknob. "I was thinking maybe you could help me. Isn't that the point of counseling? But all this talking, it's stupid, and I don't see where it's going."

"Wait," Alix said, getting out of her chair.

But Skye had already made up her mind.

TWO DAYS LATER, SKYE got Mrs. McNulty on the phone. "I have no idea," Mrs. McNulty said at first, acting as if she didn't know anything about her mother's whereabouts. Then she tried to change the subject, asking Skye about college and how she was getting along. Was she forming new friendships? How were her classes? But Skye didn't want to make small talk and pressed her for more information about her mother. "You must know *something*," she said. "I mean, is she okay?" Skye was lying on her dorm-room bed, staring at the Van Halen poster, which was already curling at the edges, the cell phone pressed between her ear and the comforter.

"I'll see what I can find out," Mrs. McNulty said, putting her on hold.

A recorded voice came on with a hotline number for reporting child abuse, cycling around with messages about parenting classes and financial counseling and affordable child care resources. It was ten minutes before Mrs. McNulty came back on the line, and by that time Skye had almost memorized the phone numbers and the information.

"You didn't get this from me," she said, giving Skye the phone number for a rehab facility in northern California. "Besides, I'm not sure she's still there."

"Thanks," Skye said.

"Don't thank me yet," Mrs. McNulty said.

Skye opened up her laptop and did a search for the facility. On the Internet, Bella Vista wasn't like the fancy private resort/hospital Skye had seen in an infomercial on TV but a state-run diversion program. Not giving herself long enough to reconsider, she entered the number into the keypad on her phone. When the receptionist answered, she asked to speak to Eva Hughes.

"Who are you?" she asked.

"Eva's my mother," Skye said.

The receptionist paused, and Skye could hear her rustling through papers. "She hasn't earned phone privileges. Call back in a week."

"Wait," Skye said, fearing dead air at the end of the receiver. "Can't I talk to her doctor?"

Skye heard the click of the hold button and soothing music along with advertising for Bella Vista. *The only fully accredited rehabilitation center in northern California for treatment of dual-diagnosis polysubstance abuse.* Did that mean her mother was using more than just prescription pills?

A woman with the raspy voice of a smoker came on the line. "This is Lydia."

Skye explained again that she was looking for her mother. "Are you her doctor?"

"The doctor is busy," Lydia said. Without pausing, she continued, "So Eva has a daughter." She seemed to think this was an amusing discovery.

"Why's that funny?" Skye was pacing the small aisle between her bed and Evelyn's, alternately looking at the heavy wooden door of her dorm room and out the window toward campus. A student with a skateboard had just been stopped by campus police, and he was getting a talking-to from the officer. Skateboards weren't allowed on the main road circling the campus. The student was feeling in his back pocket, presumably for his ID.

"How long's it been since you saw her?" Lydia asked.

Skye didn't feel much like explaining herself to some know-it-all bitch. "So can I talk to her or not?" It was obvious the conversation was going badly off course. Skye had imagined that when the time came and she located her mother, she'd convey a more neutral attitude, as if she didn't mind waiting until Eva was ready to see her, however long that might take.

"It won't help being pissy with me," Lydia said.

"I'm sorry," Skye said, in case Lydia had some actual rather than simply perceived authority. "She's my mother. I just want to see her."

"Write her a letter," Lydia said. "If she wants to see you, she'll contact you."

The phone went dead before Skye had a chance to ask anything else.

MOSTLY IT WAS THE free pizza that drew them in. Matt and Skye had gone to a noon lecture on gender identity sponsored by the philosophy department. A colleague of Dr. Morris's from UCLA was doing research on transgender individuals and health care. Matt wasn't interested in the topic, but as an incentive, Dr. Morris was giving out extra credit for attending the lecture and writing a one-page opinion piece; Skye convinced him he could use the extra points. Afterward, they walked back to the dorms. Matt was kicking a stone down the walkway with the side of his foot, as if it was a miniature soccer ball. He wanted Skye to kick it back to him, but she was too distracted.

She told him about the phone call to the rehab facility, how she had to write a letter, like some extra-credit homework assignment. Ever since Matt's snarky comments in the library and Skye's minimalist explanation, he'd been more attentive, even thoughtful. He was the only one of her college friends she trusted with any of the details of her past.

"A letter? Really?" Matt asked. "So what're you going to say?"

Skye kicked the stone—too hard, and it flew off into the bushes. Matt bent over and picked up another stone.

"I wish I knew," she said. "I'm hoping it'll just come to me."

Skye had already drafted two attempts. The first letter had turned out to be an angry rant: *What about me? Were you even thinking about me and how it felt to be dropped off at some stranger's house and left there? Not knowing if you were dead?* Admittedly, it felt good at the time, like throwing her cell phone against the wall. That had felt good, too, except she'd only done it once. Grace had made her pay for a new phone out of her own money, hard-earned money she'd made working at the sporting goods store weekends and summers. The second attempt was more solicitous: *I know it wasn't easy being a single parent, and I'm learning in my psychology class how addiction is a disease. Maybe you couldn't help it.*

Later that afternoon, reading over the latest draft, Skye decided it sounded like she was giving her mother a pass on any responsibility. She sat in front of the laptop, staring at the screen, then got up and made her bed and put clothes in the laundry basket in her closet, washed out the dirty bowls and spoons from making ramen the previous night. Evelyn was popping in and out of their room, and each time she opened the door, Skye toggled the computer screen and nonchalantly pulled up the paper she was writing for her philosophy class on Thomas Aquinas's *Five Proofs of the Existence of God.* "The notion of *faith* is troubling to us as philosophers," Dr. Morris had said, "but even so, we can sense the inexplicable in the world around us." Skye didn't necessarily believe in God, but she thought that some outside force must have moved her life off its intended course. In retrospect, she'd felt it that very moment the car had flown off the shoulder of the road, through the narrow gap between the trees into a snow-covered clearing, a moment that had revealed to her the thin line between extraordinary and disastrous.

Evelyn was opening and closing drawers, dragging out half her wardrobe. She finally put on a short skirt and matching tank top and then picked up a book and her laptop, announcing she was going out to study on the front lawn. There was more scurrying around in the room, and then the door closed and she was gone.

Skye toggled back to the letter. *Dear* ___ (she'd left this blank for now, not sure how to address her mother: Mom? Mother? Eva?), *I heard you were in treatment, and I hope it's helpful. Some woman named Lydia said I should write you a letter and maybe I could come see you. I started college in September and I really like it here, except I'm not sure about what to major in. I'd like to visit you sometime when you're ready, I'd like to know what happened. Why you didn't come back to get me. I'm sure you have some good reasons, but for the life of me I can't …* (Skye deleted this last part.) She signed it *Skye.*

Instead of *Dear Mom,* she decided to just write *Hi.* At the bottom of the letter, she included her e-mail and snail-mail addresses at college but not her phone number, not being ready for her mother to call, even if that was an option. She printed out and addressed the letter and on her way to class swung by the campus post office and slid it into the mail slot. Later that night, unable to concentrate on a calculus assignment, she reread the letter and thought maybe she should have said something about Grace and Jackson. And the part about wanting to know what had happened—it was probably too soon to ask about that. And she should have shown it to someone first, maybe Sylvia or Matt, but it was too late now. Drifting off to sleep, she could only hope that her mother would want to see her, even if she hadn't said it perfectly.

THREE IN THE MORNING. Skye abruptly woke up. Glare from the streetlamp flooded the room. Evelyn was mumbling in her sleep again, something about losing her keys—which she frequently did in her waking life.

Skye's stomach was twisted into a knot; her arms and legs were twitching, and her heart was pounding as if she were sprinting uphill. It wasn't the kind of nervousness she felt before a test or meeting new people at a party; it felt bigger, out of control, explosive, like a tornado or an earthquake. The first time she'd felt a real earthquake, Skye had been about five years old. She was watching TV; her mother was making dinner. When the first wave struck, they hid under the dining room table, which seemed like a bad idea, but her mother insisted. Soon after that, Skye learned about duck-and-cover in an earthquake drill at school and realized her mother had been right. But her mother was afraid to get out from under the table, and it was Skye reassuring her, telling her it was going to be okay. Her mother was afraid of the aftershocks, so they ate dinner under the table and then pulled blankets off the bed and even slept there until the next morning.

Skye sat up in bed and tried to take a deep breath, but the inhale was wiry and thin, and when she breathed out, the air came out in patchy bursts. Throwing off the blanket, she stretched her legs out and tried to focus on slowing her breathing, like they'd done in her psychology class when a guest speaker came to teach them about meditation. *Just breathe in cool air,* she thought. The electricity in her arms and legs began to subside. But then she was thinking about last weekend, when she'd gone with Matt and Casey and Sylvia and Alison and Jonathan to a battle-of-the-bands free concert in the gym. She'd liked how the music vibrated in her body. Growing up in Oakdale, she hadn't had much chance to go to concerts. Senior year, she and Jasmine and Jason had driven to the State Fair in Paso Robles to see Aerosmith, but that was the only time Grace and Jackson had allowed her that kind of freedom.

After the concert last weekend, she and Matt had come back to her room and fooled around on her bed. She wasn't sure how far she wanted to go; it felt good, kissing him, his hands slipping under her shirt, but it scared her, too, so she told Matt that Evelyn would probably walk in on them at any minute.

Suddenly she felt the screeching run through her body again. She tried to take a deep breath, but she couldn't fill her lungs. Evelyn rolled over in bed and pulled up the covers. It felt like the room was turned sideways. *The breath,* she thought. *Go back to the breath.* She counted more slowly, forcing herself to take a deep breath. *Let it go.* Her mother used to whisper "I love you" in her ear just as she was drifting off to sleep. Jackson said those words so seriously it made her smile. Grace, always more cautious, never said "I love you" but instead "Skye, you know we both love you," which seemed diluted and noncommittal.

Calm down, she thought again, but her in-breath was hot and jittery, and she threw off the covers and jumped out of bed, suddenly finding herself standing in the middle of the room. She put on her sweatshirt and ran down the hall to the bathroom. The lights in the public areas were on all night, although they didn't seem half as bright as the streetlamp streaming into her room.

In the bathroom, she sloshed water on her face and hands and waited while the water got warmer. It felt good. She turned down the mix of cold, letting the heat absorb into her hands. Leaning over, staring into the stream as it flowed from the faucet, she watched the water swirl in the sink and flow down the drain. It seemed trippy to her that water drained in the opposite direction south of the equator. Maybe sometime she'd get to see it for real.

She turned off the cold faucet. The steam rose, settling on her face and the mirror that reflected her hazy image. The neck and sleeves of her sweatshirt were damp. Her hands had turned pink, and she could vaguely feel the scalding heat accumulating in the palms of her hands and her fingers. But the hands weren't her hands. She stared at the long, untended fingernails and red knuckles. It seemed strange—the fingers were red and swollen. Turning the hands over, she studied the palms with their three sharply defined lines.

Outside the bathroom door there was a scuffling of slippers, and the door swung open. It was Vanessa from down the hall. Skye instinctively pulled away from the stream of water and looked down at her hands, now burning hot and tender. What had she done? She knew you should run cold water over a burn, but she didn't want Vanessa to see, so she hid her hands, fiery raw, cradled underneath her arms.

On the way back to her room, Skye realized she hadn't turned off the water. She thought Vanessa had asked her something. What was it? Something like, was she okay? She'd been too distracted by the water and her hands, which were burning now like hot pizza stuck to the roof of her mouth.

The pain was so bad that she had to pull her sweatshirt down over her hands to open the door. The sheets were cold when she climbed back into bed. Spreading her fingertips out, she tried to breathe in, one deep breath and then another. Her forehead was sweaty, her body feverish, and she tossed and turned with her hands above the sheets, trying to get comfortable.

"You weren't there," she muttered. On a vacation they'd taken to Stinson Beach, her mother had given her strict instructions about how far she could venture into the surf alone. "No further than your knees," she'd told Skye, and each time the waves doubled up against her thigh, her mother would call out, "Come back in, Skye, that's too far." But by midafternoon, her mother and Melanie and Julie were immersed in their conversation and whatever they were drinking from the cooler and not sharing with Skye. It was a broiling-hot day, and she must have wandered farther out, up to her waist. Then a wave smacked her in the face and knocked her down. She tumbled around on the sandy floor, her nose and her knees scraping against swirling seashells. She was choking on seawater. By the time Skye was able to stand up again, her knees were bruised, and salty mucous was dripping from her nose, stinging her nose and eyes and lips. The tide had dragged her what seemed like a long way down the beach. Suddenly she realized she could have drowned, and she wanted to find her mother, didn't want her mother to worry about her. A lifeguard found her standing alone, shivering, pebbles embedded in her knees, her lip split and bleeding. She was searching for the striped orange-and-yellow blanket and matching flowery umbrella. He held her hand, and they walked down the beach until she spotted her mother. "I couldn't find you," Skye said, crumpling into her arms.

"Sweetheart, I didn't go anywhere," Eva said. Her mother hadn't even realized she was missing.

Chapter Seven

On Thursday mornings, the clinical staff met for a weekly case conference. Six therapists, including Alix, who was a psychologist, three social workers, and two interns huddled together in a small group room, chairs arranged in a circle. The room overlooked a tall stand of trees and, just beyond that, the train tracks on the other side of a clearing. Nora Fielding, the clinic director, was presenting a case about a client with trichotillomania who'd pulled out so much of her hair that she needed to wear a wig. Now the client was scratching at her thighs and upper arms, raising thick welts of red and purple that had become infected. Nora was wondering if she was missing something, if the woman needed more than behavioral intervention, if perhaps her symptoms were a metaphor. Nora, usually able to mask any lack of confidence in her clinical skills, was talking about her own countertransference—the way a therapist's dynamic issues collide with the client's. She seemed especially raw and vulnerable, her voice trailing off at the end of each sentence so it was hard to hear what she was saying. One of the interns, Ted, speculated about a possible history of abuse. Of course, it was common in cases of trichotillomania, Nora said. Betsy interrupted, saying, "It's not always abuse." Scott asked about the client's relationship with her father, certain he'd been distant and critical. But Nora thought if anything he'd been overly attentive. The other intern, Monica, was dutifully taking notes. Alix could have predicted what each of them would say. It was always the same—Ted saw abuse; Betsy rolled her eyes (*Sometimes a cigar is just a cigar*); Scott pontificated about family dynamics; Nora was most interested in the therapist's own personal issues impacting the client; Monica, fearful she might be wrong, said nothing. Alix generally deferred to the clients' strengths, their resilience, the ways they overcame challenges rather than succumbing to them. But she was distracted, thinking about Skye, who'd shown up in her office the previous afternoon without an appointment, the hood of her sweatshirt pulled up over her head, her eyes puffy and red. She'd tracked down Mrs. McNulty and written to her mother. Alix wished Skye had shown her the letter before she'd sent it. At least then Alix might have been able to guide her or encourage her to wait. Then she'd shown Alix her hands, red and raw, her knuckles peeling.

"Two nights ago … uh … I don't know …" She shook her head, her eyes filling with tears. Then she bit her lip and turned her head away, trying not to cry. "I don't know. Really. All of a sudden I was in the bathroom, and the water was too hot, and it was like I went somewhere else."

Alix leaned in closer to Skye. "Let me see," she said.

Skye put her hands out in front of her. Alix looked closely at the peeling skin and raw edges around her knuckles, touching the backs of her hands softly. "Does it hurt?"

Skye nodded and pulled back. "Why would I do it?"

Alix paused for a moment, considering what to say. "It's a way of coping."

"What if she doesn't want to see me?" Skye asked.

Alix responded reflexively, not giving much thought at the time to the merits of caution over truth. "She might not." And then she walked Skye over to the Health Center so the doctor could look at her hands.

Recalling it now, Alix winced at her curt response. She wondered what the girl's mother would do with the letter. And how would Skye deal with the waiting—not to mention the aftermath?

The silence in the room startled her. Betsy and Ted and Nora were all staring in her direction; she hadn't heard Nora's question.

"I'm sorry," Alix said, shaking off the image of Skye's hands and the girl's face, tense with pain. "I'm just a little distracted."

Nora looked puzzled and asked again about the client they'd been discussing. "What do you think?"

"I'm not sure," she said.

After the meeting, Betsy was standing in her office doorway, leaning against the doorjamb. "Are you okay?"

"Not really." Alix waved her into the room. Betsy closed the door and sat down.

Alix told her about the session with Skye. It was obvious that Skye had opened a can of worms she couldn't handle—finding her mother, writing the letter. It wasn't a coincidence she'd felt overwhelmed to the point of scorching her hands in the bathroom sink. The girl had dissociated—broken with reality. It was a common phenomenon, especially in adolescents not able to handle strong emotions thrust upon them.

"I'd like you to see her," Alix said.

Betsy shook her head. "Not this time. You've been sloughing off the tough cases ever since Richard died. It's time you came back to the living."

The last couple of months, Betsy had been there for her, filling in the gaps, coaxing her back to work, seeing the more difficult, distressed clients, consulting with her, holding her hand. But lately, Alix had begun to feel impatient with anything more than the simplest, most straightforward patients, those presenting with depression or anxiety—the bread and butter of therapists. After a couple of sessions trying to sort out what might be going on, Alix found herself more and more disengaged, unable to connect with her clients, and she'd refer them to Betsy or one of the interns who seemed to have an endless supply of empathy.

"I'm worried about what's going on with this girl," Alix said. "And I'm afraid I might be missing something. You could see her—at least for a second opinion."

"Here's your second opinion," Betsy said, "sight unseen. Whether you like it or not, sometimes clients give us what we need."

"Really, Betsy, is that the best you can do? I'm struggling here, and you know it's not easy for me, asking for help. And then I get this crap from you. Like this student's been sent to see me by some unknown force, taunting me with my own inadequacies?"

"Not inadequacies. Blind spots."

ALIX THOUGHT IT WOULD be good to get out of town for the day. She called the restaurant to make sure it was open in the off-season—the fish dive where she and Richard had had their first date and where, later, at the beach across the street, she'd watched him go hang gliding. Then she printed out a map with directions, even though it was a straight shot south on the Pacific Coast Highway. By midmorning she'd arrived at the restaurant and was standing on the cliff above the beach, watching the hang gliders skim out over the ocean. It was crowded with bikers and families with young children and the hang-gliding crowd, and she had to stand in line before ordering precisely the same thing she'd ordered that first day with Richard: fried calamari and popcorn shrimp, a side of coleslaw, water with lemon, no ice. Grabbing a handful of paper napkins, she wiped the sand off the picnic table and bench and sat down, squeezed in next to a large family, across from the same back corner where they'd eaten that first time. The sky was clear, and there was a light breeze; Alix wondered if this was a good day for hang gliding or if more wind would be better, or a more steady wind. She was sorry she hadn't gone hang gliding with Richard more than just that one time. To experience it without the fear. He'd cajoled her into opening up to so many possibilities, and since his death all she'd done was clamp down again.

She set the tray down in the middle of the table, with the shrimp and calamari, as if she were sharing with someone sitting across from her. A small boy with short-cropped hair was sitting next to her, squirming, staring at her and then at the young woman next to him, presumably his mother, and she could feel his gritty legs against her, caked with sand. She tried to shift toward the end of the bench, but there wasn't much room, and he just scooted down next to her.

At first, she attributed the queasiness in her stomach to the full thermos of coffee she had drunk on the way down. Or maybe it was watching the hang gliders with a mixture of envy and trepidation, afraid they'd crash into the bluff but at the same time remembering how it had felt to soar above the ocean. It had been a moment, crystal clear, of transformation. Halfway through the shrimp and calamari, scooping up the salsa, her mouth on fire, her eyes watering, she found herself crying uncontrollably, not aloud but silently, the tears streaming down her cheeks into the calamari, her mouth soggy with breading and mucus. Each time she looked across the table, expecting to see Richard, he wasn't there. The little boy pulled on the hem of her blouse, looking up at her as if to ask, *Are you okay?* Alix shielded her face in the remaining napkins, wondering what she'd been thinking—coming here alone. Without him. She cleared the table and threw out the remaining food, purposefully leaving behind the tiny paper cup of salsa.

Out in the parking lot, Alix kept her eyes on the road, avoiding the view toward the ocean and the beach below. She quickly got in her car and drove for twenty miles along the highway before realizing she was heading in the wrong direction. That was enough for her to dissolve again, sobbing. It seemed silly, allowing a simple mistake like making a wrong turn to affect her so acutely, but after all, even a ten-year-old could figure out which direction to drive, with the ocean always westward.

She pulled into a turnout overlooking the water and watched the white crests of waves crash, one on top of another, and then disappear underneath the surface. The pain was eating at her insides, and for the first time, she understood why someone might slice a knife across their wrist not to kill themselves (although there'd been a handful of times over the years when she'd certainly thought about killing herself) but as a distraction from the pain—a pain that felt like something was tearing her heart apart one fiber at a time. She could hear Betsy, in her cut-and-dried manner, chiding her. "Yes, he's dead," she'd say. "Get a grip. It's going to be a messy ride."

She found her cell phone and scrolled through her contact list: Barry Chan, Ben Fontaine, Betsy Gardner. She must have pressed her number without realizing it.

"Alix?" Betsy asked. "Are you okay?" Her voice sounded far away; Alix put her ear to the phone.

She hadn't meant to call her—not like this. She wanted to hang up, act as if she hadn't actually phoned in a panic, but it was too late now.

"Betsy?" Alix was aware of the shaking in her voice; Betsy would know right away that something was terribly wrong.

Then Betsy was talking to her, a muddled stream of words from afar. "Breathe ... going to be okay ... all very normal ... just grieving ... Altoids."

"What?"

"Altoids. Do you have any of those really strong mints with you?"

"Yes." She kept a box in the car. "Right here in the side pocket of the door."

"Put a couple of them in your mouth. Keep your eyes open," Betsy said. "You're going to be fine. Open the windows. Tell me what you see."

Alix scanned the skyline. Dark clouds were huddled together off in the distance. The marine layer was thickening, and flames darted from an oil platform. Closer to shore, rogue waves spewed onto the rocks. She bit into the mints. A sharp, sweet taste stung the roof of her mouth and moved up into her nostrils. Pelicans were diving for food. A spray of cormorants surfed the waves. Two sailboats zigzagged through the water; a couple was strolling along the surf's edge. Alix opened the box and took out two more mints.

There were long strands of seaweed straddling the beach. A small creek trickled to the ocean.

Betsy stayed on the phone until Alix felt in control, enough to turn around and get back on the road. She made Alix promise to stop by on her way home. In the background, Alix could hear Elise and Stan having a heated discussion; jazz was playing on the radio. It was obvious that talking her down was not what Betsy had planned for the weekend.

By the time Alix got home, it was four in the afternoon. She called Betsy to apologize for creating a scene. "Sorry, I was too tired to stop by. I'll see you on Monday at work," she said.

"We're just having leftovers," Betsy said. "Come over anyway. The last thing you need is to sit there alone."

But it was easier to beg off, nuke dinner in the microwave, crawl into bed. She poured herself a glass of wine and sat in the living room, staring out the front window at the angle of light inching downward, trees lengthening, like sharp points across the evening sky.

Chapter Eight

DR. MORRIS WAS DARTING from his lectern, where he'd gingerly placed a blueberry scone and a cup of coffee, to the whiteboard, scrawling definitions and calling out students' names. He was lecturing on John Locke's notion of *tabula rasa* and identity and had sketched a surprisingly plausible cartoon rendition of John Locke with the words *psychological identity* coming out of a bubble from Locke's mouth. Morris was engaging the class via his own brand of Socratic method, posing questions and getting students to stick their answers on the whiteboard with different-colored sticky notes, grouped by theme. Skye was leaning across the small desktop. Her hands, still burning and raw, were concealed in her sweatshirt pockets. She'd told the nurse in the Health Center about the scalding water in the dorms. "Oh, my," the nurse said. "They need to turn down the thermostat." Then she gave Skye a course of antibiotics and a salve for her hands. "They're going to be quite tender for a few days, but then you'll be good as new."

One row over, Matt had his laptop open, shifting back and forth between taking notes and finishing his physics homework, due next period. Skye was still mulling over what to write on the sticky notes in case Morris called on her. She kept glancing over at Matt, who was slouched over uncomfortably, his long body barely fitting under the desk. He hadn't shaved that morning, and he looked scruffy, and his curly hair had grown down to his eyebrows. Periodically he'd shake his head and swipe the curls off his face. It was a casual gesture she thought was sexy.

"As long as we remember the past—or portions of the past," Morris said, "then we experience our identity as psychologically contiguous with the self."

Psychologically contiguous, she thought. What did that mean? There were days when she couldn't tell the difference between her mother and Grace. Not that the two of them were alike in any fundamental way, but she found herself superimposing Grace's words onto the space in between her mother's absence. She couldn't remember if it was her mother who had taught her to swim or Grace. There was just a vague recollection swirling in her head: a woman's arms gently supporting her, the chill of cold water, her new bathing suit, flip-flops that skidded on the smooth, tiled changing-room floor. Only her mother would have known how to do flip turns and would have giggled with her over smearing spit on her goggles to keep them from fogging up. But the pool in her memory was warm and sunny, the pool she'd gone to every summer in Oakdale. And Jasmine was there. They were horsing around, and Jackson taught them how to dive, jumping off the board feet first. Then he taught them to lean out over the edge of the board, the tips of their fingers piercing the surface of the water.

But it was her mother soothing her when she belly-flopped and calling out "Good girl!" and rubbing her shivering body and hair with a thick towel. What if you couldn't remember whole chunks of your past? Then what? What happened to your identity then?

She was deep in thought and Dr. Morris was calling on random students when her phone rang, and she had to squirrel around in her backpack to find the phone and turn it off. The zipper on her backpack scraped against the back of her hand, and she grimaced. On the screen, just before it turned dark, was a long-distance phone number she recognized—the rehab facility in Shasta.

Staring at her from across the room, Morris took a bite out of the scone and then washed it down with a sip of coffee. His pace never slowed, but his face took on an expression of curiosity; he smirked and then looked down at the thumbnail photos on the desk. The whole class was turned toward her, even Matt, whose eyes held a mixture of concern and pity.

"Something we can help you with?" Morris asked.

"No. Sorry. I'm fine," she said.

Morris continued with his lecture, and Skye fell into distraction, wondering if it was her mother who had called or Lydia. It was nearly impossible to stay glued to her seat the rest of class. But she didn't want Morris to catch her by surprise again or, worse yet, ask her to write something on the board, so she kept her head down taking notes, glancing periodically at Matt, who still hadn't finished his physics homework. Most days, she liked the class—and Morris. He made their discussions relevant, and he had a good sense of humor. And despite seeming overly rigid and harsh the first day of class, he was one of the best teachers she'd ever had, even better than Mr. Sullivan, who'd taught an English/history combo when she was in eleventh grade.

"Jeez," Matt said when class was over. "I thought Morris was going to answer the phone for you."

Skye had turned her cell phone back on and was staring at the missed call. "I think it was my mother," she said.

"Really?" Matt was hovering over her as if, like Morris, he might grab the phone and listen to the message himself. It was easy for Matt to embrace all of the excitement without any of the reservations.

"Hey, what happened to your hands?" he said, noticing them for the first time.

"The bathroom sink attacked me," she said, trying to make light of it. Skye held the phone up to her ear. The voice mail was from Lydia: *Call me back.*

Skye slipped the phone back into her pants pocket. "She doesn't want to see me, I know it. Why else would she sic Lydia on me?"

"That's all she said? Just call her back?"

"There might have been more."

"Let me listen."

She scrolled back to the message and handed him the phone, then packed up her notebook and shoved her pen into the side pocket of her backpack.

Matt was closing his laptop with one hand, squinting, as if it were hard to hear the message. He stood listening for what felt to Skye like a long time, then handed the phone back. "It sounded to me like your mother's happy to know you're in college," he said, "but she's not ready to see you. Maybe she doesn't have phone privileges yet. Remember how Lydia said she had to make progress in the program? Anyway, it's good she's still there. Don't you think that's a good sign?"

"A good sign, how?" said Skye.

Matt slung the backpack over his shoulder. "I don't know, it just seems like a good thing." He seemed eager for Skye to spin it a positive way. "Anyway, I gotta go. My physics prof hates it when we're late."

The hallway was dark and eerily quiet, more like an unlit cave, her footsteps echoing against the bare walls. In her head, she was finishing the conversation with Lydia.

Skye: *When do you think she'll be ready?*

Lydia: *You're going to have to wait.*

Skye: *Isn't there anything else you can tell me?*

Skye frowned, as if it were a real conversation.

But there was only dead air. And blinding sunlight as she walked out of the building.

SATURDAY NIGHT, THEY CROWDED into the lounge opposite Matt's room for a *Law and Order* marathon. Empty pizza boxes strewn across a side table, soda cans crushed and free-thrown on top of the garbage pail, the vague smell of gym shorts and shaving lotion. Skye was sitting cross-legged on the couch next to Matt, whose long legs were stretched out in front of him. Balanced atop the garbage can, Casey was bouncing gently, coaxing more trash into the bin.

"Philosophers," Jonathan said, "they're so full of self-important crap. All of them." He'd taken control of the remote and was sitting on the floor flipping channels during a commercial break, a can of beer on the floor next to him. Except for Casey, who said he never drank, they all had a beer. Skye opened a can and took a sip. They weren't allowed to have alcohol on campus, but the RA wouldn't say anything—in fact, rumor was he'd passed a joint around in his room during orientation week.

The few times he'd made it to class, Jonathan sat in the back, periodically taunting Morris with irreverent comments meant to test his patience: "What's the average salary of a philosophy graduate, anyway?"

Sylvia, sitting almost on top of Alison, was doodling in her journal, what looked like a caricature of Jonathan with his beard and thin lips drawn back in a tight sneer.

A few weeks ago, they'd been studying Descartes. Jonathan had raised his hand. "Is the final cumulative?"

Morris picked up a half-eaten lemon bar that was sitting on top of his briefcase, took a bite and then a swig of coffee. Motioning toward Jonathan with his coffee cup as if he were offering a toast, he said, "For you, yes. Everyone else gets to throw away all their notes from the beginning of the semester. Burn them if you want. I don't care."

"Wait. That's not fair."

"I suppose it isn't," Morris said, turning back to his notes and the whiteboard, which was scrawled with quotes and definitions about Descartes's hyperbolic position of doubt.

"You're just pissed at him," Skye said, "because he's smarter than you are. Besides, what if we didn't make any assumptions? Just start from scratch and see what's really there. I mean, I don't want anyone making assumptions about me or about my life or what I might be thinking. Everyone's making up stories and then acting like the story's true."

They all knew about her mother. Whatever gaps Skye had left in the story, she was pretty sure Sylvia had filled them in.

"Of course that's what you'd think," Jonathan said.

"What does that mean?" Matt said, as if Skye needed defending.

The credits were rolling, and they were waiting for the next episode to begin. Casey had his laptop out, playing Angry Birds during the commercials.

Jonathan grabbed another can of beer and turned the sound back on. "I saw this one," he said.

Matt's thigh was touching Skye's; his hand was resting on her thigh.

"We should go into the City," Sylvia said, "to Golden Gate Park. And I've always wanted to go to that bookstore, City Lights—you know, where Lawrence Ferlinghetti and Allen Ginsberg hung out."

"Did you see the movie *Howl*?" Casey asked.

"Hey, Skye, you must know great spots in San Francisco," Sylvia said. "I heard about this combination Laundromat/café where they have great burgers and an open mic every weekend."

"We could find your old apartment," Matt said.

"I was only ten when I moved away," Skye said.

Skye didn't see the point of being subjected to some other family living in their old apartment, but it could be fun to spend a day in the City. Even if she wasn't too keen on visiting her old neighborhood. "Sure," she said. "The neighborhood around Golden Gate Park is pretty cool."

They watched another two episodes; it was past midnight by the time Matt and Skye walked back to her dorm.

They were standing outside Skye's room, the hallway dimly lit, music playing a couple doors down, a heavy beat rattling the walls. Matt leaned way over and kissed her on the lips, Skye standing on her tiptoes, and then their tongues were weaving together, and suddenly they were in her room on the bed with half their clothes off. They hadn't talked about having sex. His hands were running over her breasts, his lips on her neck. And she'd never touched a guy before. He unzipped his pants, and he was holding her hand and guiding her. Touching him was scary; he was hard, and she couldn't imagine how it would fit inside her. But she felt compelled to keep going, as if a switch had been flipped on. She leaned backward, exposing her neck; his tongue was wet on her nipples. I'm not ready, she thought. But she wanted to know what her friends knew, wanted to say she had a boyfriend, to feel close and safe and wanted.

He was taking a condom out of his back pocket. At least that was what it looked like he was doing.

She pulled away, her back against the wall. "Not yet," she said, surprising herself. She turned around to see his eyes in the dim light from the streetlamp, but she couldn't read what he was thinking.

"I'm sorry. I'm just not ready," she said.

He leaned away from her toward the edge of the bed. Then he got up, zipped up his pants, and left without saying anything.

A couple of minutes later, her phone dinged. She was curled up on the bed, her head sunk into the pillow. Matt had texted her: *Sorry. Talk later.*

Chapter Nine

By the end of October, they were all in the groove of studying and going to class and a settled rhythm in their new lives. Sylvia had switched rooms, so she and Alison were sharing a room, and they were alternately hot and heavy or on the brink of breaking up. Alison wasn't sure she was a lesbian, maintaining that her relationship with Sylvia was only experimentation. Last week, in the breakup phase, Sylvia had asked Housing for yet another room change. This week, she wasn't so sure. Jonathan had dropped philosophy. Actually, the rumor was that Dr. Morris had called Jonathan into his office and made dropping the class worth his while.

Skye and Matt were studying for a philosophy midterm in Matt's room. It was past 10 o'clock, and Casey was still in the computer lab working on a programming assignment. Casey was a neat kind of guy: his bed was made, three pairs of shoes lined up on the closet floor, textbooks arranged on the shelf. He had a gold-and-green team pennant from his high school tacked to the wall. On Matt's side of the room, a pile of dirty clothes was sprawled over the chair, empty soda cans littered his desk, and they were lying on top of the blanket, loosely pulled up over the pillow. Fielding Hall, where the freshman guys lived, was older than Mary Warren. The rooms were slightly larger, and they had bathrooms in each room, an advantage only if they were kept clean. It was obvious Matt wasn't doing his share. A dingy towel was usually balled up next to the sink, plaid boxers on the floor, and streaks of toothpaste and scum on the counter and sink. It wasn't that Skye was a neat freak; even so, she tried not to use their bathroom.

Matt got up to throw a wrapper in the trash. "Hey, did you ever get hold of that woman from the rehab place? What was her name? Lydia?"

"What's the point?" Skye said. "My mother's *not ready*. Whatever that means."

"Maybe you could just show up."

"Yeah, right." They were reading about Kant and deontology. "Get this," she said, holding her finger as a place marker on the page. "Kant believed it's not the consequences of our actions that are important but our intentions. Maybe my mother had good intentions that just didn't pan out the way she planned."

"So you're just gonna wait?" Matt leaned over and kissed her on the cheek, then put his arm around her. "I'd go with you."

Skye twisted a strand of his curly hair and watched it bounce back into place. "Really?" she asked.

"Sure. I have a friend who goes to Shasta Community College. We could crash on his floor."

"You probably have to be family to get in," she said, wondering if even she qualified.

She'd reread the same paragraph three times while Matt hovered over her, drawing his fingers through her hair. He took the book from her, placed it on the floor by the bed, and then leaned over and turned out the light. "So if we do it, the consequences don't matter?" They rolled together into the tight space of his bed, side by side, his hand resting on her waist, his legs dangling over the edge of the bed.

"I don't think that's what Kant meant."

He kissed her, and suddenly, her body was pulsing, her breathing short and pressured. She slid her hand under his shirt, feeling the warmth and smooth skin of his back, and she pulled him toward her. Their legs were wound together, and he was unbuttoning her shirt, one button at a time, and then he slid off his own shirt, his lips grazing hers. His breath was sweet and moist, and he was using his tongue to tease her. She could feel her skin against his. The forward momentum was leading to the same out-of-control place. But this time she didn't want to stop.

They'd barely talked about the other night when things had gone too fast. "It's okay," Matt had said the next day. "Let's slow down." But they hadn't figured out how to stop before it got out of control. Before there was no stopping.

Skye reached down to unzip Matt's pants. It was tricky doing it with one hand; she needed his help. It felt like a spinning eddy in her belly and between her legs, and it seemed to Skye that Matt was feeling the same craving. Despite what they'd talked about, she didn't want to think about slowing down.

Then Matt put his hand on top of her hand. "Wait," he said.

Skye pulled back and looked into his eyes.

"Let's not do this," he said. "Not yet. Not before we talk about it."

They continued to kiss. Skye felt her body relax, as if she were drained of all that energy. She figured it must have been hard for Matt to stop, but she was glad he had. Skye wanted to think of herself as smarter and more cautious than her mother, who'd obviously gotten pregnant without planning on it.

Later that night she had trouble falling asleep. The excess swirling in her body. She could still taste the saltiness on his lips.

IT WAS EARLY ON Saturday when they met up at the Veranda for coffee and donuts—Casey, Matt and Skye, Jonathan, Sylvia and Alison—and walked down the tree-lined entryway that led beyond the campus boundaries. The trees had begun to turn brown, trembling in the dry wind. Skye hadn't strayed more than a few blocks from campus since Jackson had dropped her off at school. Her footsteps were crunchy on the pavement, and she picked up a handful of dried leaves, rubbed them in her hands, and watched the pieces scatter. Sylvia and Alison were giggling about some inside joke. Jonathan was trying to engage her in a debate about the death penalty. It rubbed her the wrong way; he always wanted to argue, whether he believed what he was saying or not. Why hadn't he just worked a little harder in philosophy class?

"It's punishment for evil," he said. "And don't you think there's evil in the world?"

She knew there was no winning with Jonathan. Besides, it was Saturday, and she didn't want to be thinking about class and homework and how much she had to do before Monday. Passing through the campus stone arch felt like breaking free. She was going back to the City for the first time since the accident.

Casey and Matt were leaning over the subway map. They'd figured out the fastest route to the City: take the bus to the Fruitvale station and then BART across the bay to Market Street.

An hour later, coming up from the station, there were seagulls and pigeons and the energy of a city filled with businesspeople in suits. There were women with head scarves and tourists speaking French, German, and languages Skye couldn't identify. It was a block to the Embarcadero. Fishing boats and container ships were docked along the wharf. Swarms of tourists were eating shrimp cocktail and chunks of sourdough bread.

They walked across the street to the Ferry Building and the Farmers Market, with its stalls filled with flowers, imported cheeses, breads, fresh fruits and vegetables, handmade pottery, and blown-glass plates. Wandering through the stalls, they sampled bits of cheese and olives and strawberries. Sylvia bought a pair of silver earrings, Alison a scented candle. Out on the plaza, they could see the clock tower and sculptures. A few streets over was the towering, pyramid-shaped Transamerica Building. They sat along the edge of a fountain and watched the water pouring out from massive hunks of concrete block heaped on top of each other in a sculpture. A blind saxophonist was playing jazz, his guide dog lying next to him.

Matt thought it would be fun to climb the Coit Tower for a view of the city, so they walked up the street to the cable-car junction and waited in line while the cars were manually turned on a metal disc and then filled with passengers. Skye had a vague recollection of having been at the Embarcadero. The clanging of cable-car bells, the fishy smell of the wharf, the diesel fumes and street musicians all seemed so familiar. Even the streets that headed steeply uphill and then dropped off sharply on the other side of the crest. It was slowly coming back to her. She pulled a coin purse from her backpack and got money out for the cable car. When they got on, they moved to the back of the car, where it was open, like riding in a caboose. The cable-car ground its way up Market in squealing stops and starts.

When they got off, they walked up Telegraph Hill to Lombard Street and up the three hundred stairs to Coit Tower. A tall, pencil-shaped column, the tower had been built in 1933 by Lillie Coit, an eccentric urban legend who wore men's trousers, liked to gamble, and smoked cigars. It was dark inside, but the walls were covered with vibrant frescoes painted decades earlier by local muralists funded by the first WPA Public Arts project. Jonathan was taking a political science course, and he'd read about the Diego Rivera murals. "It's about socialism," he said. "Check out the steelworks and farmers and railroad men. It's working people building California. But it's the businessmen reaping the rewards."

Skye was staring at the depiction of a San Francisco street scene; it was the corner of Washington and Montgomery. The mural showed throngs of men in long coats and fedoras, women with fur collars, children playing, a man in a uniform waving a red flag, a postal worker opening a mailbox. There was a car accident in the background, and in the foreground, a man was being robbed at gunpoint in full view. It was a messy scene full of energy and scandal and disarray. Skye felt herself being drawn in, as if she'd been jettisoned onto the street. All along, she'd remembered the city as a tangle of people rushing off to important business, and she liked the energy and commotion. But staring at the mural now, she realized her recollection had been part fantasy, conveniently omitting the times she'd felt uneasy or worried she might not be safe. Jonathan was right: it was a mural depicting inequality and worker strife, but to Skye it was about danger and being torn apart by the unknown.

She hadn't noticed that Matt was standing next to her, and it startled her when he reached out for her hand. At first she pulled away. "You okay?" he asked. Skye nodded and took his hand. They all rode the elevator to the top of the tower; it was a clear day, and the view was spectacular. Casey's family lived in the City, near Chinatown, and he'd been to the top of the tower plenty of times. He pointed out the Golden Gate Bridge and the Bay Bridge and the Financial District and the San Francisco Hills—Russian Hill and Nob Hill. Skye tried to remember if she'd ever been to the top of the Coit Tower, but her mother hadn't been much of a tourist, and the view wasn't familiar to her. She could feel the breeze in her face as she scanned the City. *Her* city, however unfamiliar it was to her now. She thought she'd like to get reacquainted with it. Except for the couple of blocks where she and her mother had lived. She wasn't ready to see her old neighborhood, at least not yet.

After coming back down, they sat on the grass in the park by a sculpture of Christopher Columbus.

Jonathan was lying on the ground, using his backpack as a pillow. "It's pretty ironic," he said. "Those murals inside about socialists and workers, and here's Christopher Columbus out front." No one else seemed especially interested in his observation.

Matt passed around a bag of trail mix. "I think we should find Skye's old neighborhood," he said.

They all turned to look at her. Skye didn't want to have anything to do with looking for her old apartment. She would have been happy to send her friends off by themselves. Maybe she should have been clearer with them, especially with Matt. Wasn't it Alix who'd implied she should go slowly? *I'm not ready*, she could have said. But that would have meant letting on that the past still had a stranglehold on her. Maybe her friends already knew that.

"Sure," she said, only because she didn't know how to say no. "Except I'm not sure where it is." She poured a handful of the trail mix into the palm of her hand and picked out the raisins and chocolate bits to eat first.

"How far is it to Golden Gate Park? Didn't you live near the park?" Casey asked. He got out his phone to look it up. "About six miles' walk or two buses," he said.

"I'd rather eat dim sum in Chinatown," Jonathan said. It was one of the few times Skye agreed with Jonathan. But he was immediately outvoted.

"It's like *Harriet the Spy*," Sylvia said. "Scope out Skye's neighborhood. Find out who's living there now." Minus Jonathan and Skye, they all seemed enthusiastic for the hunt.

They walked down Telegraph Hill through the Financial District and got on a bus heading toward Golden Gate Park. Skye sat by the window and stared out at the tall, silvery buildings next to three- and four-story apartments. There was the corner Laundromat, a liquor store, the elementary school behind a black iron fence. The apartments had tall windows with wooden frames, concrete steps leading up to the front, and small garages at street level. So far, nothing seemed more than vaguely familiar. She remembered this much: the apartment she'd lived in with her mother had been more ornate, painted green and purple—an old Victorian near Alamo Square, on Grove Street. Her mother had made her memorize the address when she was in kindergarten. Was it 1453 Grove? 1643 Grove?

The bus passed close to Alamo Park. Skye leaned against

the window to try to see it, but then the bus turned onto Fulton. She'd known—then—how to get to Golden Gate Park from her house. They'd walked there lots of times on the weekends. Toward the end, when her mother was awake all night and slept most of the day, Skye would walk by herself down the more populated streets and then across to the Panhandle, a narrow strip of grass leading to the park. She'd buy ice cream from the vendor and watch kids fly kites and bicyclists circle through the park.

Matt was sitting next to her, leaning over her shoulder. "Hey," she said, pointing out the window, "I remember that Japanese restaurant. And the used bookstore." Her mother would occasionally buy her hot chocolate at the café next door.

"Then let's get off here," Matt said. He pulled the cord, and they piled out of the back of the bus onto Fulton Avenue.

They were all hungry; Skye remembered that there had been a little Italian sandwich shop on Grove Street. Casey looked it up on his phone; it was still there, just a couple of blocks away.

"So is this near your house?" Matt asked.

She was pretty sure they just had to walk a couple of blocks farther on Grove. All the cars parked so closely together, the narrow streets and tightly packed houses, made her feel edgy. Her eyelid was twitching; she let go of Matt's hand. The house on the corner, she thought maybe a friend from school had lived there. She wasn't ready to see her old apartment, but still, she couldn't help being curious. It seemed best to let her friends decide which direction they'd head in and just see what happened. "I don't know," she said. "I think it's down this street, but I'm not sure how far."

When Skye had thought about finding her mother, she had always imagined they'd arrange to meet at the coffee shop around the corner or maybe the used bookstore. Everything would fall into place—it wouldn't be as if they'd never been apart, but it wouldn't be difficult or strained, either. They'd resume their lives in the same neighborhood. Perhaps not in the same apartment, but somewhere nearby. By the time she was in high school, when it was obvious her fantasized reunion wouldn't happen the way she'd planned, Skye thought she might simply bump into her mother in the same places—the sandwich shop or the park or the Laundromat where they'd washed their clothes on Sunday afternoons. Laundry hadn't been a dreary chore, at least not in the beginning, because her mother brought books on tape and they shared the earbuds. Other days, they wandered through the neighborhood while the clothes were drying and her mother pointed out the architectural features of the buildings—not just the Victorian houses but the neoclassical Park Branch Library, where they'd checked out books, and Our Lady of Guadalupe Church, and City Hall in the beaux arts style. Her mother also told her about Harvey Milk, the first openly gay politician, and Mayor Moscone, who'd been murdered by Dan White in the City Hall. He'd pleaded "not guilty" based on having eaten too many Twinkies. As a kid, she wasn't sure if her mother might have been making up that last part. That maybe she needed a reason for not allowing Skye to eat junk food.

But those weren't the more recent memories, the dark memories tucked away in a remote space in her mind, memories that were only now beginning to surface again. Something had happened since she'd left Grace and Jackson's and come to school. In the middle of the night now, there were dreams and vague sensations—a tender touch on her back, the tousling of her hair. Pounding on the kitchen table. Murmuring and pacing and moaning.

The sandwich shop was still there. She was surprised at

how well she remembered it: a hole-in-the-wall Italian deli with salami strung up over the counter and a meat slicer and hunks of cheese and roast beef and antipasto in the deli case. It smelled of kosher dill pickles and fresh bread. The wood floor was worn and shiny from years of polishing. They got sandwiches to go, wrapped in waxed paper, and Skye took a bottle of root beer out of the cooler, remembering how her mother used to buy it for her as a treat. She stood near the front door and stared out at the view of apartments and stray dogs sniffing at trees. A memory flitted through her mind: they'd been playing checkers at a table out front, but then her mother had gotten upset about something and stormed off toward home before finishing the game.

When everyone had their food, they stood outside the deli, debating about where to sit and eat their sandwiches. There was a park on the corner; they walked across the street and sat on the grass, looking out over Skye's old neighborhood. "I think it's a couple of blocks down," she said. But her friends were busy chomping on their pickles and chips and didn't say anything. Skye wasn't sure they'd heard her. She gently elbowed Matt. He was concentrating on his turkey sandwich, but he asked if she wanted to head that way. Skye shrugged and pursed her lips. She wasn't sure *what* she wanted to do.

Jonathan had a Frisbee in his backpack, and after finishing their sandwiches, they spread out and threw it to each other. Skye was pretty good—she used to play Frisbee with Jasmine and Seth and Jason back in Oakdale. Matt tossed it to her, but she was looking across the park at a young mother and her two kids, and the Frisbee nearly hit her in the face. She and Eva had flown kites in the same spot.

Or was that Jackson in Oakdale Park, down the street from their house?

With the sun lower in the sky, it was getting chilly; fog was pushing against the hills. Her friends seemed to have forgotten all about the hunt for her old apartment. They took the bus back to Fisherman's Wharf. Skye was quiet, distant, and Matt asked if she was okay. She nodded, but in a way that suggested she didn't want to talk. She was disappointed in her friends. They'd seemed excited about helping her find her old life, but of course, they couldn't do it without her.

They got clam chowder and sat at a picnic table along the water and watched the light fade behind the Bay Bridge. Seagulls were scavenging fish heads left on the pier, and it smelled of diesel and saltwater and fish. A ferry boat from Sausalito pulled into the dock, and passengers disembarked. Skye wished they were already back at school; she wanted to be alone. But she was sitting between Matt and Casey, who were talking over her head, something about intramural soccer.

Sylvia was gossiping about her ex-roommate, Chelsea. "She's spreading rumors," Sylvia said, "telling people I pounced on Alison." She turned to Alison. "Honey, tell them what Whitney said."

Alison looked blankly at her.

"You know, just before your econ class."

But either Alison didn't remember or she wasn't inclined to repeat it.

According to Sylvia, Rachel was still throwing up in the bathroom, claiming it was the stress of being away from home, but Heather down the hall had heard that she just wanted to be skinny for her sister's wedding in November. There was a girl in Spruce Manor, the dorm next to theirs, who'd been raped at a frat party over the weekend. The frat claimed she'd been drunk and come on to the guy. Everyone in her dorm was taking sides, and they'd had to play musical chairs with the rooms. In the end, the girl dropped out of school and went back home.

It felt to Skye as if she wasn't part of the conversation; it was just going on all around her. None of it was important, and it made her feel insignificant, as if her own past was nothing more than a juicy story to gossip about. It was obvious her friends were talking about her when she wasn't around.

In the subway on the way back to campus, Matt held Skye's hand while she stared out the window. "We can go another time and figure out where you lived," he said. He must have realized she was upset or disappointed that they'd just gone off to the park instead of finding her old apartment. Later, back in her room, maybe she'd explain it to him: how being in the City reminded her of the past, living with her mother, and how all those memories, stirred up, left her feeling rattled and unsteady, as if she'd been knocked around in an earthquake.

SKYE TURNED IN HER calculus midterm early. There was one word problem she had no idea how to solve—something about manufacturing *x* units of commodity and using marginal analysis to approximate profit and loss. Too many of the words were unfamiliar, and she fooled around with substituting a bag of groceries for the word *commodity.* Still, the question didn't make sense. Fortunately, the rest of the problems were pretty easy for her, and she'd been able to work through them without much trouble. She doubled-checked her calculations, made a couple of minor corrections, and handed in her exam ten minutes before the end of class. With the extra time, she walked over to the coffee kiosk next to the student union, got a small cup of coffee, and wandered slowly down the hill to her appointment with Alix. The line for coffee had been longer than usual, so she ended up being a couple of minutes late. She hadn't wanted to be late with everything going on and found herself running up the stairs. She was slightly out of breath when she sat down in Alix's office.

Skye set her cup of coffee on the table next to the box of tissues. Being there didn't feel as awkward as before, but still, she wasn't sure where to start. "So what're you doing for Thanksgiving?"

"Making a casserole and spending the day with friends," Alix said.

It was small talk, but Skye was surprised she'd actually gotten an answer from Alix; she was usually pretty tight-lipped about anything personal. Typically, Alix deflected the question, making it only appear as if she'd answered. Skye wondered if she did that with everyone or if she was friendlier with some of the other students.

"And you?" Alix asked.

"Waiting for my mother to get out of rehab and invite me for turkey dinner." Skye smiled at first, then her face dropped and she looked away, ran her fingers through her hair and let it fall across her face. She picked up the coffee cup, wrapping her hands around the cup, as if it were still warm. Her hands were mostly healed but for some skin that was peeling around the base of her fingers. Healed enough that she didn't need to hide her hands in her pockets. And they didn't hurt anymore.

Skye told Alix about skirting around her old neighborhood and how, at first, she hadn't wanted to go anywhere near the old apartment where she and Eva had lived. And then she'd been curious, and she wondered how it would feel when she finally got up the courage to walk farther down Grove Street. But random memories were cropping up, like the time her mother was strung out on the couch and sent Skye to the corner grocery store to get dinner. A man followed her down the street, and she had to run into the liquor store to hide. She and her friends had passed by the same liquor store and the same grocery store over the weekend, and Skye had forced herself to peer inside, even if she wasn't willing to go in. The next time her mother had wanted her to go to the grocery store, Skye had protested. But her mother never asked why, and it didn't seem like she had any choice but to go. Skye assumed these things happened to a lot of kids growing up in a city.

"I wonder if it was scary all over again," Alix said.

It made Skye think about how alone she'd been as a little kid. Even Grace would have caught on that she was upset. And Grace would have asked endless questions until she was satisfied Skye had told her everything, and probably Jackson would have talked to the police. And for sure they wouldn't have insisted she go back to the grocery store by herself.

"I don't know," Skye said. "It just feels like I'm breaking a promise or ratting her out. Wasn't she just doing the best she could?"

"Perhaps," Alix said. "But that doesn't change your experience, how scary and unsafe it felt to you."

Skye tossed her empty coffee cup in the trash can. "I've read addiction's an illness. That she couldn't help herself."

"That's not a very satisfying answer, is it?"

Skye shrugged.

"Are you still imagining you see her on campus?"

Skye thought about it for a moment, then shook her head. "Not really. Lately it feels safer on campus. I don't know, maybe 'cause I know she's two hundred miles away."

When the session was over, she collected her sweatshirt

and backpack, her hand on the doorknob as she headed out. "Some days I just want to forget. The whole thing. Like she never existed."

GRACE AND JACKSON ALWAYS called her after church on Sundays between 2 and 3 o'clock in the afternoon. They would have eaten lunch at the church, where Grace served egg-salad sandwiches on white bread, green salad, and chocolate cake. She'd have guilted Jackson into staying to clean up, even though the last thing he wanted to do was socialize with the church ladies and the deacon, a distinctly pale, middle-aged man with bad breath.

They always asked the same questions. "How are your classes? Are you studying? How's the food?"

Jackson was on the extension. "Gracie," he said, "give her a chance to answer."

She told them about going into the City and climbing the Coit Tower, leaving out the part about her old neighborhood. "The murals were really cool, and we could see the Golden Gate Bridge and all the boats out on the bay."

"That's great, sweetheart," Jackson said. "You need anything? You okay with money?"

She'd just gotten a job at the bookstore on campus. Between the job and financial aid, Skye was able to pay for everything herself. "I'm good."

There was a lull in the conversation. If Skye had been back in Oakdale, she'd have run off to her room or reached down and scratched Chester's tummy or gone to the refrigerator to make herself a peanut-butter-and-jelly sandwich. But it was different on the phone, where the silence was more obvious and inescapable. She considered telling them about Matt, but Grace would insist on knowing more, and she'd assume Skye was hiding something from her—which, of course, would be true. Instead, she told them about her mother, how she'd called Mrs. McNulty and found out she was in rehab.

"I sent her a letter," Skye said, feeling emboldened by the distance from small-town Oakdale to college near the City. She held the cell phone loosely against her ear. It would have been different sitting across from them at the dining room table. She knew Grace would have gotten defensive, as if Skye were suggesting that she and Jackson weren't enough. In the past, whenever she'd talked about her mother, they'd argued until Jackson intervened. A couple of times, Skye had heard them whispering out in the kitchen. "She's only going to get hurt," Grace would say.

"How else is she going to find out what happened?" Jackson said.

Then Grace pouted for the better part of a week, at least until Sunday church services, where she presumably sought repentance and tolerance.

One time, when she and Jackson were out in the garden, building raised beds, sawing and hammering redwood planks, he'd tried to explain that Grace just felt hurt—not that Skye was doing anything wrong, but Grace hoped she could be her real mother, that Skye wouldn't need Eva. She'd always wanted a baby of her own, but it was so hard to adopt an infant. So when Skye came along, it seemed like the next best thing—maybe even better.

Skye knew Jackson was just trying to help, but it made her feel like a consolation prize. Jackson finally said, "Maybe it's best not to mention your mother to Grace. Just for a little while."

Now, on the phone, Grace asked if she'd heard back. There was an expectant edge in her voice.

"It's too soon," Skye said, feeling defensive.

"Well, I hope she sticks with the program this time."

"You could be more positive," Skye said.

"I just don't want you to be disappointed," Grace said, leading to another awkward pause.

A few seconds later, Jackson spoke up. "We had our first frost," he said. "I had to pull up the tomato plants."

"They're hanging upside down in the root cellar," Grace said. "You remember that time we had tomatoes all the way into December? Jackson'll make you spaghetti sauce when you're home for Thanksgiving, won't you, Jackie?"

Skye was still waiting for an invitation from her mother.

Chapter Ten

SKYE RARELY GOT REAL mail. In fact, she couldn't remember having gotten anything but fliers announcing activities in the dorms, a tuition bill, and one time an overdue notice from the library. Unexpectedly, the beginning of November, a letter from her mother landed in her mailbox. *Dear Skye, Exciting news! I finished my detox program. I know it's short notice, but I'll be in the City week after next visiting a friend. Would you like to meet at the Japanese restaurant—you remember the one around the corner from our old apartment? How about Saturday at 4 p.m.? E-mail me at the address below. Love, Eva. PS I probably look a lot older than you remember, so don't be surprised.*

Skye folded up the letter and stuffed it into her back pocket, then took it out again and smoothed the paper out on the library carrel desk. She had more midterms coming up, but Matt said she'd be crazy not to see her mother. He'd go along if Skye wanted. Maybe she should talk to Alix first, Skye thought, but they didn't have an appointment scheduled for two weeks, and she figured Alix would just ask her a lot of questions, giving her the impression that it wasn't a good idea, that it was too soon to see her mother, and she'd leave the session feeling more confused rather than less. Going with Matt was a better bet. Skye e-mailed back, saying yes, next Saturday at 4 o'clock was good for her.

Skye and Matt decided to spend the day at the California Academy of Sciences before meeting up with her mother. Casey had gone over the summer with his parents and had told them about the lemurs and penguins and giant squid, and how they could sit underneath the aquarium tank and watch fish swim all around. After grabbing coffee and a couple of granola bars at the Veranda, they took BART into the City and then the number 5 Fulton bus to the edge of Golden Gate Park. This time, they didn't need a map.

The park was already swarming with bicyclists and roller bladers and joggers and cars squeezed into every available spot on the street. Vendors were hawking pretzels and ice cream, and gourmet foodie trucks were parked on the street selling good karma burgers and Asian fusion and sustainably caught wild-salmon fish tacos. They bought two hot dogs and potato chips and sat down on the grass to eat. The sun had burned off the morning fog; Skye peeled off her sweatshirt and stuffed it into her backpack. She'd worn her best button-down shirt and new black jeans, and she'd blow-dried her hair that morning, so it looked neater, even if the edges were still cut unevenly. "You look nice," Matt said.

The California Academy of Science housed an aquarium, a four-story rain forest, a planetarium, a natural history museum, and a living green roof with sky domes. They bought their tickets and took the elevator down to the lowest level, the aquarium, where they stared at bright orange jellyfish floating in the dark and eels and sharks and anemones and urchins. They crowded in close to the tank, along with the parents pushing strollers, to watch the aquarium diver scatter food from a bag strapped to her waist while she talked through a microphone about her job and what the different fish ate, how long they lived, and what happened when they slept. Skye was distracted, and it was hard to concentrate on what the diver was saying: something about endangered fish and mercury poisoning. Some fish you shouldn't ever eat, the diver said. Matt was leaning up against the tank, searching for eels camouflaged in the rocks, and he pulled her in close, making room for her against the glass. "Check out the manta rays," he said, leaning way over so he could whisper in her ear, and she caught a glimpse of their stealthy black bodies hidden underneath a ripple of sand. He pointed out fish that blended in with the coral and plants and the bright blue damselfish and butterfly fish and puffers. The diver was talking about clown fish changing their sex. "They've got limited mobility, so it's adaptive to the species." Matt had his arm around her and kissed her on the neck. She could feel herself being pulled into the moment, forgetting why they'd come into the City. She appreciated Matt's enthusiasm; it made 4 o'clock seem like a long way off.

From the aquarium, they wound their way up the ramp. It was a strange view from the very bottom of the rain forest, like some kind of optical illusion, with the aquarium below and the flooded Amazon and piranhas swimming over their heads. Farther up the ramp, they saw green-and-orange poisonous frogs and purple orchids. Their faces and clothes were damp with humidity, and they stood captivated, in awe. It reminded her of the time Grace and Jackson had taken her to the zoo in Fresno. She hadn't been able to stop talking about the toucan and mynah birds. Jackson taught her the word *aviary*, which she kept repeating all the way home in the car in a mimicking tone, as if she were a parrot. It must have made them crazy, she thought. But she remembered that Jackson kept laughing; it was Grace who wanted her to stop.

In the penguin exhibit, Matt did his impression of a waddling penguin, hunched over, his long arms dangling by his knees. It was silly, like a video clip she'd seen on the web that looped over and over, of one penguin slapping another with its flipper, knocking it down.

They held hands on the rooftop.

"Maybe she won't show up," Skye said. They were standing on the green dome they'd seen from the outside of the building, a living roof blanketed with native plants. Leaning against the railing, they were looking over sea pink and wild strawberry and miniature purple lupine. And Golden Gate Park and the Japanese Tea Garden below.

"You sound like you want her to flake," Matt said. He seemed confused, but Skye thought she detected a hint of scorn in his voice.

Of course, it was true. Part of her was hoping her mother wouldn't show. Then she'd have her answer—a different sort of answer, but one that wouldn't make her stomach tighten and twist. It would make it easier for her to be angry at her mother. *See, she really is a loser.* Then Skye could stop wishing it would be different and she could move on with her life. Without her mother. And there was the dinner itself. Skye was anxious about what they were going to talk about over dinner. She remembered her mother had been a good conversationalist, at least when Skye was younger. But her mother would likely want to know about Skye's life and what had happened in the intervening years. And how could she talk about Grace and Jackson without being angry at her mother?

Skye wanted to tell Matt, *You're right. After all this time, I finally get to see her. It'll be great.* But it wasn't how she felt.

Matt looked at his phone, as if he were the timekeeper. "We should go," he said.

THE RESTAURANT WAS ON Haight Street, on the south side of the Panhandle: a tiny, well-kept, family-run business with booths along the walls and round tables in the center, smelling of miso soup and cabbage and bleach. They had walked over from the park, getting there on time, but Skye insisted they circle around the block again. She wanted to be a couple minutes late—just enough so her mother might worry she wasn't going to show up.

The owner, whom she recognized from years before, was a short Japanese man with a round face, a stubby pencil behind his ear. Skye scrutinized all the customers, but no one even vaguely resembled her mother. She and Matt sat down on a bench next to the cash register. Matt was checking his e-mail and reading online news. Skye had a ragged thumbnail and was tearing at it, only making it worse.

The door opened several times—an elderly Asian woman with a cane and her frail husband came into the restaurant and were seated by the owner. Two gay guys who'd ordered takeout were standing over them, waiting for the owner to ring up their bill. In the letter, her mother had said Skye might be surprised by how much older she looked. It made Skye wonder if she would even recognize her mother.

Skye figured her mother would be about forty now, younger than Grace and Jackson. But her life hadn't turned out to be easy, and probably the drugs would have had an effect on her looks. At the time of the accident, she'd had shoulder-length blonde hair and light blue eyes, and she wore eye makeup and dangling earrings bought at street fairs from local artists.

By 4:20, it seemed that her mother might not show. Skye wasn't sure if she was disappointed or not. She kept looking over at Matt, who'd moved on to checking football scores on his phone. "Give her a couple more minutes," he said, "until 4:30."

Then a woman opened the door who was the right height. But her hair was cropped short, and there was gray at her temples, and she seemed shorter than Skye remembered her mother being. Shorter, or stooped over in a way that suggested weariness. The woman paused at the entrance and looked around, her eyes falling on Skye for a moment, and then on Matt. Then she looked at her watch. Skye wanted to be sure it was her mother before saying anything. Of course, her mother wouldn't have known that Matt was coming with her. Eva looked around again.

Matt nudged Skye, and she stood up.

"Skye?" the woman asked.

Skye took a step toward her, hesitant. Her mother had her arms open, but Skye wasn't ready for her mother to hug her. Eva stood expectantly, then dropped her arms. "I'm sorry I'm so late. The bus got stuck in traffic and, well, I'm sorry. I ..."

"This is my friend Matt," Skye said, interrupting.

Eva reached out and shook his hand. "Nice to meet you."

The owner seated them in a booth. Skye and Matt sat next to each other, Skye edging close to him. The waiter brought ice water and a pot of hot tea and three menus.

Eva was wearing a worn green turtleneck sweater and dangling earrings, eyeliner and pale red lipstick. There were tiny creases in the corners of her mouth and around her eyes, and her skin was tan and leathery. Skye had her mother's nose, which was small and sharp, but otherwise Skye couldn't detect any resemblance.

Eva poured tea for all of them, spilling some as she reached across the table, and then she looked up and stared at Skye. "It's been so long, but it's so good to see you. I know it's silly to say, but you've grown."

Skye winced.

The waiter brought miso soup and pickled vegetables, wooden chopsticks in paper sleeves. Skye scanned the menu; it was hard for her to concentrate. There were a lot of options on the menu, foods she'd never heard of and couldn't imagine eating, like quail eggs and squid. Just thinking about it made her stomach queasy. Her mother was reading the menu out loud, mostly mumbling to herself in a carefree tone, her words filling the space between them in a way that was awkward. Suddenly, Skye wished she hadn't contacted her mother; it was tense, and she couldn't imagine how she would even get through the meal. She didn't have anything superficial to say to her mother, at least nothing remotely cordial or uncomplicated.

Skye looked back at the menu and tried to focus on choices she recognized. Not feeling adventurous, she decided on vegetable tempura. She picked up the miso soup and took a sip. It was too hot to drink, so she put it down and looked over at Matt, who was still studying the menu. What was he thinking? Matt was more accepting of other people's quirks than she was, and later he'd probably tell her it had obviously been hard for her mother and to give her a break.

Eva looked up from her menu. "So you're in college," she said.

That didn't give Skye much of an opening. She nodded,

leaving more uncomfortable silence. Eva smiled weakly. What was Skye studying? she wanted to know. How were Grace and Jackson? Polite banter, as if they were strangers—which, of course, they were.

It was obvious that Skye wasn't making things any easier, so Eva turned to Matt. She wanted to know where Matt was from and how he liked college. Did he play sports?

Skye stared at her mother. But when Eva's eyes met hers, she'd turn away. She felt an odd sense of familiarity at surprising things: the way her mother stirred her miso soup before drinking it, how her eyebrow arched when she spoke, her excited tone, how she smiled in awkward moments, how her voice went up at the end of a long sentence.

The main dishes arrived.

"Vegetables in batter. That's what you always ordered," Eva said. "I guess it was the closest I let you get to french fries."

Skye couldn't remember what she'd ordered ten years ago, but she was sorry she hadn't picked out something different to let her mother know she wasn't the same Skye. Her mother didn't know her, couldn't know her after all these years. Skye had been little more than ten years old the last time they'd seen each other. She tried to picture herself as that ten-year-old. Skye had been feisty, with an attitude. That attitude still came out—often at the wrong time, like with Alix when she was only trying to help. But it made Skye mad, her mother thinking she could possibly know anything about her.

But now wasn't the time to let her mother know how upset she was with her. It might be the last time she got a chance to see her. Skye wanted to ask her about the last ten years, but she didn't know how to start. She didn't know anything about her mother, even where she was living. It was hard to be patient.

Eva had ordered soup. There was a slight but noticeable tremor in her right hand. The thin, long string of udon noodles fell off her chopsticks, and she called the waiter over and asked for a fork.

"I've thought about this conversation over and over," Eva said, "and it never comes out right."

"Maybe because you never had the conversation," said Skye.

Matt poked Skye under the table, and she glanced over at him. Even though she was angry with her mother, the tone in her voice had surprised her. "Sorry," she said.

A mom and dad and two kids walked in and were seated next to them. The little boy looked about eight years old, and he'd brought a book with him that he opened as soon as he sat down. The little girl was older and had a Sudoku puzzle.

Skye was distracted, watching the family get seated.

"I'm living with friends in Healdsburg, north of Santa Rosa," Eva said. "Going to meetings and doing some drafting work."

Skye hadn't quite caught what her mother said but then realized she'd been talking about going to AA meetings.

"That's great," Matt said. "My uncle used to have a drinking problem, and he says AA saved his life."

"It's been three and a half months," Eva said. "I can tell you, three and a half months feels like a long time."

The mom at the table next to them was talking about weekend plans with the dad, who was mildly attentive. "We should take the kids on a hike. Maybe Mount Tam," she said.

Skye had heard about Mount Tamalpais. On a clear day, it was possible to see snow on the Sierra Nevada mountains 150 miles away. She wondered what it was like to be a kid in a family like that. The little boy looked really small. And vulnerable. It was hard not to picture him in the back of a car, alone.

"They're too young," the dad said. "Whitney's going to whine, and I'll end up carrying Garrett. Besides, I told my brother I'd help him set tile in the bathroom."

Skye looked around. The restaurant seemed dingier than when they'd first come in, before her eyes had had a chance to adjust to the dim light. Paper umbrellas hung from the ceiling. There was a faded scroll on the wall with a geisha girl in a garden. The smiling Buddha in the corner needed dusting.

The conversation shifted. Matt was telling Eva about the aquarium, and she wanted to know their favorite exhibit. "What do you think?" Matt asked, touching Skye's arm and trying to draw her into the conversation.

She thought it was a stupid question. "Maybe the rainforest canopy, with all those birds and butterflies. Right there."

Matt and Eva weren't having any trouble talking to each other—spy movies and the San Francisco Giants and Billy Collins's poetry. Matt could strike up a conversation with almost anyone. Skye was glad he was there. But she didn't want him to make it any easier on her mother. Matt was telling Eva about how he and Skye had met and about their philosophy class. Her mother was talking too loudly.

"For a while I was really into Buddhist philosophy," Eva said. "That probably would have been a better path than drugs."

Skye glanced over at the family next to them, hoping they hadn't heard her mother talking about drugs. The dad had a smirk on his face; then he looked away. Even Matt wasn't sure what to say to that.

Her mother apparently hadn't noticed their reaction. She asked if they wanted dessert. "How about green-tea ice cream? I always thought it was dreadful, but you used to love it."

Skye had eaten her meal too quickly, especially with her stomach in a knot, but she wasn't ready to go, not having asked the most important questions. "Sure," she said.

The family next to them had ordered a chicken-and-vegetable platter they were sharing. Matt's phone rang; he took it out of his pocket to see who had called, then pressed the off button. He put the phone back in his pocket.

"You're awfully quiet," Eva said.

Skye looked at her mother and frowned, not knowing how to respond.

"Hey," Matt said, "tell your mother about how we were trying to find your old apartment."

Maybe this was a way to get her mother talking about the past, Skye thought. "I couldn't remember the address. Wasn't it on Grove?"

Her mother thought for a moment. "Grove Street," she said. "That does sound familiar. Or was it on Hayes? It was such a great neighborhood. But I've lived in so many apartments and halfway houses since then. There's no way I'd remember the number of the house."

Skye wanted her mother to notice how important this tiny bit of information was to her. It seemed like such a small thing to remember. But then the waiter brought out Skye's dish of ice cream; it seemed Eva was more interested in tasting it. She reached over to Skye's bowl. "May I?" she asked. "Maybe, after all these years, I'll like it." At first, Skye pulled the bowl back, but then she pushed it toward her mother. Eva took a small spoonful. "Nope," she said, smiling. "Still not my thing."

"What happened?" Skye asked, almost in a whisper. "That's what I want to know."

Eva put her spoon down and looked across the restaurant at the front door.

"You have every right to know," she said. "But I'd like to take it slow."

"I just want to understand," Skye said.

The little boy knocked over a container of soy sauce. The mother was grabbing all the napkins to mop up the brown slippery mess, and the father had pulled both of the kids out of the booth. The whole restaurant was looking in their direction. It suddenly occurred to Skye that probably her mother had planned on their meeting in a public place. So she wouldn't have to reveal too much.

"There's lots of time for that," Eva said. "Besides, it'll give me a chance to see you again."

Skye wasn't sure whether or not she should be relieved. It seemed her mother expected they'd be seeing each other again. But it could be a long time before Skye got any answers from her.

When the bill came, Eva grabbed it with a flourish, as if paying for them should have been unexpected. But then she took wadded-up bills out of a small change purse and counted them out carefully. Skye wondered how Eva was supporting herself.

Then they were standing in front of the restaurant, near the curb. It was almost dark, and the sounds on the street were loud and penetrating. Skye could feel her chest contracting.

When her mother had first walked into the restaurant, it had been obvious that she was trying to appear cheerful, but now she seemed worn out and limp, as if she'd been stirred and overcooked in a thick pot of stew. She shook Matt's hand again and then reached out to Skye, who reluctantly consented to be hugged, her arms rigid at her sides.

"I've missed you so much," Eva said, clasping her arms around Skye, cinching Skye's body close to her chest. Her hands were trembling, and it was obvious that she was shaking with tears. "I screwed up, I know. And I want to make it up to you."

Skye extricated herself from her mother's embrace, but still, Eva held her shoulders tight, staring intently into Skye's face. Her mother's makeup was damp, and the lines around her eyes were filled with black, inky mascara, making her look like an overdrawn caricature. She took out a tissue and wiped her eyes, blew her nose, then wrote her phone number on a scrap of paper. "Will you call me? Or you can e-mail me. Okay?"

Skye took the piece of paper and stuffed it into her pocket without looking at it. Stepping away, she turned in the opposite direction, not even waiting for Matt, who was standing closer to Eva. He was thanking her for dinner.

"Maybe next time I can visit you at school," Eva said.

A bus heading toward Union Square passed by. It was a bus they could have taken, if only she'd been able to get away sooner. Skye reached out for Matt's hand, tugging at him.

"Sure," Skye said. "Only I have midterms now, and then I'll be going home for Thanksgiving." It was the first time she'd called Oakdale *home.*

They crossed the street and sat down on a bench in the bus shelter. Eva was still standing in front of the restaurant as if she were unsure which way to go. The restaurant's neon sign was flashing an eerie light onto her face. Then she clenched her purse under her arm and disappeared around the corner.

"She seemed nice," Matt said.

"I never said she wasn't."

"You don't have to take it out on me."

THE SUBWAY WAS NEARLY empty on the way back to campus. Skye and Matt sat next to each other, two seats facing toward the rear of the train. Lights flashed through the windows as the train left the station. Skye watched her reflection appear in the glass and then disappear into the darkness, repeating itself again and again. She wanted to whisk away the evening to some unknown time in the future when she'd know more about her mother and how it all ended, like skipping ahead in a book to find out if the protagonist dies.

They sped under San Francisco Bay; Matt held her hand in the tunnel while the train rocked in disjointed rhythm. With her other hand, Skye steadied herself on the seat.

They didn't talk, except for Matt asking if she was okay over the clacking and squealing of the wheels. Skye shrugged or nodded. She didn't want to talk. Her thoughts weren't sorted out in a way she could put into words. They were confused, swirling around in an eddy.

The train emerged from the tunnel, and Matt took out his phone; he was playing a game, checking Facebook. Would she post something about the evening? Probably not, given how quickly information spread in the dorms—their own private off-line social media platform.

"Don't tell anyone, okay?" she said. "Especially not Sylvia."

It was the first time Skye had smiled since the museum.

They pulled into the 19th Street station. A middle-aged couple, well dressed, got on. And two tall men. The couple sat across from Matt and Skye. The young men stood near the doors. They were wearing black jackets, wool caps, and sneakers, carrying what looked like rifles in heavy vinyl cases. But then Skye realized they were probably pool cues. She was daydreaming in their direction, what might have looked like staring, thinking about her mother and how fragile she'd looked and how, at the last moment, her mother had clung to her.

The train collected steam again. She looked at the map above the windows. Two more stops. Suddenly, she felt exhausted; then Matt was pulling on her.

"This is our stop," he said. She grabbed her backpack, unprepared for the rush off the train.

Outside the station, the street was desolate, and there was an overwhelming odor of motor oil and damp sewage. They walked quickly, looking around. Skye wondered if this was the part of town they'd been warned about. A couple of high school kids on the corner ahead of them were smoking cigarettes and swaggering, scuffing their feet against the pavement.

They could have waited for the bus to campus, but instead Matt grabbed her hand and they crossed the street, walking the mile back to school. At the stone entrance to the college, Matt loosened his grip. They walked up the hill to Skye's dorm room. Evelyn's father had driven up earlier in the day to take her home for the weekend. Her bed was made, the pillows fluffed and ready for her return on Sunday night.

"Want to watch a movie or something?" Matt asked.

Skye flipped on Evelyn's TV and turned out the lights. They sat side by side on Skye's bed. She surfed the channels: *Law and Order*, a *Seinfeld* rerun, an old black-and-white romantic comedy, a cops-and-robbers movie, college football, an infomercial for the perfect abs.

"I didn't want to feel sorry for her," Skye said, leaning against the wall. She hit the mute button on the remote. "It just would have been easier if I could stay angry. But she seemed pathetic and sincere at the same time, and now what? Are we friends? Maybe we're just distant cousins. I mean, what if I hadn't gotten Mrs. McNulty to tell me where she was?"

"But you did," Matt said. He rested his hand on top of hers. "And the drug thing is behind her. And she said she wants to see you again."

Skye turned the sound back on, then leaned over and kissed him. In the background, two men were chasing a woman down a dark alley, shouting at her to stop. "Hey," one man yelled, "don't make me shoot you."

Skye got up and cranked open the window.

A gunshot went off, then another.

She grabbed the blanket and pulled it up over them.

The woman was hiding behind a storage shed on the roof, wounded, her breathing shallow, the lights of the city dim and shadowy. Sirens screeched in the background.

Matt put his arm around Skye. She leaned her head against his shoulder, her eyes on the TV. A police car raced around the corner; the sirens grew louder. She was rooting for the woman, but it wasn't clear why they were pursuing her, if she'd even broken the law.

After all these years of wondering, she'd finally gotten up the nerve to find her mother. And now there were even more unanswered questions, and an edited image of her mother to compare with the past.

Eva seemed trendy and smart, like Skye had remembered, but there was another side to her: tentative, self-protective, as if she'd recently recovered from surgery or a long illness, protecting a wound still raw and vulnerable. Her words had been direct and convincing, but her voice had been shaky, and her hands kept dropping the chopsticks, and she'd brought the teacup to her lips deliberately, as if she was afraid she'd spill it. On the way out of the restaurant she had almost tripped over the door sill.

"Why didn't I just ask her?" Skye said.

"Ask her what?"

"Why she never came back."

"You did. Remember?"

It was obvious to Skye that she'd been too nervous to even remember what her mother had said. Her mother probably had a whole other way of seeing their situation, but it was going to be hard for Skye if she couldn't even hold on to what was said during their conversations.

Morris's last lecture had been on Nietzsche and absolute truth. He'd pointed out that perceptions and ideas and standards are constructed, made up. Stories people tell themselves about what's right and wrong. Of course it was true, Skye thought, that values changed over time, but wouldn't it be easier to live in a world where you could depend on people acting in a certain way, where everyone could agree on what was right and wrong?

"Values and cultural mores outlive their usefulness," Morris had said. He'd been wearing a red bow tie that day in class. "There is no absolute truth."

Skye pushed the mute button again, leaving the room a timid shade of blue. There was a heavy-metal concert going on in the gym, and the dorm was eerily quiet but for the sound of an occasional car driving by on the street below. A commercial on TV showed an oversized burger dripping grease and ketchup. She'd read an article about how tricky it is to get two drips timed exactly. And they weren't even using real ketchup but some fraudulent, red syrupy lookalike.

Matt reached over and kissed her. He started to unbutton her shirt, but she held his hand in place.

"Not now," she said.

Matt pulled away.

She didn't mean it the way it felt, like disapproval. "I'm sorry; I just feel weird is all."

Half expecting he'd go back to his room, she turned the

sound up. But he didn't go; he just sat there. It felt uncomfortable, and he didn't say anything to make it easier, but he reached out to hold her hand. She'd been acting weird all day long, and now he knew just how much crap she was carrying around. The other night, she'd dreamed about the car crash, only in the dream she was driving instead of her mother. She was too short to reach the brake pedal, and the car was gaining speed, careening down the mountain while her mother was asleep in the backseat, oblivious to the danger. She'd woken up clammy and disoriented just before they crashed. The streetlamp outside her window flickered on the ceiling like emergency lights at the scene of an accident.

SKYE DIDN'T GET OUT of bed until noon, a dull ache in her head. She'd spent a fitful night, odd memories about her mother whirling around in her head. She called Matt. "I'm really sorry about last night."

"Sorry? About what?" He seemed genuinely puzzled.

"I was acting weird the whole day, and it was so great you came with me to see my mother, and I wouldn't have gone alone."

"I'm glad I met her," he said. "Hey, Casey and I are going over to Logan Field to kick around a soccer ball. Why don't you meet us there?"

She hadn't eaten yet, and it was all she could do to pull herself out of bed. "I'm not up for playing, but I'll come watch."

Armored with a protein bar and a cup of coffee from the downstairs vending machine, she sat on the grass and watched them practice, setting up goals and defending. There was a lot of jockeying and poking fun at each other. Casey ran circles around Matt, but Matt didn't seem to mind.

Her coffee was getting cold, and she finished off the last gulp and leaned back on the grass, discarding the cup next to her. Looking up at the sky, she could see clouds drifting by in puffy shapes. It was something she and her mother and Melanie used to do at the beach: point out the shapes. A dragon. Two train cars. Off in the distance, the rhythmic wallop of tennis balls, a skateboarder clunking along on the asphalt, crows cawing. Her mother, sitting on the grass next to her, was asking about college and was she making friends. And about her relationship with Matt. "He's adorable," she said. "That long, curly hair and his nose—well, he'll grow into it, I'm sure." It was not quite the same conversation she'd had reverberating in her mind over the years—now that she had an updated version of her mother with her hair cut shorter and gray mixed with the blonde and wrinkles around her eyes.

"I'm glad you found me," her mother said. "I was thinking we could go up to the mountains like we used to, maybe with Melanie and Julie. Would you like that?"

Skye pulled on a long blade of grass and wound it around her finger, like a ring. What happened to Melanie? she wondered.

In an imaginary conversation, her mother always knew what she was thinking. "We had a disagreement," she said. "Well, more than that, but I ran into her recently at a yoga class at the Y, and we talked it out. She was asking about you and wants to see you." Her mother seemed confident and poised; her voice was steady. "I'd like us to visit more often," she said. "I'll take you to the farmers market. We can cook together, like we used to before …"

Skye wanted to play coy, test out her mother to make sure she really meant it, that she wasn't just reeling her in until things got rough.

"I'm not going anywhere," her mother said. "Not this time."

MATT AND CASEY WERE standing over her, blocking the sun. "Hey," Matt said, "let's get something to eat before the game." They were all going to a basketball game: Matt and Casey, Jonathan, Sylvia and Alison. The women's team was on a winning streak, and lately the bleachers were packed. Matt reached down, took Skye's hand, and pulled her up. Her back was damp, and there were grass stains on the bottoms of her jeans and the knees.

They walked back to the dorms, where Skye took a shower and changed. Three other girls, Jen and Sara and Emily, were getting ready for the game, putting on makeup and false eyelashes and blow-drying their hair. Even with the water running, Skye could hear them chattering about ideal boyfriends.

"They're all either geeks or doughy," Jen said.

"Or gay," said Emily.

"How does a guy who's twenty already have man breasts and love handles?" Sara asked.

Matt was tall and lean, and probably these girls would say he wasn't muscular enough, but Skye thought the really buff guys at the gym were intimidating and unapproachable. She liked how patient Matt was with her, not like the stories she'd heard about getting drunk and hooking up. She put on a clean pair of jeans, a long-sleeved T-shirt, and sneakers and met up with Matt and Casey at their room.

By the time they got to the gym, the bleachers were packed, but Sylvia and Alison had saved a row of seats for them just short of the nose-bleed section. Matt and Casey and Jonathan ran off to buy hot dogs and soda. The pep band was playing a medley of disco songs: "Macho Man" and "I Will Survive." Sylvia and Alison were sitting glued to each other, holding hands.

"Hey, Skye," Sylvia said, "we were looking for you last night.

We went to the movies—girls' night out. But we couldn't find you."

"What'd you see?" Skye asked.

"*Kissing Jessica Stein.* Even if you're straight, it's a great movie."

"Matt and I went into the City." Skye didn't want to say more, knowing how good Sylvia was at broadcasting—and stretching—whatever you told her; Matt and Casey and Jonathan were coming up the bleacher steps, and the pep band launched into the school song. The two teams came out onto the court, and the crowd was cheering.

Matt handed her a hot dog wrapped in waxed paper, loaded with mustard and sauerkraut and relish. "I remembered you like everything on it," he said.

AFTER THE GAME, MATT walked Skye back to her room. He had his arm around her, and they ambled slowly up the hill, past the library and campus police and the parking kiosk, which was closed for the night. The team had been behind for most of the game, and then a spark had ignited in the last ten minutes, and the center had sunk a three-point shot to win by two. Matt leaned over and brushed his lips against her ear; his breath was warm and moist. He wanted to know if she was ready.

"Sure," she said. "I mean, yes, I want to."

She pulled the key out of her pocket and unlocked the door; she didn't turn on the light. They stood in the middle of the room, their eyes adjusting to the darkness and a streak of light from the streetlamp that entered through the window. It was hot and steamy in the room from the murmuring radiator. Matt leaned down and kissed her, and he began to peel off her coat and his jacket.

They lay down on the bed, Matt on top of her, and he took off his shirt and then Skye's shirt and unhooked her bra. They lay still for a couple of minutes, just kissing and holding each other. His heartbeat, the damp rhythm against her ear, his chest rising and falling, his warm body, their jeans legs like strands of DNA wound together in a helix.

"Just a sec," he said, and he got up and fished around for something in his wallet, and he took off his jeans and unzipped Skye's pants, and they were kissing again. Skye ran her fingers through his hair. She could feel her body shift, as if a long, electrical circuit that ran from her lips to somewhere between her legs had been all of a sudden switched on; and the gentleness turned liquid and shimmery, and their bodies were moving against each other, and it was all they could do to undress fast enough. She could see in the shadows that Matt was putting on the condom. At first he had trouble getting inside her, and Skye wasn't sure if he was inside or not. She felt a slight stinging pain and cringed, and then he was moving up and down on top of her, and the wave of energy moved through her body. For a moment her eyes went blank and her back arched, and the liquid froze and melted. Afterward, he was still holding her tight, and they lay there entwined. Skye pulled up the blanket, and they dozed off, Matt's arms around her, his breath against her neck. He whispered, "I love you" just loud enough to be unmistakable, and she wanted so much for it to be true.

Chapter Eleven

THE DAY BEFORE THANKSGIVING, Jackson picked her up near the off-ramp at the same gas station in the same seedy-looking neighborhood in Merced. He was waiting for her when they pulled into the parking lot. They all got out of their cars, and Jackson shook hands with Matt and his friend Tanner, who knew Matt from physics and had a car. Then Matt kissed her, and he and Tanner made a U-turn back onto the highway. Skye glanced at Jackson to see if he'd noticed, but he was leaning over, unlocking the passenger-side door.

She got in the truck; the heat was turned up. It smelled familiar, like sawdust and varnish. Jackson didn't look much different. He was wearing stained jeans, his long hair tied back with the same leather cord, the same stray hairs fluttering. "Sorry I didn't get to change before coming to get you." He started up the truck and merged back onto the highway.

"We've been cooking up a storm," Jackson said, his eyes shifting between Skye and the road. "I hope all that studying makes you hungry."

Grace had been calling more frequently, not just on Sunday afternoons, asking if there were special dishes she wanted Jackson to cook for her; and Jasmine, impatient to see her again, had orchestrated uninterrupted plans for them to hang out together. Skye found herself faking it, pretending she was looking forward to seeing everyone but feeling detached, like one of those failed miter joints Jackson had shown her that didn't quite match up.

Jackson was holding both hands on the steering wheel, but his fingers were restless, tapping at the wheel. He was talking about the early snow a couple of weeks ago, all but gone with the unseasonably warm weather, and now the tourists were staying away, waiting for better snowpack. "Guess who I ran into?"

She didn't want to play any guessing games. "I don't know," she said, trying not to sound testy. "Who'd you run into?"

"Mrs. Reed, remember? Your fourth grade teacher? She was asking about you."

Skye couldn't remember any of her teachers before she'd come to Oakdale, only the ones who'd come after: Mrs. Shaw, with her long red fingernails and thick mascara for fifth grade; Mr. Ridley, whose wife was friends with Grace, had been her sixth grade teacher. Then in middle school, there was … Of course she remembered Mrs. Reed, her first teacher at Oakdale Elementary, where it was supposed to be temporary, who had taught her long division and let her take a stack of books home to Grace and Jackson's. (The other kids could only take home one at a time.)

"You okay?" Jackson asked.

Skye leaned against the passenger door and closed her eyes. She wasn't sure what was stopping her from telling Jackson about having had dinner with her mother. Jackson would be a better bet than Grace, for sure. "I'm just tired, I guess," she said.

They were starting up the steep incline to Oakdale, where the highway turned into a two-lane mountain road. Dingy scrub brush gave way to grassy hillsides. Water trickled down muddy shoulders, and there were thick stands of evergreens and sprawling oak and sycamore, open space turned inward. The last time she'd been here, the hills had been crusty brown, the trees sagging with drought. Their leaves had been a dusty green. And there was so much about her mother she hadn't known.

Taking his eyes off the road, Jackson glanced in her direction again, then adjusted the heat. His hands squeezed the steering wheel. "Hey, did you ever hear from your mother?"

It wasn't lost on her that Jackson referred to her as "your mother" and Grace called her "Eva." She told him about going into the City with Matt and then meeting Eva at the Japanese restaurant, how she'd seemed older and had been sober for three months.

"It must have been kind of strange," Jackson said, "seeing her after all those years."

THANKSGIVING AFTERNOON, SKYE AND Grace and Jackson crowded into the front seat of the pickup and headed over to the Millers'. They were all sitting around the table: the Millers—Sally and Jerry, Jasmine and her brother, Jake, Grace and Jackson, Skye, and Mrs. Miller's mother, who lived a few doors down, in the house where Sally Miller had grown up. Jerry Miller was already red-faced from too much bourbon.

They were passing around dishes of green beans, Jackson's fresh-made cranberry sauce, stuffing, sweet potatoes, and the platter piled high with turkey.

"Don't you remember?" Sally Miller said. "You were both in fifth grade and joined at the hip. You even brought Chester that first Thanksgiving, and he followed you around like a lovesick puppy—which I guess he was."

Mr. Miller had deep-fried the turkey in a vat of oil in the backyard. He was about to take a bite out of a turkey thigh. "Back then, I thought maybe we'd adopted three kids instead of just two."

"The year Jerry's dad passed away," Grace said. "I think that was the only year we missed having Thanksgiving together."

Skye counted back, realizing she'd celebrated the same number of Thanksgivings with Grace and Jackson as with her mother, and for sure she remembered a lot more of them with Grace and Jackson and the Millers. It seemed like an awful lot of years wishing it could be different. Suddenly, she realized she didn't know what her mother was doing for Thanksgiving. Why hadn't she asked?

Jasmine was sitting next to her. That morning, they'd ridden their bikes out to the stables, and the owner, Shelley, had let them take out two of the older horses. They got as far as Sunken Creek before turning around.

"I decided not to drop out of school," Jasmine said. "I mean, what am I going to do, work at a movie theater the rest of my life? I only wish I had a plan, you know, like you."

"I don't have much of a plan," Skye said. "I just like going to school."

"Well, anyway, I'm applying to a four-year school next year." And then Jasmine added, "I really miss you."

"Me, too," Skye said. It surprised her how this time she really meant it.

Skye told Jasmine about seeing her mother, and Jasmine couldn't believe that Mrs. McNulty had finally spilled the beans. But then Skye didn't have to explain anything else because Jasmine already knew the whole story—almost as if she'd met Eva.

"And what about that guy Matt? You still seeing him?"

"We slept together." Skye was trying to act nonchalant about it.

"You've been holding out on me," Jasmine said. "Miss Goody Two-Shoes. I wanna meet him."

Mrs. Miller was talking about the time they'd had Thanksgiving dinner in Sequoia National Park at the family camp. There'd been an early snowstorm, and they'd all gone cross-country skiing. "I think Skye was the only one who knew what she was doing."

It was Mrs. Miller who'd given them the contraception talk. They were in tenth grade, and Jasmine was already hooking up with guys. Skye was surprised—and embarrassed—by how Mrs. Miller used all the correct terms, like *penis* and *vagina* and *menstruation,* unlike Grace, who, if she mentioned anything at all, used expressions like *Aunt Flo* and *your privates.* Grace was just as likely to make believe Skye hadn't ever reached puberty. It was something else she assumed her mother would have been better at—if only she'd been there.

"More stuffing, anyone?" Mrs. Miller was passing the dish around again. She turned to Skye. "So how's college life?"

"I like it," Skye said.

"What are you studying?" Mr. Miller asked. "I hope it's something more useful than cardboard packaging. Or, what was that we saw on the news? Video-game design? Although I guess that could make you quite a bit of money."

"I haven't decided on a major," Skye said.

"We're so proud of her," Grace said. "Even with all the studying, Skye found a job. Sweetheart, tell them where you're working."

"In the bookstore, stocking shelves," Skye said. "It's no big deal." She wanted them to change the subject, talk about something that didn't involve Grace getting to take credit for Skye's boring job on campus. It was annoying how she made a big deal over nothing.

Skye and Jasmine and Grace helped clear the table while Jackson brought out the two pies he'd made—pecan and pumpkin. Jake grabbed the can of whipped cream, shook it up, and squirted a stream into his open mouth. Mr. Miller laughed, then told him to cut it out. Over dessert, they talked about the crazy weather and climate change and the off-roaders who were ravaging the cross-country trails and how the housing crisis would affect the seasonal rentals.

"Did you hear? Bruce Wilding's retiring as sheriff," Jackson said, dishing out seconds of pie.

"Hey, wasn't it Bruce who found Skye down in the gully off Highway 49?" Mr. Miller asked, swishing the remaining bourbon in his highball glass. "Criminy. That was a long time ago. Whatever happened to your mother? Who does that? High on drugs, driving down those mountain roads."

Mrs. Miller threw him a stern look.

"I'm just asking. I mean, the woman drives off the road with her kid in the backseat, and then you don't hear from her again." He motioned toward Jake. "Son, hand me that whipped cream, will ya?"

Jasmine said, "It's not Skye's fault, you know."

"No one's saying it is," Mr. Miller said.

"My mother just got out of rehab," Skye said. "I met up with her in the City."

IT PROBABLY WASN'T THE best way for Grace to hear. Out of the blue. That her mother had written back, and they'd even met at a restaurant. The rest of Thanksgiving dinner, Grace was stiff, sullen. She took a small piece of Jackson's pecan pie and stabbed at it, picking off the crust and then nibbling at the filling. They all talked around her, except Mr. Miller, who was too drunk to realize what was going on.

"The more the merrier," he said, taking another gulp from his glass. "Maybe your mother'll join us next year."

Grace started to clear the table, and Mrs. Miller got up to help her. "Hey, I'm not finished yet," Mr. Miller said, grabbing his plate and the near-empty glass of bourbon from his wife.

"I think you are."

After all the dishes were cleared away, Mrs. Miller sent Jasmine and Skye and Jake into the kitchen to wash the dishes. They could hear Mrs. Miller saying in a conciliatory voice, "Grace, she loves you, but it's just something she has to do. It was the same with my kids."

"You didn't tell her?" Jasmine said. "Shit, Skye. What did you think would happen?"

"She always gets so wonky about it. I figured Jackson would tell her."

"Yeah, and then what?"

On the way home, it seemed like Jackson drove especially slowly, edging up against the side of the mountain around every turn. Grace was doing a lot of sighing and slow simmering, and Skye thought, for sure, any minute, she would explode. But nothing happened until they got inside the front door, just when Skye figured she was in the clear. Grace switched on the floor lamp, and they all took off their coats, hanging them on the hooks by the door. She hadn't looked at Skye, not once, since she'd found out.

I didn't do anything wrong, Skye thought. Except she had to admit—to herself—that Jasmine was right. It would have been better to have told Grace earlier.

Chester must have sensed that there was going to be a scene because he whimpered, and, even with the nighttime chill in the air, he slunk out the back doggie door. "How could you?" Grace said. "Humiliate me. In front of our closest friends." It all came out in a well-controlled stream, like a row of punctuation marks. "Your mother's not the kind of person who can follow through on her word," she said. "I haven't had the heart to tell you, all these years. But maybe it's best. If you find out for yourself." With that, she stomped off to bed. Skye could hear the TV go on in Grace and Jackson's bedroom, louder than usual.

Skye went into her room. It felt weird being back in her bedroom, as if nothing had changed and she hadn't been away at college. The room smelled the same, with the pine tree shedding needles that had piled on the windowsill outside, the old quilt on her bed, and the same laundry detergent Grace used to wash the sheets. Grace had left a few fliers on her desk—the sporting-goods store was having a sale on sweatshirts, ten tips for how to avoid Black Friday shopping madness, the Christmas play at the church. Lying on her bed, she tried to read finish her calculus homework, but the page blurred. She could hear rustling in the trees, the last of the fall leaves clinging to the branches. Tomorrow she and Jasmine and a couple of her high school friends were thinking about hiking up near Yosemite. She missed the mountains and the alpine meadows and knowing that most everyone here had her back. *Maybe it's best if you find out for yourself.* But Grace was thinking about the Eva she'd heard about a long time ago. She didn't know how much Skye's mother had changed. And wasn't it worth another try?

The rest of the long weekend, she hung out with Jasmine and her other friends from high school, Amanda, Seth, and Jason. They never made it up to Yosemite but instead went to the movies and scarfed down burgers and fries at Pete's, drank coffee from the drive-through espresso bar on the main drag. Sitting outside in Seth's backyard, they passed around a joint. Jasmine had this belly laugh Skye had forgotten about that sounded like a coyote caught under a car wheel. Without her noticing when it happened, Skye suddenly felt as if she'd never gone off to college, and Oakdale was her real life. Her high school friends didn't ask any uncomfortable questions about her mother or her friends at college. She could make believe she lived in the space between, without any past or future.

JACKSON DROVE HER BACK to Merced to meet up with Tanner and Matt. Grace had gone to church at the crack of dawn to help arrange the flowers on the altar for Sunday services, so there hadn't been much of a good-bye. All the way down the mountain, Jackson avoided saying anything about Grace or her mother except for asking if she'd be home for Christmas.

"I know Grace is upset with you," he said, "but I'm sure she'd want you home."

"I'm sorry," Skye said. "I should have told her about seeing my mother."

"Well, I could have told her, too. But you know, she'd appreciate hearing you apologize."

They turned on the radio and listened to Sunday gospel music until Jackson pulled into the parking lot next to Tanner's car. Matt barely looked up. He was sitting in the front passenger seat, his feet up on the dashboard. The CD player was turned up loud, playing a local indie band Skye recognized, a fusion of rock and jazz with horns.

Tanner got out to say hello to Jackson and put Skye's duffel in the trunk. Skye slid into the backseat behind Matt. It wasn't until they'd reached Route 99 that she asked Matt about Thanksgiving.

"The usual," he said.

On the way home he'd talked nonstop; he'd been upbeat about going home and seeing his family and friends from high school. Skye wondered what was wrong, whether he was thinking they should just be friends. Or whether he was mad that she hadn't called him on Saturday, like they'd planned. He hadn't been doing well in school, so maybe he was just worried about finals.

Tanner looked over at Matt, puzzled. "Did you hang out with your high school buddies?"

Matt shrugged.

Skye hated silence; it made her feel uneasy. Whenever Grace was mad about something, she'd pout and run off to her bedroom. Her mother had been the same way. Skye would have preferred something more clear-cut, unequivocal, than stony silence.

If he wouldn't talk, then she would. "We had Thanksgiving at Jasmine's house," Skye said. Then she launched into how Grace had had a conniption when she'd found out Skye had seen her mother. Grace had pouted the rest of the weekend, made excuses so she didn't have to sit down to dinner with them. "Oh, then she tried to ground me, told me I couldn't go out Saturday night with my friends because I hadn't spent enough time at home. Why should I stay when all she does is pout?" Skye said.

Matt let out a brittle sigh. "My mom suddenly turned vegetarian," he said, "so we ate this tofurky crap. What's the point of having something that's pretend meat?"

"That stuff's gross," Skye said.

More silence.

Tanner said he'd had Thanksgiving dinner with his mother and stepdad and then a second Thanksgiving dinner with his father. "It used to be pretty awkward, but now it just seems normal."

They spent the rest of the trip talking about finals and soccer and whether the cafeteria would serve turkey soup, like having leftovers from home. Skye dozed off, woke up and peered out at the flatness of the valley, the aqueduct with a trickle of water and garbage, the cattle grazing, the orchards of avocados, figs, and walnuts. Tanner was concentrating on the road, merging onto the main highway junction heading west, where the landscape morphed into cement pillars and shopping malls, car lots, Denny's and the Olive Garden and gas stations with towering signs. In the reflection of the window, it seemed as if Matt's eyes were moist and he was wiping his nose with his sweatshirt sleeve. She wanted to ask what was wrong—something more than having to eat tofurky—but she didn't want to embarrass him.

"Hey, Matt," she said, tapping him on the shoulder. "Jasmine's mom packed a turkey sandwich for me, and I kind of OD'd on turkey. You want it?"

"You sure?" he asked, wiping his eyes and then turning around. He peeled back the waxed paper and took a bite. "Mmm, I missed this. Thanks."

When they got back to campus, Tanner parked the car, and they walked up the hill to the dorms. Evelyn wasn't back yet; Skye unpacked her clothes and tossed her books onto the bed. At home, she'd found a thin silver ring Jasmine had given her for her last birthday that she'd decided to wear again, and she'd brought back her senior yearbook, a high school soccer trophy, and a snow globe from a trip to Utah with Grace and Jackson. She'd wanted to make believe she could have both lives: the one in Oakdale and her new life with her mother.

Doors were opening and closing up and down the hallway. She could hear Sylvia giving someone an earful about visiting her Mormon cousins in Arizona. Sylvia's parents had given her explicit instructions forbidding her to mention anything gay-related. Not ready to face Sylvia or any of her other dorm friends, Skye kept her door closed. Of course, her visit to Oakdale had been just that, a visit; Morgan College was her home now. But she wanted to hold on to the past just a little bit longer.

An hour later, she was sitting at her desk, reading and taking notes. Matt knocked on the door.

"I'm sorry," he said, hunched over in the doorway.

"About what?"

"I was a jerk in the car; I just wasn't ready to talk."

To Skye, it sounded like the prelude to a breakup line. "Oh," she said, certain she knew what was coming next.

He sat on her bed and leaned against the wall. He was looking down at his lap, biting the side of his finger.

She wasn't prepared for what came next.

"My parents are getting a divorce," Matt said. "My dad wasn't even in town for Thanksgiving. I can't really blame him. I mean, my mom's a pain in the ass; it's always gotta be her way."

He was picking at a piece of loose rubber on the bottom of his sneakers. "I'd sure hate to be married to her, but I thought they'd worked things out. At least, that's what my dad said when he dropped me off in September. He promised they would go to couples counseling. Now, all of a sudden, everything's changed. He's moving to Portland to be with his new girlfriend."

She could feel a knot in her stomach and wished she'd asked him in the car, "How come you're so quiet; what's up?"

"They're not sure they can afford to pay for college after this year," he said.

"That sucks," she said. "I'm sorry."

Matt shrugged.

"I know it's selfish," he said, "but honestly, I don't care if my parents are happy. I just don't want them to split up."

Chapter Twelve

BETSY WAS RIFLING THROUGH the hangers in Alix's closet, tossing outfits on the floor, clothes in one pile, hangers in another. Pantsuits, sweater sets, an array of silk blouses Alix had bought in New York and San Francisco, blazers, leather pumps, dresses with ruffles and capped sleeves. It was part of Betsy's strategy to get her to move on, like a Hollywood makeover. Alix regretted having acquiesced.

"This is passable," Betsy said, holding up a pair of tailored pants, "but I'm not seeing anything to go with it." She set it aside on the bed. "And you're the only person I know who doesn't own a pair of jeans."

Alix hated to admit being so elitist as to snub jeans. Something about her Upper West Side grooming. "My hips are too wide," she said. "It's impossible to find jeans that fit."

"Likely story," Betsy said, tossing a hangerful of belts onto the floor.

"Hey, that's alligator," Alix said, pulling a thick, olive-green belt from the stack. How had she gotten herself into this position, defenseless with Betsy at the helm? She held up the belt, but then realized Betsy was right and tossed it onto the Goodwill pile.

As something of a distraction from the clothing debacle, Alix told Betsy about Skye's ambivalence, thinking maybe seeing her mother wasn't such a great idea. But Skye had located her mother at a rehab facility in northern California and written to her. In their last session, the girl had talked about wandering around her old neighborhood with her friends, which had brought up a host of traumatic memories. As far as Alix knew, Skye was still waiting to hear from her mother.

"She ended the session with a doorknob comment about just wanting to forget the whole thing. And honestly, I think she's right."

"After all these years, she's found her mother," Betsy said. "What's the worry?"

"I just don't see this going well."

"Since when did you start playing God?"

"Oh, get off it, Betsy. You of all people. As if you don't maneuver and scheme and bulldoze your way toward an intervention."

"Life's a bitch," Betsy said, pulling a stack of scarves from the shelf. "Here," she said, tossing them on the bed. "Make yourself useful."

Alix was staring at the heap of clothes on the floor. She sat down on the side of the bed and flipped through the scarves. With every session, it was becoming clearer to her that Skye had been better off placed in foster care with

Grace and Jackson. Of course, it could have turned out differently. If Grace and Jackson hadn't been so steady. If Eva had managed to overcome her addiction. But that wasn't what had happened, and Alix found herself asking the same question: What good could come of Skye finding her mother? In her own research, she'd located a handful of characteristics that fostered resilience—the ability to bounce back from negative experiences, self-esteem, stable social supports, and persistence, or what in the psychological literature was lately called *grit*. As far as Alix could tell, *grit* was the only one of these characteristics that she could clearly discern in Skye. And frankly, she wasn't so sure that in Skye's case, it was at all helpful.

Betsy was flipping through the meager outfits left in the closet. "You need a new wardrobe."

"No thanks to you."

Betsy smirked with what she took as a compliment, then grabbed a black plastic garbage bag and began stuffing clothes into it. Alix held the bag open for her.

"And what about scalding her hands in the bathroom sink?"

"She's fragile," Betsy said. "I get it. But this isn't any different from a host of clients you've seen over the years. Ambivalent. Reactive. It's messy. One week she's writing to her mother, the next week she imagines having been immaculately conceived."

"She doesn't know what she wants," Alix said.

"Of course not. That would make it much simpler, wouldn't it?" Betsy said. "Carefully tied up and never look back." The plastic bag was full; Betsy was forcing out enough air so she could knot the top of it. She tossed the bag toward the bedroom door. It landed with an exhale.

"Okay, now on to Richard's clothes," Betsy said.

"That's where I draw the line," Alix said.

But Betsy had been eyeing the closed closet door, and she opened it before Alix had a chance to get up from the bed.

There were clothes piled on the floor and in the laundry basket, a clean pair of jeans, a blue button-down shirt still on the hanger—presumably what he'd intended to wear the day he'd died. Unlike Alix's closet, which faintly smelled of rose petals, Richard's had a distinct odor of dirty laundry and disuse. It was obvious nothing had been touched since he'd died.

"Oh, honey," Betsy said.

Alix sat limp on the bed and watched as Betsy pulled out the laundry basket and then lifted up all the shirts and pants hanging on the clothes rack and stacked them on the bed. On the shelf were his wedding ring and a few pieces of jewelry—a gold stud earring he'd occasionally worn and a pair of cufflinks with his initials, an anniversary present from Alix. Betsy took down the one suit Richard had owned. He'd worn it to his sister's wedding, an elaborate evening affair in Oakland at Jack London Square. He was in the wedding party and wore a white rose in the lapel, the first and last time he wore the suit. His parents wanted him cremated in it, but Alix insisted it wasn't what he'd have chosen. Instead, she pulled out a pair of navy cotton slip-on pants he'd bargained down in the market in Chichicastenango and his favorite shirt, a gaudy Hawaiian print she'd purchased for him in Maui.

She didn't want Betsy to say anything. Not about the clothes lingering in the closet or how paralyzed she felt, believing Richard might return and need his threadbare jeans and slippers and books, the hiking boots, and his camping gear.

Betsy stuffed the clothes into the black plastic bags and dragged them downstairs. By the time she got back, Alix had dusted all the shelves and was moving her summer dresses and sandals and light jackets into the closet, instantly annexing the empty space, filling the shelves and hangers as if her clothes had hung there all along.

THE TRAIN, RUMBLING THROUGH town so close to the counseling center, always interrupted her sessions. Today it gave them both a chance to think back on the last couple of weeks since Alix had seen Skye.

"Did you have a nice Thanksgiving?" Skye asked.

"Yes, I did. Thank you." It was a lie, but that wasn't the point. She'd made a sweet-potato casserole and gone to Betsy and Stan's. Their daughter, Elise, had been home from college, and Betsy had invited a gay couple she'd met at the dog park, along with Stan's partner, Carl, and his wife, Rita. And Ken, a recently divorced accountant-turned-contractor whom Betsy had been dying to introduce to her. Alix found him dull and overly solicitous, and the dinner conversation centered on Rita's claim that the homeless over in Aptos were scamming the government and making out like bandits. "I personally heard about one family. The husband's panhandling, making five hundred dollars a week; his wife's doing drugs, and the daughter got herself pregnant so they could get more welfare."

Alix pictured Richard, who had thrived on confronting that kind of naive idiocy, sitting across from her at the table, smirking. "I know that family," he would have said. "Saw them parked out in front of the natural foods store on Soquel Drive." He would have paused long enough for Rita to believe that finally someone was going to back her up. "But that guy, dressed in a suit and tie, told me the panhandling was clearing closer to *seven* hundred a week."

Alix smiled to herself and looked at Skye. "And you? How was the holiday?"

"Good," the girl said, pausing to add, "We did our usual at my friend Jasmine's—even her father getting drunk was the same."

"And your friends?" Alix asked. "How was it being home?"

"Good." Skye took out a piece of gum, popped it in her mouth, smoothed out the wrapper on the top of her thigh. "But then Grace got really mad."

"Hmm. About?" The girl was leading up to something; it was obvious that Grace having been mad was just a starting point for whatever the girl had on her mind; perhaps something had happened over the Thanksgiving holiday.

Skye shifted in her chair and looked around Alix's office. "I don't know why she hates my mother."

"Hates?" Even Skye wasn't that naive, Alix thought.

"She's never given her half a chance."

"I imagine she feels pretty protective of you."

Alix waited, assuming Skye would fill in the blanks.

"I should have said something. I don't know, I just figured Jackson would talk to her."

The girl was looking down, avoiding her eyes. Alix could feel they were getting a little closer to the issue.

"I don't know why it's so hard. To tell you," she mumbled.

Earlier in the week, Jeremy had reappeared in her office. This time, it seemed he *wanted* to talk, but he'd hemmed and hawed the entire session. They'd exhausted all the safe topics; then he'd gotten up out of his chair and stood by the open window, leaning his head out as if he were looking to see if the bus had arrived. Alix had been distracted by her own speculation about what could be so painful to reveal. Contrary to the police report, maybe he *was* still stalking the ex-girlfriend. Was he having suicidal thoughts? Had he had a drunken mishap? Maybe he was flunking out of school. Something was troubling him, but she had no idea what.

Then, with three minutes left to the hour, he had whispered, "My stepfather messed with me. I've never told anyone."

Of course, Jeremy imagined he was one of only a handful of boys to have been molested. Alix had heard similar stories countless times. It used to break her heart. Now it was just a crime scene, lots of broken glass and blood on the walls that needed cleaning up.

Alix could see that Skye, too, was struggling. Her hands were clenched together, and she was biting down on the end of her thumb. Alix figured the girl and her adoptive mother had had some kind of blowup over Thanksgiving.

But then Skye blurted it out: "I saw my mother. She's been clean for three months. Grace was mad—it was stupid how she found out."

Alix listened as Skye told about having seen her mother and how she had told Jackson about the meeting but not Grace. "I told myself she couldn't handle it, let Jackson dodge the bullet. But I was just being a coward."

Alix tilted her head and tried to look impartial, refraining from saying what she really thought—that Skye was in way over her head, that she needed to slow down and consider the consequences, that a lot of people were going to get hurt in the process.

"You're right. That wasn't fair to Grace," she said.

Skye frowned, as if she were trying to translate what Alix had just said. "I thought you were supposed to … I thought you were on my side," she said, sounding angry. "Isn't … isn't that the point?" She was stuttering, trying to get the words out as fast as she was thinking them.

"No, not really." Alix paused to gather her thoughts. She could explain that therapy meant holding up a mirror so

Skye could choose rather than react—but that would probably sound even more condescending. Her head felt clogged, and she could hear Betsy's throaty laugh down the hall. *Damn you, Betsy.*

"I thought at least you ... saw how much I needed to see her." Skye's face was tense, her forehead drawn, taut; she was reaching for her sweatshirt, getting out of her chair.

"Wait," Alix said. "You're angry."

But Skye was already out the door.

THE FOLLOWING WEEKEND, ALIX and Betsy went to Nordstrom's in the City to replace Alix's clothes—the ones Betsy had discarded in the three black plastic bags to be taken to the thrift shop downtown. They took the escalator up to the second floor and browsed the active-wear and the trendy designer clothes. The store smelled of evergreen and spiced cider, and there were tinsel and flocked trees and ornaments on display. A pianist seated at the grand piano downstairs was wearing a red blazer and playing Christmas tunes. The lilting notes and fake optimism were getting on Alix's nerves.

"How's it going with that client of yours, the one who's looking for her mother?" Betsy asked.

Alix hadn't wanted to tell her about their last session, but it was inevitable Betsy would find out. She was pretty sure Monica had seen Skye leave the session early, and of course, everyone had heard Alix calling after her down the hallway. She relayed the meager details of their session: the girl's impulsive reunion with her mother and the adoptive mother's reaction.

"What are you? A size six?" Betsy was flipping through the sales rack. "And what do you mean, she stormed out? What happened?"

"Ten," Alix said. "Remember? The hips."

Betsy looked at her suspiciously, then slung a couple of pairs of jeans and leggings, size eight, and three brightly colored no-iron linen blouses over her arm for Alix to try on.

"They're only no-iron because the wrinkles are permanent."

"Yes, that's the point," Betsy said, coaxing her into the dressing room. "You need to loosen up. Wrinkles are in." She ran her hand along her neck as if she could iron out the loosening skin.

"And I don't like those colors. They're garish."

"You think black and drab gray suits you? Honey, you're not winter. You're what: spring? Maybe summer?" She held up a pastel green against Alix's face. "Go look in the mirror. See how that brightens up your face?"

Alix didn't want to look in the mirror. And she didn't want to talk about Skye, either, but she couldn't figure out how to dispense with their conversation. "On the surface, she appears self-contained, quite capable, but she's moving too fast."

"Too fast?" Betsy said. "How many years has she been waiting to see her mother?"

"Yes, but …"

The salesclerk, whose nametag said "Whitney," was unlocking the dressing room and hanging the clothes on a hook. "I'll come back in a few minutes to see how you're doing," she told them.

Betsy sat on a cushioned bench just on the other side of the dressing-room door. "And I want to see everything," she called out. "Even if you don't like it."

Alix took off her slacks and tried on the jeans. She avoided looking in the three full-length mirrors until she had the pants on. "They're too tight," she said.

"Let me see."

Fortunately for her, Whitney reappeared. "I'll get you the next size up," she said.

Betsy kept talking in a hushed tone while Alix stood naked in the dressing room, waiting for Whitney. "I'm not saying you shouldn't caution her, but this young woman's got a lot of moxie. Do you know how few foster kids make it to college? Something like three percent. What are the odds? And she left your office thinking she's a coward. Besides, aren't you the guru of resilience? I'd think you'd have figured out a way not to undermine her confidence."

Despite her supposed expertise, it hadn't occurred to Alix that Skye was breaking the odds. Instead of feeling more secure about seeing the girl, it made her feel even worse.

"But I thought …"

"In any case, good for you. Seeing her through this."

In the end, Alix agreed that the brighter colors were flattering. She bought three blouses—not the wrinkly no-iron but two silk button-down blouses and a flowing polyester with cap sleeves and a draped neckline—and two pairs of jeans, one hunter green and the other black. They went to the shoe department, where she bought a pair of suede low-wedge pumps and walking shoes.

Alix handed the salesclerk her credit card.

"That wasn't so painful, was it?" Betsy said.

Of course, it wasn't the price of the clothes that was bothersome, but the makeover Betsy was intent upon rendering.

They took the escalator upstairs to the café, the two shopping bags overflowing with white tissue paper. At the front register, Alix ordered a niçoise salad, hold the anchovies, with basil lemon dressing and raspberry iced tea; Betsy order a BLT and iced coffee.

They sat down in a booth.

"I can't imagine what you do all weekend long," Betsy said.

"Maybe I should take up golf; I hear it's very meditative." Alix knew she was being childish, but it felt good. She'd caved in when it came to Betsy's wardrobe choices, and even if she knew Betsy was right—not necessarily about the wardrobe but about finding a diversion—she had no intention of admitting it.

Betsy apparently didn't catch the sarcasm. "I hear all the mucky-mucks on the fifth floor play, although I suppose a woman would have a hard time inserting herself into their coterie. How about gardening? You have all that space for flowers and a vegetable patch."

Alix could hardly imagine all that soil underneath her fingernails. "What, and stain my new jeans?"

THE CLINIC WAS IN disarray. There'd been a student suicide on campus—a physics major with a history of drug use and numerous hospitalizations. He'd been seen in the counseling center over the summer by one of the interns and the staff psychiatrist. The parents had insisted he return to school for fall semester, something they'd been warned against by the psychiatrist.

Nora called an emergency staff meeting to debrief the incident. "I know we're all feeling strained beyond our limits," she said, "with the number of students calling to schedule appointments. And there aren't enough of us."

It was a frequent topic of discussion, with the level of distress of the students coming to see them: eating disorders and bipolar illness and OCD and alcohol and drug use. Following the suicide, Alix had gone to the residence halls with Ted to talk about coping with loss—the irony of this not lost on her—and she'd come home especially tired and drained and hadn't slept well, waking up to an image of Skye holding her hands in the sink—not under the hot water but with a razor blade. Of course, she couldn't force Skye to come in—certainly not because of a dream. And it was Alix's dream, not Skye's. Only Betsy or Nora would think it meant anything of substance.

"Could we have followed up better?" Nora asked. She wanted to know whether there was anyone else they were seeing now who might be at risk. Alix didn't want to talk about Skye—not with the entire staff. They'd all have predictable opinions about how she should be approaching the treatment. After they'd made the rounds, Nora turned to her.

"Alix," she asked, "how about you? Any at-risk clients?"

Alix didn't have much of a choice; she couldn't very well lie. She told them about the case: a freshman, mother abandoned her when she was ten, recently renewed contact. Alix gave them a perfunctory summary of the foster parents, the recent episode of self-harm.

"I doubt she's in any immediate danger," Alix said, soothing her own uneasiness. "Not really. But she stormed out of my office. A misunderstanding."

Nora said, "I would imagine you're seeing her through your own lens of loss."

Ted wanted to know if the student had been abused by the foster parents. "Grace. Is that her name? It sounds like she's acting as if she has something to hide."

"An only child," Scott said. "She's probably got overly high expectations for herself."

"Did you call her back?" Nora asked.

"She's not ready to do the work," Alix said. "I'm not sure how calling her would be helpful."

Betsy was staring at a scrub jay tapping at its own reflection in the window; she didn't say anything.

Alix resented the intrusion from Nora and Betsy and from the other staff even while admitting to herself they were probably right to insist she contact Skye. Later that afternoon, Alix called and left a message. *I'm just checking in to see how you're doing. I think we had a misunderstanding the other day. I'd appreciate hearing from you.* Alix paused for what would certainly be perceived as a long interval, then said, *You have a lot of courage, and I wouldn't want you to feel otherwise. Please call me.* She hated conducting therapy via voice mail, but even so, she hoped Skye would make another appointment to see her.

Chapter Thirteen

SKYE AND MATT WERE walking back from the bookstore, up the steep hill to their dorms; she'd been working all afternoon, unpacking and shelving new books for the next semester, and then she'd bought two reams of paper, a couple of blue books for finals, and a package of highlighters. Matt was carrying one of the bags for her. Skye was talking about her last session with Alix, how Alix had sided with Grace and hadn't even asked her about her mother.

"Wow, she really doesn't get you," Matt said.

It was true. Since their last session, when Skye had walked out, she'd been thinking the same thing. Was she supposed to get Alix's *permission* to see her mother? Skye knew she'd screwed up, not telling Grace about seeing her mother, but she'd assumed Alix would give her at least some credit for finding her mother, that she'd say something like "good job"—

couched in some kind of therapist noncommittal double-talk. She'd expected to spend the session talking about how it was for her, seeing her mother after all those years. But Alix just sat there in her oh-so-proper sorority-girl clothes and perfect hair and manicured nails. And those high heels and the diamond bezel watch. Then Alix had called and left a message, something about them having had a "misunderstanding." It didn't seem like a *misunderstanding* to Skye, so she hadn't called back. One of the other counselors—she thought his name was Tom or Ted—she'd seen him in the waiting room, a young guy with spiky hair and a tattoo on his arm, someone who looked like he had a past. Maybe all along, Skye should have been seeing him.

Still, Matt saying that Alix didn't understand her rubbed Skye the wrong way. "How could she?" Skye said defensively.

"I'm just saying," Matt said, his voice retreating. "Or maybe she just wants you to think about what might happen."

Skye was walking ahead of Matt, her footsteps pounding the sidewalk in a way that made it obvious she was mad.

"You sound just like her. And Grace."

"I don't know, maybe she's—"

"You're an idiot," Skye said, expanding the distance between them. She glanced behind; a bicyclist on the path nearly ran her over.

Matt stood watching her, stunned. "I didn't mean anything; it was just a question."

Skye quickened her pace, crossing the street without looking. A car slammed on its brakes and swerved, barely missing her. She stared blankly through the windshield and continued onto the sidewalk. The driver rolled down his window and shouted something like "What, are you crazy?" Skye ignored him.

Out of the corner of her eye, Skye could see that Matt was

walking down the sidewalk on the opposite side of the street, still carrying the plastic shopping bag with the two reams of paper. He stopped for traffic to clear so he could cross. "Wait up," he shouted.

On the next block, Skye let him catch up. She stood staring at him, waiting impatiently.

"What?" he said. "I mean, I'm sorry, can't we talk about it?"

"Sorry about what?" she asked.

"I don't know," he said, "but I must have said something wrong."

"I'm pissed off," she said, "and the last thing I need is having to explain myself. Can't anyone get me? I mean, is it that complicated?"

"I just wanted to help." Matt reached out to touch her hand, but she stepped back.

"I don't need your help," she said. Skye released a blast of air from her pursed lips. "And what are we going to talk about? Philosophy and how hard the midterm was? Or Jackie Barber in the front row sucking up to Dr. Morris, like we're still in high school?"

"I didn't know I was so boring," Matt said.

Skye tightened the straps on her backpack. "You're not boring," she said. "That's not what I meant."

"What did you mean, then?"

"Just forget it," she said, turning her back on him.

Without thinking, she started walking up the hillside behind the dorm. The few times she and Matt had hiked up the path, she'd liked hovering above the campus, seeing the big picture of their lives from a distance. The steps were damp, and she slipped on the granite stones, skinning her knee against a rock. She rubbed her knee; there was blood on her palm, but she continued up the hill past century plants and prickly cactus. Each breath was labored, as if she were hiking at high altitude, her lungs struggling for air. But she kept running, even though her legs ached and her shoulders hurt from the weight in her backpack. She took off the backpack and left it on the side of the path, figuring she'd find it on the way down, and continued running alongside the tall grass. At the top, she turned around to look at the view, perched over campus, and then sat down on a flat, cold rock. The dampness seeped through the seat of her pants, and her lungs fought to catch up. Her knee was throbbing, and her pants leg was torn. Over and over in her mind she heard Matt's voice saying, "I just wanted to help." The sky was purple and gray. Amber streetlamps glowed; she could hear air drafting between the parked cars. A horn honked; someone shouted. She pictured Matt standing frozen, wondering what had happened, holding the plastic shopping bag. He'd walk back to his room, and Casey would ask, "How's Skye?" He'd shake his head in disbelief, realizing he'd gotten in out of his depth.

THE NEXT MORNING, SHE regretted running off and making it seem as if it was Matt's fault that she was upset. She texted him: *Sorry. Hope ur not mad.* When she didn't get a reply, she called him. "I was just upset about seeing my mother, and I shouldn't have taken it out on you."

He didn't answer the phone, but later, when they saw each other, Matt said he'd figured it was something like that, but he seemed distant. After that she felt unsettled, her schoolwork drifting along with her thoughts, something she couldn't afford, given that finals were coming up in less than a week.

She didn't know whom to talk to, so she scheduled another appointment with Alix. "I'm not stupid," she told Alix.

"I get why you want me to be careful and not have big expectations about my mother. But I need you to be on my side, whatever happens. Even if I screw up. Even if this all goes to shit, and my mother disappears again."

Alix paused, her head leaning in thought. Skye knew she wasn't really giving her much choice, but she didn't want to keep talking and poking at her feelings if she couldn't be sure Alix would help her out. No matter what happened. It was obvious Alix didn't want Skye to look for her mother, didn't want her to complicate her life. Maybe Alix didn't want to complicate her *own* life. It was pretty clear Alix thought she couldn't handle the truth. And who could blame her with Skye burning her hands and storming out of her office whenever she got mad? But she wasn't weak, not with everything that had happened in her life. She just needed to know Alix wouldn't cave in or disappear.

"Well?" she asked.

"Yes," Alix said. "Of course."

THE ENTIRE THREE WEEKS Skye was home for winter break, Grace didn't ask—even once—if she'd heard from her mother or whether they were going to see each other again. Skye figured she was done with her pouting, at least for now. Between volunteering for Meals on Wheels and arranging the flowers for Christmas Eve at the church, knitting scarves for the troops, and decorating a float for the Christmas parade, Grace was out of the house most of the day except for dinner.

It was Jackson who asked if she planned on seeing her mother again. Not knowing, Skye shrugged. She didn't want to admit how much she'd been thinking about her mother, wondering if she'd ever see her again. She hung out with

Jasmine and her other friends from high school. Matt came up a couple of times from Visalia, and they all went skiing.

Two days before Christmas, Skye was sitting in the living room, watching TV with Jackson and Grace—a Christmas show with Tony Bennett. Bored, she was scrolling through old messages on her phone, checking Facebook, watching YouTube videos. Suddenly a new e-mail popped up, an e-card from her mother. Skye was stunned, and she had a hard time tapping the small icon, her fingers shaking with nervousness. At first, the e-card wouldn't open. Then she watched little elves stowing presents under a tree and a written message appeared in sparkling tinsel:

Dear Skye,

It was wonderful seeing you! I hope you'll give me the chance to be there for you. Wishing you and Grace and Jackson a Merry Christmas!! Love, Eva

Grace must have seen the panicked look on Skye's face. "What is it?" she asked. Grace was leaning over Skye's shoulder, trying to see the screen.

Skye pulled the phone out of view. "Nothing," she said, heading for her bedroom. She texted Jasmine, but it was hard to wait for any response, so she called her. Jasmine didn't pick up the phone.

Skye wasn't sure why, but the message made her mad; her mother wasn't acknowledging any of Skye's questions. As if they could just move on without an explanation. What had happened to all her questions? And then she'd tacked on a "Merry Christmas" as if now everyone could be one big happy family.

She forwarded the e-mail to Matt and then called him.

"What are you gonna do?" he asked.

They'd gotten over their last fight after her session with Alix, but still, he'd been more cautious when it came to saying anything about her mother.

"I mean, is that the best she can do?"

There was a long pause, and then Matt asked if she wanted to get one more day of skiing in before they went back to school.

"Sure," she said, but it wasn't the same as getting an answer to her question, so she pressed him.

"I don't know, Skye," he said. "I just don't want to be arguing about your mother. I liked her; she's trying to say she's sorry, wants to be a part of your life. Isn't that what you want? I think you should write her."

Skye went back to the living room, where Grace and Jackson were still watching TV. Slumped on the couch, she stared at her phone, replaying the little video clip of the elves, watching as they lit up the tree. Their own Christmas tree was flashing on and off with blue and red and green LED lights. Earlier in the day, Jackson had put Christmas music on the stereo and baked ginger cookies. The Millers came over, and they spent the afternoon drinking eggnog and hanging tinsel and ornaments. It was hokey, but they all had a good time.

Now Grace wanted to know what was going on.

"Nothing."

"Well, it's something,"

"Gracie, it's okay," Jackson said.

"It's from my mother. She e-mailed all of us a Merry Christmas."

"That's nice. Is that all?"

"She wants to make up for the past." Of course, that wasn't exactly what her mother had said.

Grace didn't say anything, but she went into the kitchen,

and they could hear her unloading the dishwasher, cupboards slamming, dishes clattering against each other.

"Why does she do that?" Skye asked.

"The same reason you keep egging her on," he said. "When you know perfectly well how Grace will react. She's been your mother all these years, and it hurts her feelings. But do what you need to."

That night in bed, she lay awake wondering what her mother was doing for Christmas, if she had friends who'd invited her for the holidays or if she spent them alone in her apartment or maybe with her AA friends, who Skye imagined were mostly estranged from their families. It was becoming more and more obvious that there wasn't any point in Skye asking what had happened. Her mother's whereabouts all those years were a tightly held secret, and there was little hope she'd be successful in unearthing the truth. The only remaining question was how much longer she was willing to be strung along.

IT WAS 1:30 WHEN Skye got out of the subway and walked down Third Street to the museum. She hadn't intended to be late, but it had taken her longer than she'd expected, with having to take the bus to the Fruitvale station, and then she'd just missed the train. When she finally got there, her mother was sitting on a bench in front of the museum reading the newspaper, one of those throwaway alternative papers.

A few weeks into the new year, her mother had e-mailed again. She'd been busy working on a drafting project with a deadline and was sorry she hadn't gotten back to Skye sooner, but she was going to be in the City again, for work. Would Skye like to go to an exhibit at the MOMA? Architectural photos of San Francisco. They could meet at the museum and have dinner together afterward. Skye tried not to get her hopes up.

"Sorry I'm late," she said.

"I just got here myself."

Skye didn't remember her mother always being late, but maybe she had been too young to notice. Or maybe it was a more recently acquired habit.

Her mother hadn't gotten up from the bench, and Skye wasn't sure if she should sit down next to her, but then Eva stood up and gave Skye a hug, less clingy than the last time, and they walked together toward the front of the museum. Her mother was tall, but her stride was short and out of sync with her brisk pace. It made walking next to her unpredictable. Skye found herself jogging ahead of her mother and then stopping to wait for her. They walked through the tall museum glass doors and stood in line behind an elderly woman in a long wool coat and a family with two little girls, one in a stroller. Skye grabbed a brochure and looked through the list of exhibits. Eva took out her wallet and paid her own entrance fee, then seemed to think twice and pulled out another bill to pay for Skye. "Two, please," she said to the cashier.

Skye would have liked to get the audio tour. She'd done that one time with Jackson when they'd gone to an exhibit of Diego Rivera paintings at the art museum in Fresno. Judging from how her mother had been handling money, she figured it was probably too much for Eva to spend.

They entered the gallery. The photographs were mostly black and white, highlighting architecture of famous landmarks, taken from unusual angles: aerial shots, close-ups accentuating gargoyles or concrete figures or the dramatic lines of bolts in the Golden Gate Bridge. There were photos of the Coit Tower, where she and her friends had seen the murals depicting working-class California; the Transamerica Building; the War Memorial, home of the San Francisco Opera. These buildings were familiar to her. Skye scanned the descriptions. *Home of the San Francisco Opera, originally built in 1932, a fine example of Beaux-Arts style ... Roman Doric order ... sustained major damage during the Loma Prieta earthquake in 1989 ... major retrofit and remodel in 1992.*

Skye looked over at her mother, who'd taken out a pair of brightly colored reading glasses from her shoulder bag, the kind of plastic glasses sold in the drugstore. She was studying a photograph of Our Lady of Guadalupe Church. The details of the buildings and the photographs didn't interest Skye, but Eva was preoccupied with the photographs, inspecting them up close and then backing away to view them from across the gallery. Skye thought their visit to the museum was an excuse, that the real reason was for them to see each other again. It seemed odd wandering from one photograph to the next with her mother as if they were well acquainted with each other and didn't need to talk.

It was crowded in the museum, and there was a lot of jostling to get close to the photographs. Two children were playing tag, their parents apparently oblivious to the disturbance they were causing. Skye found herself glancing over at her mother, keeping track of her so they wouldn't get separated from each other. Eva walked around the corner to the next set of photos; Skye followed. San Francisco City Hall. *Located in the Civic Center, yet another magnificent example of Beaux-Arts style ...* Raiders of the Lost Ark *was filmed in the rotunda, ... In 1978, Dan White murdered the first openly gay politician in California, Councilman Harvey Milk, and Mayor George Moscone.*

Skye pointed to the description. "I remember you told me about Harvey Milk."

"Really?" Her mother sounded surprised that Skye remembered anything she might have said. "Such a tragedy." Then she turned the corner into the next gallery.

The Painted Ladies of Alamo Square. *While the Painted Ladies of Alamo Square may be the most widely recognized and frequently photographed of the Victorian homes in San Francisco built beginning in the late 1800s, there are actually some 48,000 of these Victorian and Edwardian style homes in the City.* They stood in front of three photographs, familiar buildings around the corner from their old apartment, houses from a previous life where they'd stop on walks to the grocery store or the park. Funky buildings, they were brightly painted with elaborate scrollwork in blue and yellow and orange and red. *During the war, painted battleship gray with surplus paint … Also known as Postcard Row, featured in the opening credits to the popular television series,* Full House.

Skye sat down on the bench opposite the photos; her mother sat down next to her, staring at their life as it had been. Before.

"Jesus," she said. "There it is, staring me in the face." Her voice was shaky, and out of the corner of her eye, Skye saw that the tremor in her mother's hand was worsening. Her mother was trying to hold her hand steady; she looked away, and then she took a tissue out of her bag and wiped her eyes, apparently forgetting she had mascara on. "I thought this would be a good idea, you know—somehow nostalgic. But I've misjudged. Again. I'm sorry," she said. "Apparently I keep screwing up." She kept looking at the photos and then turning her whole body away from them, like a young child playing peek-a-boo.

Skye's shoulders stiffened. "What did you think? That it wouldn't matter that you left me behind? That we could start all over again?"

Eva looked up, her face tense, as if she were squeezing the sadness from it. "I don't need you to judge me. I'm perfectly capable of doing that on my own."

Without giving Skye a chance to respond, her mother stood up and walked away. Skye saw that she was heading for the restrooms down the hallway. Was she supposed to go after her? Skye looked around the gallery to see if anyone had been watching them. No one seemed to have noticed. She had a dull, tense pain in the pit of her stomach; it felt like guilt, as if she'd done something wrong. If Matt had been there, he would have poked her in the ribs or given her a disapproving look. It made her mad, thinking about how she felt trapped into making believe everything was okay with her mother.

When Eva came back, her face was devoid of smears and lines, her lipstick freshened. Only the way she was stuffing a used tissue into her pants pocket revealed that she'd been crying just minutes before. She twirled around, giving a quick look at each of the walls. "I've seen enough," she said. "How about we get a bite to eat?"

Skye shrugged. She was feeling dragged around, the promise of something better held out like an ice-cream cone.

They took the number 30 bus through Chinatown, up Columbus Avenue toward Russian Hill. The streets pulsed with late-afternoon activity—couples strolling, women going home with shopping bags from fancy clothing stores and gourmet food markets, unshaven men pushing carts filled with aluminum cans and old clothing. The bus was packed, and they stood side by side, steadying themselves on the metal bar hung from the ceiling. It was an easy reach for her mother, but Skye had to stand on her tiptoes. Eva pointed to her favorite Chinese restaurant and the Coit Tower they'd seen in the exhibit. "I went there with my friends," Skye said. "They have really cool murals painted on the inside."

But her mother was concentrating on not missing their stop, and Skye wasn't sure she was listening.

"This is it," her mother said.

They pushed their way through the crowd and hopped off the bus.

IT WAS A HOLE-IN-THE-WALL Eritrean restaurant off Lombard. Skye had no idea what that meant. Was Eritrea even a country? When she ate out with Grace and Jackson, they usually went to the local Italian restaurant: lasagna, eggplant parmesan, cannelloni, antipasto, red-and-white-checkered tablecloths, paper napkins, empty chianti bottles with half-burned candles for decoration. It always smelled like marinara and garlic and olive oil, with a slight bouquet of disinfectant.

The light here was dim; there were woven carpets covering the floor and low, round tables without chairs; Middle Eastern–sounding music played in the background. They sat down at a small table in the corner.

The waiter came to take their order. Skye scanned the menu: *Kelwa, Kitfo, Alicha-beggee, Vegetable sambusa.* The names of the dishes were meaningless to her. But her mother was familiar with the menu, had been to this restaurant several times before. She ordered for both of them.

"Matt seems like a very nice young man," Eva said.

"Is that who we're going to talk about?"

Her mother frowned. "It's awkward, don't you think? Let's not make it any harder.

"Are you still vegetarian?" her mother asked. "You used to be adventurous when it came to food. Not like other kids who refused to eat anything but spaghetti and meatballs and white bread."

Skye remembered making macaroni and cheese and tater tots—nothing she'd classify as adventurous.

The waiter brought their food: garbanzo beans with onions, tomatoes, and bell peppers; a cauliflower-and-potato curry dish; and some kind of pastry filled with peas and carrots and onions. There was a basket of bread they used to dip into the bowls. Everything smelled of exotic spices.

"I hope Grace and Jackson have been good parents," Eva said.

Skye tilted her head, thinking for a moment. "Sure," she said. "Just a little on the boring side."

"I guess it wasn't the same as growing up in the City. That must have been a shock." Her mother dished out a second helping of cauliflower. "I always wondered what it would be like to grow up in the mountains. Ride your bike, hang out without worrying about muggers and rapists and crossing highways—not that bad things don't happen out in the countryside. But growing up in Boston, my mother was always on edge, certain that something bad was going to happen. It wasn't until college ..." Eva stopped and waved her hand.

Skye was mopping up the curry with a piece of bread. It wasn't as if nothing happened in Oakdale. There'd been random bullying, fights in school—the kids knew about her mother, and early on Skye had felt compelled to defend her. But her mother's comment made Skye think about the freedom she and her friends had had in Oakdale. They rode their bikes all over town, went horseback riding at the stables, ice-skating on the pond. Of course, she'd had a lot of freedom in the City, but that was only because her mother had been strung out on the couch. "Grace used to tell me there was no point in trying to hide anything. For sure, someone in town was going to see me and report back."

"You were always so responsible," Eva said, "and I asked you to do way more than I should have. I'm sorry."

This time her apology sounded sincere. Skye almost said, "It's okay," but pulled back. "You can't keep saying you're sorry," she told her mother.

"You're right," Eva said, ignoring Skye's bratty tone. She pushed her plate to the side. "It's a nervous habit." She was nibbling on a piece of bread, dipping it in the sauce left on her plate. "Hey, I have an idea. You up for a walk?"

"Where to?"

"It's a surprise."

Eva paid the bill, and they walked down Columbus Avenue with the Transamerica Building in the distance, past a tailor, cafés with small tables and chairs out front, a real estate agency, a tattoo parlor, the neighborhood park. There were rails running down the middle of the street, curving around the corner, and electric lines overhead. A trolley passed by, the wheels squealing. The streets were humming with cars and young men walking arm in arm, an old woman pushing a walker. The restaurants and bars and cafés were overflowing; dance music poured into the streets. When Skye had been younger and Eva had still had a grasp on her life, they used to walk all over the City—grocery shopping, library books, a video for Saturday night. With their arms full of packages, they'd take the bus home.

"Here it is," Eva said, standing in front of a small neighborhood bakery. It was painted green and red and white like the Italian flag and smelled of sweet dough and butter and chocolate. Inside was a deli case filled with cakes and pastry and bear claws and cookies. They had to take a number. Customers in line were buying packages of fancy exported cookies and cold-pressed virgin olive oil. Everyone else was milling around, waiting their turn. The man behind the counter was taking orders and shouting to the side. Another man in a white shirt and apron was squeezing cream into a pastry shell. "Fresh-made cannoli," her mother said. She ordered a plain and a cherry-filled for them to share. "You drink coffee?" she asked.

"I'm a college student," Skye said.

"And two espressos."

They sat outside at a small round table along the sidewalk. It was getting dark. Random sprays of purple and orange clouds painted the space above the skyline. "I'd never let you eat these when you were a kid—too much sugar. So I'd sneak out at lunchtime." Eva laughed. It was the first time Skye had seen her smile, and Eva suddenly looked younger, more carefree. The cannoli was made of fried dough rolled into a tube, stuffed with ricotta cheese and fruit filling. Powdered sugar was sprinkled all over and chocolate drizzled on top. Skye cut into the cannoli with her fork, and the ricotta and cherry filling squeezed out the back.

Eva was watching, and she scooped up the filling from Skye's plate. "You remember that time you ... What was your friend's name—Whitney? or Heather? You had some science project, had to launch eggs in some kind of parachute contraption to see how far they could go without breaking."

Skye took another bite of the cannoli. "Hmm. And we hit a car on the other side of the park."

"What were you supposed to learn from that project?"

Skye shrugged. "I don't know. How to break an egg?"

They both laughed. Skye noticed she and her mother had the same self-effacing kind of laugh.

Skye took another bite of the cannoli. "I remember all those little dollhouses and miniature furniture we made out of balsa wood and scraps. You dressed up nails with ribbons and torn sheets to make them look like people. And remember, you came to my class on Career Day to talk about being an architect? And you taught me how to fly a kite."

"That's nice," Eva said. "I've been worried you might have forgotten some of the good memories." She picked up her coffee. Skye thought she was pausing, considering whether she should say anything else. "Anyway, that wouldn't leave you with much—the good memories." She put the cup down. "We never flew kites together; maybe that was Grace. Or Jackson."

Skye frowned. "I get confused. Did you teach me how to swim, or was that Jackson?"

"Jackson, probably, although there was that time we went with Melanie and Julie up to Huntington Lake. You might have learned how to float on that trip."

Skye had a vague memory of someone's steady arms underneath her body, the smell of cold water that was momentarily warm in random spots, the sun on her face, the oily smell of motorboats buzzing in the distance, kids' voices, stepping on rocks, the muddy bottom, silt stuck to her bathing suit, potato chips and lemonade. But she'd also gone to the lake with Grace and Jackson most summers, and sometimes with Jasmine's family. It was the first time she'd had a hot dog—a real one—grilled on the barbecue, with mustard and relish squeezed out of a bottle. For sure, that wasn't her mother.

"And I'm not really an architect," Eva said. "With everything that went on, I never did pass the exams."

Her mother's admission disappointed Skye, but at the same time, it cleared up some of the mystery. Skye had always wondered if her mother had been a designer or if she'd done drafting or if maybe she'd been the office secretary.

"When are you gonna be back in the City?" Skye asked.

"I'm not sure. Soon, I hope." Eva's firm was working on a condo remodel with retail space on the first floor. "For now, they're letting me do some drafting, until I get back on my feet. And I'm helping out with filing the permits—grunt work, really."

They talked about Skye's classes and what she wanted to major in. Eva wanted to know what it had been like growing up on a farm with chickens and a goat.

"It's not really a farm," Skye said. "We just have some animals and a big garden."

"Sounds like a farm to me, but what do I know?"

They bused their dishes and walked over to Greenwich Street and then down toward the Embarcadero. "Where are you staying?" Skye asked.

"Not too far from here. With a friend."

Skye assumed her friend was a guy because her mother didn't say anything more about it.

"Thank you," her mother said. "This was sweet, spending the day with you," and she kissed Skye on the cheek. "I'll e-mail you when I'm back in the City."

Skye walked down the subway stairs, the cement steps cold underneath her feet, the damp air seeping through her jacket. She was suddenly immersed in the memory of her mother pulling the covers up at night, leaning over, and kissing her on the cheek. It was just a kiss, but still, she could feel the softness of the sheets, see the dim light from a living room lamp. The smell of the lavender lotion she'd used suddenly came back to Skye, and the sounds of her mother straightening up the living room, the scuffle of her slippers—fuzzy purple slipper socks with leather soles. Skye touched the side of her face, damp from her mother's kiss.

Chapter Fourteen

ALIX'S DESK AT HOME was wedged into an alcove next to the kitchen. A layer of dust had accumulated on the desk, along with a stack of file folders, journal articles and overdue library books crammed with sticky notes, an array of scribbling and lists of imagined chapters, outlines, and assorted drafts on her computer. Saturday afternoon, Alix sat down in front of the computer, research piled up next to her. The washing machine was swishing dirty clothes, making a gurgling sound from the laundry room. She'd made a pot of coffee and got up and poured herself a second cup with a splash of half and half. She played around with possible titles, scrawled and then scratched out on a legal pad: *Defense Formation in the Recovery of Multiple Traumata: A Case Study Approach.*

Too clinical. She was trying to write a mainstream book that would appeal to the broader public.

Before moving to California and the college clinic, Alix had spent five years working at a mental health center in Washington Heights, one of the seedier neighborhoods in Manhattan. From her patients, she'd heard down-and-out stories about broken radiators in the dead of winter, diabetes and untreated cancer, rotten teeth needing to be pulled, kids playing ball gunned down on their front stoop. One of her first clients at the clinic, Cornell—not his real name—was an Iraqi veteran who'd just come home with classic symptoms of PTSD. The blasts had left him with an ever-present ringing in his ears. And there were mood swings and blurry vision, sleepless nights, chronic pain. And ghosts. They'd been ordered to clear out a compound of suspected insurgents, but after the smoke settled and the rubble was carted away, they saw that it was women and children they'd killed. Limbs scattered, a face split apart, a young boy, terror frozen on his lifeless face. It was the face he kept seeing, and he described it to her in detail: dark brown eyes, a thick brow, the blue-and-white-striped robe stained red, intestines exposed. And there was the stench, and the incinerated schoolbook resting in the boy's remaining fingers.

In high school, Cornell had pressured his father. "I want to enlist. It's not fair—letting others fight and die for my freedom."

"Have you ever seen combat?" he asked Alix. She paused long enough to construct some flimsy platitude and reassure him she was trained to deal with all sorts of trauma.

"That's what I thought," he said.

But he stuck it out, showing up every week for his appointment, sometimes two or three times a week. She convinced him that medication might help, and he started going to a support group with other veterans. He got a job at a homeless shelter, work he found meaningful, that kept him in touch with other veterans struggling to keep their heads above water. The ringing in his ears never stopped, but the mood swings and the flashbacks slowly lessened. When she asked if he'd ever thought about taking his own life, he blanched. "I'm always suicidal," he said. He'd just made up his mind it wasn't an option.

Twenty Stories of Resilience.

Except they weren't all stories of resilience. There was Tim. He'd come into her office in the counseling center, distraught, sleepless, overcome by guilt. He'd struck and killed a pedestrian—the man was drunk, disoriented, wandering down the middle of a dark, rural highway at 2 in the morning. The police investigated and cleared Tim of any wrongdoing, but he kept replaying the incident in his head, wondering why he couldn't simply have avoided hitting the man, why he hadn't swerved at the last moment. She listened attentively; it was shortly after Richard's death, and it was clear to her that the young man had been the unfortunate victim of bad luck, of fate, of nothing more than the fact that sometimes bad things happen. When she tried to reassure him, point out his lack of culpability—in reality, what else could he have done?—he simply said, "In the end, I'm the one who killed him." Despite her calling him numerous times, urging him to come back to the clinic, he refused further treatment and dropped out of school. Later that semester, she was crumpling up the newspaper for kindling in the fireplace and saw his obituary in the paper. He'd driven off the highway in the middle of the night. A single-car accident. Only Alix knew there was more to the story.

The Risk-Takers. Boring.

Leap of Faith. Trite.

It was impossible to settle on a title when so little of the book was complete. And the profiles—of individuals, some courageous, some ordinary—compelled her to dig beneath the mantle of losses that dotted her own life. Of course, her own story of loss was unexceptional—so ordinary as to be pathetic. And yet, it was a mystery how some people withstood so much pain and assault on their psyches for years on end. Holocaust survivors, the Dalai Lama, torture victims, women subjected to genital mutilation. But there was a limit. A colleague had once told her, "Everyone has a breaking point." The real question wasn't why some people broke; that seemed patently obvious. No, the real question was why others languished with nothing more than a series of commonplace disappointments.

The washing machine clunked and then whirred to a stop. She got up and relocated the wet clothes to the dryer, then poured herself another cup of coffee. The cup had been a gift from Richard, brown and white rabbits with hints of pink. Alix had taken the cup to work numerous times until one morning she'd noticed her client, an especially sheltered young woman, staring at the cup. The rabbits, Alix realized, were all fornicating in a variety of imaginative positions. When she confronted Richard, all he could do was laugh. "I just figured you knew," he said.

She leaned over the keyboard, her fingers poised above the keys, suddenly remembering a dream she'd had the previous night, waking up feeling as if she'd been punched in the stomach. It was 3 in the morning. She'd dreamed about a dead pelican on the beach. In the real-life event the dream was based on, she'd gone with Richard to the beach. While he was off hang gliding, she walked along the surf. It was early in the morning, and there wasn't anyone else out on the beach. She came upon a dead pelican washed up on the shore, sand flies swarming over the feathers and guts, blood oozing, gulls pecking at the innards. When she walked by, Alix noticed the pelican tied up with fishing line, a hook embedded in its throat. She gagged on the stench and slowly backed away. But in the dream, Skye was hunched over to get a closer look. The pelican was still alive. Painstakingly, she was disentangling the fishing line, and Alix bent down to help her. As they worked side by side, she was aware of Skye's breathing, the awkwardness of their hands and bodies so physically close. When she woke up, Alix felt ashamed by her lack of compassion and the fear that was strangling her. It was Skye who'd reached out to rescue the bird.

She picked up the coffee cup and took a sip. Before even swallowing, she was hurling the coffee cup across the room. It splintered in a series of loud cracks, knocking over a wine-glass drying on a towel by the kitchen sink. The stem snapped from the glass and sputtered around on the tile floor like an off-kilter top. Alix closed her eyes and bit the inside of her cheek. *Don't*, she thought. *Don't do it.* But she was out of her chair, picking through the coffee cups in the cabinet. An old Audubon cup of Richard's, with two great blue herons and a chipped rim, another from the Sierra Club with birds of California. She took them outside, rolled back her arm, and lobbed the Audubon cup against the Douglas fir. The handle flew off, but the rest of the cup remained intact on the grass next to the exposed tree roots. She ran over and picked it up again and this time threw the cup against the storage shed, shattering it into pieces. The second cup sailed across the yard and hit a concrete retaining wall. She was out of breath with the emotion and the exertion, but she spied an empty pottery planter, green and gold with flowers, that she'd never liked, and she tossed it into the air. The planter landed on the patio with what Alix detected as a bounce before shattering.

Alix had her hand over her mouth, stunned at the damage she'd wrought, staring at the broken pieces. She went back inside the house. The walls were streaked with brown liquid, the floor strewn with slivers and broken shards, the refrigerator, the ceiling, in a watery Jackson Pollack motif. A rabbit's head from the first coffee cup was dislodged from the rest of his body. White ears, slivers of red and black, a curved piece that had been the handle lay on the floor. She grabbed a cardboard box from the garage and began picking up the pieces, tossing the remnants of birds and lettering into the box. Broken wings, a cracked beak, a body separated from the head. She went outside and picked through the tall grass, revealing chunks of glassy birds, adding them to the shattered remains.

It wasn't until the next morning that she fully assessed the damage. The coffee had dried to a sepia-toned stain on the walls, and there were slivers of pottery strewn across the tile floor all the way into the living room. She'd inadvertently left the half-and-half on the counter, and the kitchen smelled of stale coffee with a tinge of sour milk. She swept up and vacuumed and then got out an oversized sponge, a bottle of spray cleaner, and the six-foot ladder Richard had bought to paint the cathedral ceilings. She cautiously climbed halfway up the ladder, which was as far as she was willing to venture. Starting at the ceiling, she began wiping down the walls—coffee and years of grime and splattered tomato sauce. It didn't take long for her arms and neck and shoulders to ache, but she paused only long enough to make another pot of coffee and a couple of pieces of toast. By lunchtime, with daylight streaming in through the front windows, the kitchen walls and counters had been resurrected. In the living room, there were spots on the ceiling that wouldn't be cleaned until several months later when she hired a handyman to scale the ladder.

But the broken remains of coffee cups and handles were staring at her. She took the box out to the side of the house and was about to dump it into the garbage can when she saw a shard with one of the hummingbird pairs split from its partner, a beak reaching out into vacant space. She took the box back inside, placed it on the kitchen table, and carefully sifted through the broken shards, picking out anything recognizable. Like a jigsaw puzzle, she began to rearrange the bits of bird to fit them back together. A red wing split in two, talons and a severed leg, a snowy plover foraging in the sand, a red flower, two yellow eyes. Only a thin, ragged border separated the segments of bird. It was painstakingly slow, and she had to be especially cautious not to cut herself on the sharp edges. Her fingertips turned tender; specks of red welled up. For dinner, she heated up a can of soup. While she ate, she continued to work, arranging and rearranging the pieces.

When all the birds and the coffee cups had been restored, she stood back and admired her work.

AND THEN, SATURDAY MORNINGS, it became something of a ritual to thwart writer's block. Sitting down at the computer, her thoughts frozen, she'd grab two or three mismatched mugs out of the cabinet, a few decorative plates, run out the back door, and throw them against a tree or the wall. Or the storage shed—this being riskier since she might inadvertently hit the side window, making for a much lengthier cleanup. It wasn't that different from target practice, she thought, and she'd collect the pieces in a wooden salad bowl—something she wouldn't be tempted to throw against the wall. She donned heavy gardening gloves to avoid cutting herself. Then she'd take the broken ceramic pieces inside and reconstruct the birds or flowers or pithy coffee-mug adages on the dining room table like a globe flattened into a

Mercator map. Her collection of broken shards was growing, quickly taking over the portion of the table she'd allocated for her emerging project, but no matter. She hardly ever ate her dinner seated at the table.

Unfortunately, in the process, tiny pieces of glass had blown all over the yard, and she was afraid some innocent bird or a raccoon or the neighbor's cat might inhale a sliver and choke to death right there on her back patio. After each episode, she was forced to sweep and hose down the patio. Clearly, she couldn't keep breaking dishes like this, and besides, the mugs were really too thick to break into the size pieces she found most aesthetically pleasing. And yet, it was gratifying, like yelling "Fuck" when she was momentarily frustrated, when she wished for Richard's help fixing a leaky faucet or getting the lawn mower to start. Or changing the batteries in the smoke alarms. Or when she woke in the middle of the night, huddled on her side of the bed, cold and lonely, her skin coveting his touch. She'd recently discovered there was a word for the satisfaction one feels hurling an expletive. *Lalochezia.* Surely there was a word for hurling pottery or a ceramic dish against the wall, listening to the sound of broken glass. To relieve oneself by throwing an object, perhaps related to the Greek root *ballo,* as in "going ballistic." Of course, it wasn't like her to be so outwardly expressive—and that was the pleasure of it. Alone, behind her house, the thwack and tintinnabulation. The finality of seeing an unmarred whole broken into pieces, strewn across the yard, a muted battle scene.

Walking downtown after one such episode, she noticed a sign in the café window advertising a pottery class. "Learn how to throw pottery." It was the word *throw* that drew her eye to the poster, and she smiled at the image of a whole class throwing pottery against the wall, then reassembling the pieces to create a larger work. Of course, she understood that throwing pottery had to do with a potter's wheel, but still, the image made her smile. Create pottery and then break it, feeling no guilt or remorse about destroying her own work. Ashes to ashes, dust to dust.

Chapter Fifteen

"EITHER I HAVE FREE will or my actions are predetermined. Both cannot be true," Morris seemed quite pleased with himself. He picked up his coffee cup and took a sip, waited for a response from the class. There was a rustling of notebooks, unimpressed eyes staring back at him. Philosophy 211, Ethics and Philosophy. They'd been studying the so-called compatibilists, David Hume and Thomas Hobbes, who argued that free will and determinism, if defined more generously, were in fact quite compatible. Skye missed having Matt in the class, but he'd gotten a C first semester. His requirement for philosophy fulfilled, he'd enrolled in accounting instead.

Morris continued with an example from the news: the case of a young man accused of killing his wife and three sons. At first blush, it appeared to be nothing less than the wanton murder of innocent family members. "The court," Morris said, "will certainly find him culpable, and perhaps he will even receive life in prison." What later came out in the news was a history of drug abuse. The young man had only recently been released from the hospital following a voluntary stint in rehab. "Furthermore, we learn he was a decorated veteran who had served in Afghanistan, had been seriously injured, and was suffering from post-traumatic stress, and we immediately begin to believe this is not as straightforward as initially assumed. We have an emotional reaction to the circumstances, and likely as not, we are inclined to sympathy for his circumstances, particularly because he attempted to alert his drug counselors that he was not ready to leave the hospital. Then there is evidence that the physicians on the army base denied his request for continued inpatient treatment. ..."

A student in the front row raised his hand. "But not all addicts commit violent crimes."

Morris agreed that of course, there were many complicating factors. "Certainly, this young man was free to act. No one was forcing him to shoot his family, and yet, given the circumstances of his recent past, the alleged addiction and psychological trauma, we understand that his actions might even be said to have been predetermined. And if his actions are predetermined, then how can he be held blameworthy?"

If she were more bold, Skye might have offered up her mother as an example.

IT WAS A SATURDAY WHEN they met downtown at the Embarcadero station just after 1 o'clock. Eva wanted to show Skye the building her architectural firm was renovating; when Skye emerged from the subway, her mother was standing at the top of the stairs, wearing layers of clothes—a maroon sweater and green peacoat, a knitted scarf that was wound several times around her neck. The colors clashed, and her hair was windblown, giving her a frazzled appearance.

Eva gave her a hug, and they quickly walked the half block along Market Street, then waited for the light rail heading south. With the sun shut out by tall office buildings, it was cold and darker than the other side of the bay. Skye pulled up the zipper on her jacket.

"It's an old warehouse we're converting into lofts and retail space. In the Dogpatch district—not sure why it's called that except it's pretty seedy. Now, anyway." The owners of the architectural firm had snatched up the building, certain the entire neighborhood would be gentrified. Her mother was talking fast, sputtering out the words, something about it being a historic district and Abe Lincoln had signed the Pacific Railway Act and how artists and craftspeople had been attracted to the area and you could see the harbor. "It survived the 1906 earthquake and fire that leveled most of the City, and the Museum of Craft and Design is moving into warehouse space nearby."

It occurred to Skye that when she was little, her mother would occasionally get frantic about work or the apartment being dirty, and she'd go on a wild cleaning binge. At the time, Skye didn't think much about it because most of her friends complained that their parents yelled about a messy room or tripping over toys in the living room. And the binges were more tolerable than the dark Eva that followed. But now Skye could see that there was a frenzied quality to her mother's monologue; she hadn't been just a normal parent upset about a cluttered house. Skye wondered if the dark Eva would appear again. And then what?

They got off the train in a neighborhood with abandoned cars on the street—stripped of tires and mirrors and anything electronic—and storage warehouses with broken windows, worse than near the Fruitvale station in Oakland, where there were some remodeled houses and apartments on one side of the station, and if you walked in the right direction, it felt okay. But Eva seemed to calm down once they were walking, and her speech slowed. She was just nervous, Skye told herself, and the thought reassured her.

They passed a construction-rental business and a lumberyard, and there were lots of signs for space available and bulldozers and semis parked on the shoulder of the road. With no sidewalks, they had to walk on the street. They came to a small park with a community garden and benches to sit on; a young woman had her two small dogs on a long leash. Across the street was a warehouse painted in retro shades of brown and green with old-style metal-framed windows.

"Here it is," Eva said, taking a bulky key ring from her purse. She fumbled for the right key, her hand trembling, but finally got the door open. There were building materials everywhere: stacks of drywall and plywood, cans of paint, spools of electrical wire, a table saw, and a tile cutter. It smelled of sawdust and the dampness of cold concrete. Coffee cups and soda cans and fast-food wrappers were strewn on the floor, but there was lots of light inside through the high windows. With all the carpentry work Jackson did, the tools and the smells were familiar to Skye.

Eva showed Skye the ground floor that would become retail space, and then they climbed the stairs to the lofts and walked through each of the apartments. There were holes for where the toilets would go and stubs for plumbing; loose wires dangled out of the walls. Eva told Skye the plan was to stain the concrete floors and leave the ceilings open, and then Skye and her mother stood out on a little balcony, and it felt like they were trespassing, sneaking around deserted apartments, even if they weren't.

Eva excused herself to make a phone call and walked into the next room. Skye couldn't hear everything she was saying, but her mother's words were pressured. She could tell whoever was on the other end of the phone was interrupting her mother, trying to keep her focused. Her mother was pacing back and forth. "Yes," she heard Eva say, "in a week. It looks like they'll be ready to drywall in a week." Her mother kept saying "okay, okay" into the phone in a way that suggested she was apologizing. Just before ending the call, Eva said, "I promise. I'll be there next week."

When she came back, Eva was smiling, although she seemed a bit rattled. Skye didn't want to ask if everything was okay, afraid she might embarrass her mother or upset her even further.

Eva took Skye up to the roof of the building, and they could see the vacant lot next door that her mother said would eventually be more apartments, and the tops of ships in San Francisco Bay, and tankers, and Alameda in the distance. On the opposite side of the building was the highway. Eva pointed out the Potrero Hill neighborhood.

After walking through a couple more of the apartments, they headed over to an ice-cream and frozen-yogurt shop. The owner, a bald man with hair coming out of his ears, seemed to know Eva. He asked how the renovations were going.

"Who's your friend?" he asked.

"Skye, this is Eddie," she said.

Skye wondered if her mother thought about introducing her as her daughter, but maybe she didn't want to risk getting into explaining the complicated circumstances.

They ordered two scoops of ice cream each and sat by the window.

"It's still mostly industrial down here, but there's a great café across the street and a couple of terrific restaurants," Eva told her.

Skye figured this was as good a time as any to ask her about the past, especially since she didn't know how many more chances she'd get. But she wasn't sure where to start.

"How was it being in rehab?" she asked.

Eva's eyes narrowed, and she put her hand over her mouth. Of course, Skye knew little about her mother, but it occurred to her that given Eva's history of relapsing, she was probably suspicious of anyone asking about her past.

"What difference does it make? Besides, it's nothing to be proud of." A semi was driving by, and they could feel the vibration of the floor as the truck rumbled down the street.

Skye shrugged. "I just want to know ..." She stopped herself from finishing the sentence: *I just want to know ... what happened.*

Eva scooped out a spoonful of ice cream, but she let the spoon dangle in the air without eating it. "This one was better than most. There was a view of Mount Shasta out the dining room window, and they had a library and a gym with hand-me-down exercise machines from the state prison. But you can't ever sleep with the lights on all hours of the night, and there were birds squawking, and, depending on the direction of the wind, you could smell decomposing garbage and manure from the cattle ranch next door. Nobody wants a rehab with drug addicts and ne'er-do-wells in their neighborhood, so mostly they're built in godforsaken places out in the middle of nowhere."

Skye didn't care much about what it looked like. She wanted to know if her mother was going to stay sober. "Did you go to counseling?"

"Sure. Mostly groups and AA twice a day. And you have to see the shrink for meds." Eva's right hand was trembling more than usual. She put down the spoon and put her hand in her lap. "You have to bare your soul or they accuse you of not really being serious about working the program." Her tone had turned resentful. "There are a lot of really messed-up people in those places. Crazy people. Really crazy. They need a whole lot more help than I do."

"Do you think it helped?"

Eva frowned. "Yeah, sure. It always helps. Every time I've been in rehab. It helps for a while."

Skye wanted to tell Eva that she hoped this time was for good and she wouldn't ever have to go back to rehab. That seeing Skye would be some kind of incentive. Maybe this time she could be enough of a reason for her mother to stay clean. But Skye *didn't* say any of those things; she could see how vulnerable Eva was and how much her mother needed to believe she wasn't like the other addicts in rehab. Her mother seemed determined to put one foot in front of the other and keep going. Something Skye could appreciate, even applaud.

"It's different this time," Skye said. "I'm sure it is."

As if Skye could prove to her mother that this time there would be no relapsing, no disappearing, she wrote her phone number on a scrap of paper and handed it to her mother. Eva took the number and stared at it for what seemed like a long time before putting it carefully into a side pocket of her purse. Of course, her mother had already given Skye her phone number that first time they'd met at the restaurant, even if Skye hadn't used it.

They took the train back and walked over to the ferry building for clam chowder in sourdough bread bowls.

"You know the way back to the BART station?" Eva asked.

Skye nodded.

Eva said she hoped they could get together again soon. "This was fun," she said. "I've always wanted to go to Alcatraz Island, you know, where the old prison is. How would that be?"

Skye nodded, relieved that after their short talk, her mother still wanted to spend time with her. Apparently, Skye hadn't pushed too hard, hadn't asked too much. Eva didn't give her much of a chance to say *Thank you* or *I enjoyed seeing the renovations.* Her mother was already explaining that she was late; she was staying with a friend, and the keys, she needed to get the keys. But it must have been a different friend because after a quick hug, she hurried off in the opposite direction.

AS IF THEIR VISITS were becoming a habit, the following week, Eva called Skye to ask if she and Matt wanted to go with her on a tour of Alcatraz Island. "It'll be cold and windy on the ferry," she said, warning them to bundle up. Saturday morning, Skye and Matt met her mother at Pier 33 in front of the ticket office for the ferry; she'd already picked up their tickets. Apparently, her mother hadn't taken her own advice and was wearing jeans and a light windbreaker, but she seemed full of energy—enough to fuel her body heat without a jacket. Eva introduced them to Joanie, a woman about the same age as her mother, with short, highlighted hair; she was overweight, which almost went unnoticed given the perky smile and loose-fitting clothing she was wearing. Eva didn't say anything else about how she knew Joanie, so Skye assumed she was an AA friend. Joanie had dressed more sensibly, in an oversized jacket with a hood.

There was a crowd of people, more than Skye would have expected in February. When they boarded the ferry, they went up the stairs and sat on the deck that was outside but covered with a canopy. Sailing time to the island was fifteen minutes; it was noisy and rocky on the way, but they could see the Golden Gate Bridge and, looking back, the City skyline with the steep hills arching up from the wharf. The skyscrapers dwarfed what had seemed like daunting hills when they'd walked up them. Matt had a camera, and he and Skye stood at the railing. He took her picture with Alcatraz in the background, and the tall lighthouse that looked something like the circular-shaped Coit Tower, and a huge tan-colored structure that was the prison. As the boat approached, they could see that most of the buildings were burned out and crumbling from neglect. Eva ran downstairs to the snack bar and bought them a bag of pretzels and a package of mixed nuts and cheese crackers—junk food she swore she'd never allowed Skye to eat when she was a kid—and two cups of coffee for Skye and Matt. ("I sure don't need any more caffeine," she said.)

Skye had told Matt about how her mother had been wound up when they'd visited the renovation. She gave him a knowing look. *See what I mean?*

"Stop worrying about it," Matt said. "We're gonna have a good time."

A ranger met them when they got off the ferry, mostly to tell them about the bathrooms and about the rare flowers and plants, the marine wildlife and nesting seabirds, and not to pick up anything or leave trash behind. "You all saw the sign at the entrance," he said. "'United States Penitentiary,' with the graffiti 'Indians Welcome.' In case you wondered why we left the graffiti, in 1969, when the prison was closed, a group of students, mostly from San Francisco, occupied the island for almost two years in protest of US policies discriminating against Native Americans. It's not so much graffiti now. It's more like history."

Eva got the audio tour for all of them, and they put on the headsets. She dashed up the steep walkway to the prison, but at the top she turned around; she saw that Skye and Matt and Joanie were walking more slowly, and she waited for them to catch up. Inside, the prison looked pretty much like what Skye had expected—dark, with exposed lightbulbs hanging from long wires, the solitary-confinement cells, and two-story cell blocks with small wire cots, a toilet and sink, peeling green and gray paint, and a concrete exercise yard overlooking the expanse of choppy, frigid water. "The Rock," as Alcatraz was called, had been home to Al Capone and "Birdman" Robert Stroud and James "Whitey" Bulger and had appeared in a bunch of films, including *The Book of Eli* and *Catch Me If You Can* and *Birdman of Alcatraz*. They were all listening to the same number on the audiotape, except Eva was having trouble being quiet during the explanations, parroting the audio guide and fidgeting with the headset and the cables. When they learned that in 1846, John Fremont, leader of the Bear Flag Republic, had bought the island for the US government for five thousand dollars, Eva said, "I think he overpaid." It was annoying and funny at the same time. Eva reached out for Skye's hand and then put her arm around Skye's shoulder, and they walked back outside together.

The sun was peering through the clouds, and it was bright with light reflecting off the waters. Skye squinted until her eyes adjusted to the light. They all walked back down toward the wharf and sat on a bench. Matt was showing Joanie the pictures he'd taken on his camera. The hillsides were covered with wildflowers and orange-and-yellow-flowering bushes, purplish ground cover, and hundreds of gulls and cormorants nesting on the island. The contrast seemed strange to Skye, the birds and plants mixed among the crumbling concrete walls with their missing windows, the roofless buildings, and the fencing with the wide, gaping holes—as if nature were taking over for all the mistakes made in the past.

Eva pulled out the snacks, and she had sandwiches and some oranges to share that she took out of a large shoulder bag. Joanie had brought along a thermos of hot chocolate. "All these years, I've lived in the City and never came out here." Joanie said. "It took Eva dragging me along." She was pouring hot chocolate into the cups. "You remember that time ..." Then she stopped, as if she needed to concentrate on not spilling the hot chocolate. She didn't finish her sentence.

The ferry pulled into the wharf, and they got back on and sat down at a table. Matt and Joanie were both Giants fans and were talking baseball and how it would be great if they all went to a game. "They start playing the beginning of April," Joanie said. That meant they'd still be spending time together in another two months, thought Skye. The ferry picked up speed, and it was hard to hear over the noise of the motor and the wind. Eva wanted Matt to take a picture of her with Skye, and they went outside with the skyline approaching. Months later, when Skye looked at the photograph again, her mother's arm around her and the sun lighting up their faces, Eva smiling and leaning her head toward Skye, it would seem as if they'd belonged together.

LATER THAT NIGHT, SHE called Grace and Jackson. The RA had left a note pinned to the message board outside her door. *Grace is worried. Call home.*

"Sorry," Skye said when she got them on the phone. "It's been crazy busy here, and my boss gave me extra hours at the bookstore."

Grace was more understanding than Skye expected. "I think maybe you needed your space," she said, "seeing Eva again after all this time."

It wasn't the reaction she'd expected. So she told them

about Eva taking her to the construction site and then out to Alcatraz. "She's funny. I didn't remember that about her, I mean, maybe 'cause of everything that was going on back then. And you should see this renovation her company's doing. Maybe you guys could come see it."

"My, we have been busy," Grace said.

Skye started to argue with her, but Jackson interrupted. "Gracie, remember that time we went out to Alcatraz? We were first married? Took the ferry there at night and got to watch the sunset."

"And we stayed in that funky hotel just off the highway," Grace said. "With the cage elevator we got stuck in."

They were laughing at their inside joke, which gave Skye time to think about spring break and how she was going to tell them Eva had asked if she wanted to spend the week in the City. She could lie and say she was working in the bookstore. Or she could wait until the last minute and say she was finishing up an overdue assignment. Grace would be upset if she didn't come home for Easter. That and Christmas were the only two holidays when she insisted they all go to church. Every year, she took Skye shopping for a new dress and new shoes. The rest of the time, going to church was optional since Eva hadn't taken her and Grace didn't want to impose any particular religious beliefs on her.

Jackson was asking her about classes, telling her something about not getting too distracted. "I know you want to spend time with your mother, and that's really great, but—"

"I know," she said, cutting him off. "I'll talk to you next week."

Chapter Sixteen

There hadn't been much rain that season, but February was making up for it with torrential downpours and flooding on the walkways and side streets and overflowing storm drains. Alix found that getting around campus was a soggy proposition of weaving through the buildings instead of walking around on the muddy paths, and shaking out drippy raincoats, and squeaky shoes. Every day they were discovering new leaks in the clinic ceiling and window frames. The facilities staff had strategically positioned buckets and large garbage pails, making it obvious the campus was better prepared for drought conditions.

There were still ongoing reverberations in the clinic from the recent student suicide. The vice president was micromanaging in anticipation of an impending lawsuit, which meant Nora was pulling files and calling emergency staff meetings.

She wanted to revamp their entire intake system and set up an ad hoc committee on assessing risk. She had them calling every no-show to get them to reschedule, and she was driving Candy crazy with scheduling and rescheduling her appointments for out-of-the-office meetings with attorneys and disquieted administrators.

At Nora's insistence, Alix and Betsy were reviewing charts, assessing for any overlooked at-risk issues. File folders were stacked on the conference-room table. A large bucket was stationed near the window; a steady drip made splattering noises.

"Ever think you could be wrong about her mother?" Betsy asked. "And about Skye?" There were sticky notes marking sections of the table for the different degrees of risk. She tossed a folder onto the pile labeled *Minimal.*

Alix raised her eyebrows. "Hardly likely."

At their last session, Skye had told Alix about their excursion to Alcatraz Island and about their plans having expanded into April: future plans implying that her mother was serious about being there for Skye. Eva wanted Skye to spend spring break with her in the City doing touristy things—going to museums and concerts in the park and Chinatown. At first, these new developments made Alix consider the possibility that she'd been overreacting, not allowing for the chance of a rare event actually occurring—Eva following through.

"That's terrific," Alix said, wondering if Skye was letting her mother off the hook, not asking the tough questions about why she'd abandoned Skye, imagining her mother as too fragile to confront.

"I *have* been asking about the past. Slowly. I just want to give her time to adjust," Skye said, as if she sensed what Alix was thinking. Apparently, Eva had confirmed she'd injured her shoulder while skiing back in college and had had trouble getting off the pain meds. She'd been clean and sober for varying periods of time until the car accident, and then there'd been four surgeries to put pins in her tibia and repair a broken pelvis. The medication had kept her going, but eventually she'd been forced to detox all over again. Alix had had a few clients at the community mental health clinic in New York who'd been addicted to prescription medication. The meds often caused insurmountable cravings and jittery nerves and paranoia. Sometimes it was hard to know which was worse—the never-ending pain or the wrenching side effects.

"I know it sounds stupid," Skye said, "but all along, I knew I just needed her back. Even Matt thinks she's going to stick around. And we haven't been arguing lately. I just have to figure out how to tell Grace I'm not going to Oakdale for Easter. I'm even thinking about staying at school this summer. You know—work or take classes."

If only Alix could believe it were true. After all, wasn't she in the business of helping people change? Shouldn't she, of all people, believe it was possible, despite the odds, for Eva to re-create herself?

Betsy grabbed another file and flipped through the initial assessment and ensuing case notes. "And why should you know better about her own life than she does?"

"That seems a strange thing to hear—from you, of all people," Alix said.

Alix had asked Skye about school and how she was sleeping. Clients going through tough transitions—gay students coming out, students working through past abuse, addicts getting clean and sober—she knew from experience their concentration and schoolwork almost always suffered. The transition was disorienting, like an out-of-body experience, leaving the client suddenly unsure of what life might have in store for them.

"Fine," Skye said. Everything was going fine. But her hair was even more straggly than usual; there were dark circles underneath her eyes; the hem of her jeans was smeared with mud.

Alix pressed the girl further, and Skye finally admitted that she wasn't sleeping. Lying awake at night, she found herself listening to the wind and the water pouring out of the drainpipes. Her body was feverish and restless, but she didn't dare get out of bed, fearing she might end up standing over the bathroom sink. And then she was exhausted during the day. It was hard to concentrate, and she was having trouble keeping much down except crackers and frozen yogurt. At work, she'd shelved two boxes of books in the wrong sections, so it looked as if the orders hadn't come in. Another student, Melody, had had to hunt around for the missing books. Yesterday, Dr. Morris had called out her name twice before she'd realized he was asking her a question. She wasn't sure what was going on in her head—mostly a torrent of imagined conversations with her mother about what had happened and why she'd never come to collect her from Grace and Jackson.

Betsy's certainty was annoying, even if Alix was too hesitant to argue. She obviously didn't grasp the complexities of this case.

"It must be entertaining for you to watch me struggle," Alix said, "and offer your easy platitudes."

It was one of the few times Betsy didn't have an instant rejoinder.

SOON AFTER, SKYE SCHEDULED another appointment with Alix. "I was afraid to like her," she said. "All this time, tracking her down. She's no Claire Huxtable, but she isn't Betty Draper, either."

Alix must have looked puzzled.

"You know, *The Cosby Show. Mad Men.* By the way, you look nice."

Alix wasn't wearing her usual tailored gray or brown slacks and sweater set but the greenish-blue, loose-fitting silk blouse and straight-legged black pants she'd bought on the shopping trip with Betsy. Alix said thank you and looked down, then tugged at her pants and adjusted the blouse. "Of course, over the years, you've filled in the gaps," she said. "Made your mother into something that couldn't possibly fit reality."

Skye squinted. It seemed to Alix she was about to react defensively, but then she shook it off. "I just want you to believe in her," Skye said. "That it's going to be different this time."

Alix fingered her gold bangle, slipping it on and off her wrist. "Yes, of course," she said. "I remember."

Skye bit off a piece of her fingernail and then bent over and fiddled with the zipper on her backpack as if she were preparing to get up and leave. But instead, she looked around the office and her eyes landed on the black-and-red cover of a book on Alix's shelf. *Love at Any Cost.* She pulled it off the shelf, scanned the book jacket, flipped through the pages. It was about domestic violence and the urge many women felt to stay despite years of suffering physical and emotional abuse. She closed the book, resting it on her lap. "If it's too hard, I mean, if you can't ..."

It *was* too hard, Alix thought, but that was becoming increasingly irrelevant. She wanted to explain how everything happening in their sessions was replicating—like a clone—Skye's emotional life outside the therapy. Like Skye's certainty that Alix couldn't be there for her—it was exactly what Skye feared most about her mother, that ultimately, her mother would disappear all over again. The extracted promise to be there for her, no matter what. Wasn't that what she wanted from her mother? And Skye storming out of their sessions, staying two feet ahead of rejection. In therapeutic parlance, it was called *transference*, and Alix liked to explain the process, to help her clients go deeper in understanding their own dynamics. Normally, she would have felt free to explain, knowing her own feelings weren't muddying the process, but with Skye, it was tricky. Alix had been ambivalent from the start, wanting to refer the case to Betsy, afraid she couldn't cope with the inevitable messy ending, the self-harm that was likely to intensify, the disintegration and primitive decompensation when Skye's mother abandoned her all over again. Of course, Alix didn't want to diagnose Eva sight unseen, but the signs weren't encouraging: the wavering moods and labile affect, numerous relapses, the history of chaotic relationships, the rapid speech and tremor.

So Skye was right to question her less-than-unwavering commitment.

Suddenly, Alix recalled her dream from the other night about the pelican, and she looked up at Skye with the odd sensation of having shared something intimate with her. Which one of them was the pelican? she wondered. But of course, they both were. That's how it worked in dreams.

"You can do this work with me. Or with someone else," Alix said. "But neither of us really has a choice except to see it out."

Later that afternoon, reviewing her notes, Alix realized she'd included herself, as if she, too, were being forced down the same narrow path.

ALIX SIGNED UP FOR the pottery class, four consecutive Tuesday evenings at the art center downtown. The class was at the back of the building, a large studio with wooden tables and pottery wheels and jars of glaze and paintbrushes and clay. Everything in the room was covered with a thin layer of grayish silt. Fifteen minutes into the class, Alix felt light-headed from the gassy, hot smell of the kiln. Their instructor, Sally, was a large-chested woman with knobby hands and dangling earrings. She had them slice off slabs of clay with a thin steel wire, knead it into a ball, and then roll and pinch the clay into bowls. She encouraged them to score the sides in free-flowing designs, and she laid out an array of wooden and metal scrapers along with trimming and forming tools and textured sponges. There were six other women in the class, mostly older, retired women with gray hair and arthritic hands who chatted with each other. Alix kept to herself, occasionally smiling at the women, just enough to appear mildly congenial. Frank Sinatra and Connie Francis tunes were playing in the background. "I Did It My Way." "Strangers in the Night." "Don't Break the Heart That Loves You." By the end of class, Alix had pinched and prodded the clay into two soup bowls and a misshapen pitcher. Sally admired each of their creations, holding them up for everyone to see. The next class, she said, she'd teach them about bisque firing and then glazing their pottery. Alix's hands felt rubbery and dry, and the lines on her palms were accentuated with grayish-colored clay embedded in the folds. She'd only broken one nail, but it was obvious that if she were to continue, her manicured nails would be the first casualty.

On the third Tuesday, Sally demonstrated how to throw a pot on the wheel. "Before you even sit down," she said, "you must center yourself." Sally demonstrated the appropriate posture, how to place their feet and hands. "Use your core," she said, bracing her arms against the wheel. And then she closed her eyes and took in a deep breath. Sally moistened the bat and dropped a three-pound ball of clay into the center, talking them through the steps while she pulled the clay into a cone and then pressed the cone down evenly into a flattened mound. She wanted them all to try it. "Remember to breathe," she said.

Alix, of course, was listening for bona fide technique, ignoring the new-age jargon about centering her qi and breathing from her core. She sat at the wheel, moistened the bat, and threw down her ball of clay. It missed the center, and she had to pry it off (breaking yet another nail) and start again. This time, the mass of clay lodged itself approximately in the center of the bat. She started the wheel, gently pressing the pedal, except it revved out of control into high gear and the ball of clay flew off, hitting the side of the wheel. On the third try, she was able to center the clay and secure it to the wheel, pulling the clay into a cone, just as Sally had demonstrated, and then forcing it down onto the bat. She pulled up the sides of the clay into a small, respectable-looking bowl, but then the wheel flew into top speed again and the rim of the bowl twisted off center and collapsed. "Relax," Sally said. "Be one with the clay." Toward the end of class, Alix reluctantly took Sally's direction, breathed in, and focused all her attention on the clay, not trying to wrestle with it but firmly cajoling it into form.

Her pot was lopsided, but even so, it was a pot. Her hands were slimy, her arms had streaks of slurry up to her elbows. She was wearing one of Richard's old button-down shirts, her new jeans, and a cheap pair of sneakers she'd bought especially for the class. Everything was spotted gray. She took home two more bowls and a large plate glazed purple and cobalt blue from the previous week, placing them on the kitchen table along with the broken pieces of mugs and plates.

Certainly worthy of throwing against a wall.

Chapter Seventeen

OVER SPRING BREAK, EVA took Skye to the San Francisco MOMA, where they saw an exhibit of minimalist painters and a performance piece with a mime throwing paint onto roofing felt. Then they bought sandwiches and hung out in Yerba Buena Park and listened to a street musician playing jazz on his saxophone. Eva threw five dollars into the case. She'd been to a poetry reading in the park in October, and she rattled on about a young spoken-word poet and how she'd love to be able to read like that.

It seemed to Skye that her mother talked rapidly enough and was dramatic enough that she'd be good at spoken-word poetry, though obviously, it was more than just the delivery. It was cool but sunny, and the pigeons were pecking at crumbs. Yellow daffodils were pushing up from the ground. Skye wasn't used to winter being over so early—or never really happening at all. After lunch, they walked up Kearny Street to City Lights Bookstore on Columbus Avenue and browsed the poetry section and recent fiction, and Eva bought her a copy of *The Joy Luck Club* because she said it was set in San Francisco and was about families—especially about a mother and daughter. Waiting in line at the register, Eva ran into a friend, a man with a beard and a thick neck, a construction contractor, whom she must have known from work. They talked about the building in Dogpatch. When Skye asked about him later, Eva looked puzzled and said no, she hadn't known him. "He just had a wonderfully open face and deep-set eyes." On the way out, Eva told her about Lawrence Ferlinghetti, who had founded the bookstore, and about the Beat poets, like Allen Ginsberg, whom Skye had already heard about from Sylvia. Eva took her around the side of the building to Jack Kerouac Alley. The walls were brightly painted with women working in the fields and a macabre mural about the "shadow of the grasshopper." There was a plaque with a quote by Ferlinghetti embedded in the walkway: *Poetry is the shadow cast by our streetlight imaginations.* Her mother thought the plaque said a lot about their relationship. "All that time we spent apart, but we kept thinking about each other. Even in the darkest times, I saw you. In my imagination." Eva took out her phone and got a stranger to take their photo, standing behind the plaque.

They walked back out to the main intersection; Skye couldn't keep from thinking about what her mother had said: *I saw you. In my imagination.* She wondered if that could possibly be true. And what would that mean? To be seen in someone's imagination.

EVA WAS STAYING IN Joanie's guest room when she was in the City; Skye was crashed on the living room couch. It seemed that Eva knew her way around San Francisco without looking at a map. She must remember from before, Skye thought, because they used to walk everywhere. There was a mysterious side to Eva. Skye kept reassuring herself that she'd learn more about her mother when the time was right. Every afternoon, Eva went to an AA meeting, and a couple of mornings she rushed off to work. Skye stayed in the apartment or went to a café to catch up on schoolwork, especially calculus and philosophy, because she'd had trouble concentrating on the details with so much going on. Eva would come home early, and they'd find a little neighborhood restaurant or they'd go to Chinatown for dinner. One night they went to the farmers market and bought ingredients to concoct a broccoli-and-cheese-and-quinoa casserole. They never talked about the past. Even when Skye ventured a question, Eva would deflect it, waving her hand as if whatever had happened was uninteresting or too tedious to explain.

Thursday afternoon, Eva wanted to go to a new Japanese restaurant that had just opened. They were walking down Post Street toward the Japantown Peace Plaza, the five-story pagoda a few blocks ahead. "I know you don't believe me, but I've thought about you every day," Eva said. "This whole time, I never forgot about you." When Skye looked at her, puzzled, Eva changed the subject, telling her about the nutritional value of green tea and how doctors thought it was one reason the Japanese were so healthy. "And sushi," she said. Eva asked if she liked sushi. Skye made a face.

"It can be an acquired taste," Eva said. "We'll work on it."

That night, out of the blue, Eva said she'd done everything Social Services wanted. "Rehab and AA meetings and parenting classes and counseling. But they weren't satisfied, no matter what I did and how much I promised. I even thought about kidnapping you and moving to some remote area of the country, making a fresh start for both of us. Except it's not really kidnapping when it's your own kid."

"Really?" Skye wasn't sure how she would have felt about being scooped up and transported across the country like a fugitive, even by her own mother.

They were sitting in Joanie's living room, on the couch/Skye's bed, watching whatever crime show happened to come on, passing the carton of Chunky Monkey ice cream back and forth.

"Did you think I'd forgotten about you?"

For a moment, Skye felt defensive, thinking her mother was shedding responsibility, turning it around so Skye was to blame.

Eva handed the carton back to her. "Of course, you couldn't have known what I was going through. And sure, I kept relapsing, but who wouldn't? They were watching my every move. I know I sound paranoid, but it's true. Even if you're paranoid, it can still be true." Eva laughed at the overused joke. "One time—just one time—I ate a poppy-seed muffin from the bakery near our apartment on Fulton Street. You know, the one with the red-and-blue banner across the top of the door? And my luck, of course: that was the day they called me in for one of their random pee tests. And I failed it. I tried to tell them, but that Mrs. McNulty—nothing got past her. She just rolled her blue eyes, wrote it all down in my file, and I was back to square one. You can't imagine how demoralizing that can be."

Skye wanted to ask about all the missed birthdays, and the cards and phone calls that had abruptly stopped, but Eva already seemed over-the-top upset.

"It wasn't fair. Everything was stacked against me. Against us. And then I'd get out of rehab, and I wasn't strong enough. I wasn't ready, and I was afraid if I took you back,

I'd screw up again." Her mother's eyes were watery. She was holding the carton of ice cream, her face turned away. "I know I screwed up, but you remember Mrs. McNulty? How she'd bring you for those supervised visits at the hospital? I just didn't want you to see me that way. Then I'd hear from her that you were doing well in school, that you'd made friends. That you were happy with your adoptive parents. You had a father and a mother and a stable home life. The longer we were separated, the more it seemed like there was no good time to return from the near-dead and say, 'You're my daughter. I want you back.'"

Skye wondered if anyone had thought about asking her what *she* wanted.

Before she could say anything, her mother continued, "But it's different now, isn't it, baby? She was staring not directly into Skye's eyes but off to the side. "I'm ready now, and nothing's going to change that."

Skye lay awake most of the night on the couch. Outside the window, street traffic skirted by parked cars with a whooshing sound. The foghorn exhaled. Music blared from a neighbor's window. They'd watched TV until close to midnight. Before going off to bed, her mother had held Skye's face in her hands and kissed her on the cheek. Skye had looked away.

She wanted to believe her mother, but there was so much that didn't add up. There was a photograph on the dresser in the guest room of her mother and Joanie and a couple of other friends—no one Skye had met. And her mother's clothes. She wasn't living out of a suitcase, but where was home? Joanie hadn't been back to the apartment the whole week. Eva said she was at a training in Sacramento, and hadn't that worked out perfectly? They had the whole apartment to themselves. And how she knew her way around the City after all this time. And the poppy-seed muffin. She rolled over and found her phone, Googled *poppy-seed muffins and urine test.* Snopes.com said it was *true*: poppy seeds really could make someone drug-free look like a heroin user. She scrolled down the information on the site; there'd been plenty of lawsuits won on the basis of false drug charges, children taken into emergency protective custody, jobs lost. In fact, the Federal Bureau of Prisons required inmates on furlough to sign a form agreeing not to consume poppy seeds. Including poppy-seed bagels. Skye felt bad for doubting her mother. And then the drugs and Social Services. She was pretty sure Social Services could make everything worse, requiring her mother to jump through lots of hoops. One time Alix had asked her, "Do you think you've been better off? Without your mother?" Skye had immediately shot back a defensive "No." It wasn't anything she wanted to believe. There were times Skye had wondered if Mrs. McNulty really wanted Skye back with her mother. Grace and Jackson looked way more like most people's idea of parents. But the drugs. Skye kept going back to the drugs. No matter how hard it had gotten, her mother had had choices.

THE NEXT MORNING, SKYE made herself coffee. There was a note for her on the kitchen table. *I have to go to work and then an AA meeting. See you for dinner.*

Skye grabbed her coffee and ambled through the house, looking at the prints on the walls, the knickknacks on the shelves, the books. She went into the guest room, where Eva had pulled the blanket up over the pillows. A nightshirt and pajama bottoms had been flung onto the chair back. She shouldn't have, of course, but Skye felt drawn in, as if she were mindlessly wandering through a museum or a modern archaeological site. She couldn't figure out why Eva wasn't living out of a suitcase. She opened the closet with shirts and pants and skirts hung on hangers. The dresser drawers were stuffed full of underwear and bras, jeans, T-shirts, but then she saw two photographs tucked underneath the socks. They were old photographs, faded and dog-eared with fingerprints and something tacky like orange juice spilled across one of them so there were bubbly stains in one corner. A much younger Eva was holding a tall plastic cup in her hand. It was obvious she was drunk; her eyes were half open, and she had a goofy smile, her tongue sticking out to one side. Her mother, in a dress with spaghetti straps and a trendy layered haircut, looked cute but sloppy drunk. She was leaning against a man with black hair and olive skin, a deep cleft in his chin, and dark eyes. And Skye's same slightly overlapping front tooth. Even Skye could see that he looked so much like her, it was uncanny.

She cleared away the magazines and books from the coffee table in the living room and placed the photos next to each other in the middle of the table to look more closely at them. Then she sat down on the couch, trying to read her philosophy textbook, but she couldn't concentrate knowing the photographs were just lying there on the coffee table, without an explanation. She imagined a conversation with Alix. What would Alix tell her to do? Alix was cautious. It was obvious in the careful, limited way she handed out tidbits of advice. She thought Alix would tell her, *Go slowly.* That seemed helpful, except with the knot in her stomach and anger simmering in the back of her throat, Skye wasn't sure how that was possible.

Later, Eva came back from work and her AA meeting. She'd gone to the farmers market and picked up homemade vegetarian tamales and gelato for dessert. Skye followed her into the kitchen.

"Would you make the salad?" Eva asked, taking out the knife and cutting board for her. Skye sliced up carrots and a tomato and bell pepper, washed the lettuce. Eva was steaming the tamales. She slid a Melissa Etheridge CD into the player in the living room and turned up the volume. Eva had a strong, throaty voice, and she was belting out the lyrics and pointing the wooden tongs in the direction of the speakers and then toward Skye, dancing while she shook the vinegar and oil in a small glass jar. Skye wished she could be so carefree and not worry about her mother seeing the photos laid out on the coffee table.

It wasn't until Eva had set the table with purple calla lilies and the fancy water glasses that she put down the tongs and walked toward the guest room to change her clothes. She pushed two of the dining room chairs under the table, ran her hand over the leather back on the lounge chair, pulled down the front window blinds. Skye was watching as her mother moved closer to the coffee table. It reminded her of Grace and how she had imagined that Jackson would tell Grace about having seen her mother and how badly that had turned out. Suddenly she wished she hadn't left the photographs on the coffee table for Eva to simply stumble upon. It would have been better to talk to her directly. And she never should have rummaged through her mother's dresser drawers or closet.

Eva slid off her shoes, bent over, and tossed them under the coffee table. That was when she saw the photos.

Eva turned toward Skye. "Where did you get these? You've been going through my things." Her face had tightened in anger. Or maybe it was betrayal.

"He's my father. Isn't he?"

"It's not him." Eva said. But she didn't elaborate.

That was a blatant lie, and any regret Skye felt for violating her mother's privacy passed quickly. "How come I never met him?" she asked.

Eva had picked up the photos and was staring at them as if she hadn't looked at them in a long time. "It wouldn't help you understand anything about what happened to you. To us."

Skye followed Eva. Outside the bedroom door, she watched while her mother put on baggy pants and a sweatshirt—the ones she'd left hanging over the chair. Then Eva went into the bathroom and shut the door, and Skye listened to water running and the cabinets opening and closing. As if she'd run out of options, Eva opened the bathroom door, sighed, and plopped down in the living room; Skye sat opposite her on the couch.

"Don't blame me after you hear what happened."

For a split second Skye thought maybe her mother was right, that it would be better if she didn't hear it—but by then it was too late.

"Graduation weekend. Melanie and a couple of the other girls from the sorority—we all got invited to a frat party. Mostly guys we knew—Randy and Ken Somers and James. What was his last name? He was dating Jody … I forget. It's been so long."

Eva was rattling off the details of the story as if she were telling an old girlfriend about some funny experience from the past. Skye wanted to laugh along with her mother, but the story wasn't going to be funny. Wasn't this what she'd wanted all along? To know what had happened? But it was all Skye could do not to cover her ears. Not to get up and leave the room.

"Anyway, we'd had a couple of shots at home and … That's what we did back then. The preparty. And then the party. So I was drunk," Eva said, as if she were confessing. She laughed nervously, and then she jumped up, suddenly remembering the tamales steaming on the stove out in the kitchen. When she came back to the living room, Eva said she wasn't hungry anymore and they could eat later.

"We were all drunk," Eva continued. "But then I'm not sure what happened except I went into the back of the house to use the bathroom. And the last thing I remember, I'd passed out. Three guys took turns. At least I think it was three guys—because who was counting?"

Eva leaked out a raspy snicker and turned her head toward the window. She hadn't been sure who the father was until after Skye was born. And then it became increasingly obvious. The darker skin, the pointed chin, Skye's stocky build, the overlapping front tooth.

"Your grandmother kept warning me how hard this would be, especially as you got older." Her mother's voice was tense and edgy. "She wanted me to have an abortion, but I was naive, and I thought everything would turn out fine. And I guess it could have turned out fine."

"But it didn't," Skye said.

"No," her mother said, "it didn't. Not for me. Not for us."

For the first time since they'd sat down to talk, Eva turned toward Skye, looking pointedly in her direction. "I loved you. I really loved you. And then I hated you."

Skye was staring at her mother, and then her eyes fell. What could she say to that? Her mother hating her didn't seem like such a surprise.

"I'm sorry," Eva said. "But I told you, I'm not strong. Not like other women. Other women who would have been able to cope with everything that's happened."

In the dim light of the living room, Eva looked washed out, haggard and gray, a dingy crocheted throw hung loosely around her shoulders.

"What's his name? Where does he live?" Skye asked. But her mother's head was slumped against the arm of the couch. She had only enough energy to swat her hand in Skye's direction.

Then Skye recalled that her mother, just after seeing the photos, had gone into the bathroom, and she'd heard the cabinets opening and closing and water running. It was obvious she'd taken something. Had she been using all this time? Maybe her mother hadn't ever been sober except for the time she'd spent in rehab. Was that why she sometimes seemed wound up? Or had she been using again just recently because of the stress of Skye's visit?

That night, with Eva passed out on the couch, Skye ate dinner by herself and went to sleep in Joanie's bed, on top of the covers.

EVA WAS UP EARLY making blueberry pancakes. There was a pitcher of fresh-squeezed orange juice on the table and a pot of coffee on the counter.

"Did you sleep okay?" Eva asked. "I didn't realize how tired I was, sorry, I can't stay up like I used to." She flipped the pancakes and got a coffee mug out of the cabinet for Skye. "Get yourself some coffee," she said.

Skye poured milk in the coffee and sat down at the kitchen table in a narrow corridor of hazy sunlight. She'd tossed and turned most of the night, awake too much to dream.

"I thought maybe this morning we could either walk over to North Beach or take the bus if you're not up to it. There's a street fair going on, and this one bakery makes the most amazingly decadent pastries. And then I have to pick up something at the office. I thought we could stop by, and you could see all the progress we've made."

Skye wondered if her mother was thinking about last night. Was she wondering how Skye might be taking in this new revelation about her father? That Eva had known who he was all along—and that he'd raped her? She wanted her mother to ask, "How are you feeling about our talk last night? I know it's a lot to take in."

But Eva didn't ask. She just ate, standing up, flipping pancakes, scraping the rest of the batter out of the bowl as if she were cooking for a crowd.

"Sorry I displaced you from the couch. How was Joanie's bed? I'm so glad we've had this time together. And we had a good talk, didn't we?"

Skye was having trouble breathing, and she found herself fighting back tears. She'd been sure that in the end, it would all turn out okay, not the way Grace and Jackson imagined. Now everything she thought could be simple had become a tangled mess. She pushed the pancake around in the syrup, took another sip of coffee. Nausea roiled up into her stomach.

"I'll be back," she said, and went into the bathroom and shut the door. A burning sensation rose in her throat, and she leaned over the toilet, hoping she wouldn't be sick, taking in a deep breath, swallowing the acid mucus back down into her stomach. The room was stuffy; heat percolated from the radiator, and her neck and face felt flushed. Pearls of sweat bubbled up along her forehead. She couldn't make any noise, alert her mother that something might be wrong, and then have to explain. What would she say?

She looked over at the razor on the side of the tub but then turned away.

I want to go home, she thought, wishing she was back in Oakdale and not across the bay in San Francisco. She leaned over the sink and splashed cold water on her face. She looked in the mirror. She hoped her mother wouldn't notice that her eyes were red and swollen.

When she returned, Eva was cleaning up in the kitchen. "You okay?" she asked, not looking up.

"I'm sorry. I have to get back to school," Skye said. "I have a paper due on Monday, and I need to go to the library on campus. I thought I could finish it without that, but I can't."

Eva put two more pancakes on Skye's plate and slid the syrup next to her. "I said too much last night. That's it, isn't it?"

Skye shrugged and poured syrup on the pancakes. She cut into the pancake with her fork but then twirled the fork with her fingers and set it on the kitchen table, afraid that whatever she ate wouldn't stay down. She went into the bedroom and packed up her duffel bag and backpack with books and her laptop.

A half hour later, they were standing by the front door, her mother's hand guarding the doorknob. "I know it's been hard for you, and I'm sorry if I said too much last night, but now you know what happened, and there won't have to be any more secrets between us. We can start again. It's funny, but I feel better, like all that bad energy got released." Eva looked suddenly younger, her face glowing, as if she'd spent the morning at a spa.

"Sure," Skye said, offering a forced smile.

"Do you want me to walk to the subway with you?"

"I know the way."

Her mother gave her a hug and held on tightly. For too long. She smelled of lavender, but she felt sad, like a swollen river, overflowing.

SKYE ADJUSTED THE STRAPS on her backpack and walked toward Fulton and the park. It was quiet. Damp air dripped down streetlamps and railings; there were a few sluggish trucks on the street. She turned left and headed for the train, her pace quickening, carrying the duffel bag and her backpack and the brown paper bag her mother had held out to her like an offering just as she'd broken away. "If you get hungry on the way back to campus," she'd said.

A train coming from the opposite direction rolled into the station; Skye could feel the trembling of the platform, the stale tailwind streaming behind the tracks. Through the train windows, she could see a handful of passengers disembark. Others got on. She hadn't planned on going back to campus until the next day, but the air in the apartment had turned stifling, squeezing the breath out of her lungs. The dorms weren't even open until tomorrow, and she didn't have a plan for where she'd stay the night, but she had to get away from her mother.

Skye opened the paper bag. Inside were a sandwich and a bruised pear. She shoved the bag back into her pack and took out *The Bluest Eye.* She had an essay due on Monday. She rifled through the pages until she found the photo of her father tucked into the back of the book, the one with her mother smiling and not so sloppy-drunk. And her father, his lips and cleft chin leaning against her cheek, poised for a kiss.

About an hour later, after staring at trains coming into the station and then heading out again and at the weekenders getting on and off, Skye walked back up the stairs to the street and stood on the street corner. She had twenty bucks and change in her wallet and a debit card with whatever was left from her last paycheck. She'd forgotten to charge her phone the night before, and her battery was running low. There was a café a couple of blocks down Fillmore Street; maybe some coffee would help her think more clearly, give her time to come up with a plan for the day. She ordered a medium coffee at the front counter, then moved to the back, away from the windows, and stared at her phone, thinking about whom she could call. Casey was the only one of her friends who lived in the City, but it would feel weird calling him, and Oakdale was too far away to go home just until tomorrow, and anyway, she couldn't call Grace and Jackson, not after she'd lied to them, told them she had to stay on campus to work. And she couldn't let on to Grace that maybe she'd been more right than wrong about Eva.

It had been rape. What did that mean about her?

She drank the coffee slowly and read her book. Poor, desperate Pecola Breedlove, hoping for blue eyes, like some folks dream of being taller or athletic or having a good singing voice. Or two parents. Some things weren't meant to turn out the way you hoped.

It was a little past 10 o'clock. The coffee was already cold, and she really didn't have enough money to spend on more coffee. Better save the sandwich and the pear for lunch. She should have forced herself to eat at least one of the pancakes. She should have talked to her mother. But about what? What could she have said? That it wasn't fair to blame Social Services? Or Mrs. McNulty? That she'd chosen drugs over anything else? That she'd have been better off not knowing about her father? But now she'd probably never get the chance to find out who he was.

It was drizzling outside, and then it started to rain, huge drops slapping against the front window. What if it rained the whole day? She hadn't brought an umbrella or a rain jacket.

She buried herself in the book and didn't look up again until she turned the last page. Then she took out a pen and paper and jotted down notes for the essay she had to write. *Pecola Breedlove is a lot like all of us, wanting something we can't have. Except Pecola can't hide her differences—everyone sees the color of her skin and makes assumptions about who she is.* Skye had spent her own life pretending she was no different from anyone else.

She gulped the last of the cold coffee and put the papers and book into her backpack. There was a bus stop in front of the coffee shop with an overhang and a bench. The rain was letting up, but it was still drizzling, and her sweatshirt wasn't enough to keep her warm. Skye wrapped her arms around her body and waited about twenty minutes for the next bus, not even knowing where it was going. The bus was about half full; she sat down near the back. Two women were sitting across from her, one with a small baby in a front carrier, the other, presumably the grandmother, overloaded with a diaper bag and stroller and purse. Skye wondered why they weren't sitting near the front of the bus, where it was easier to get on and off.

They passed a thrift shop, a florist, a locksmith, apartments, a school. The neighborhood looked familiar to her, but she wasn't sure if it was from before. Or the time she and Matt and her other friends had come into the City. They'd taken the same bus to Golden Gate Park.

She got off and looked around—it was the corner of McAllister and Divisadero. There was a liquor store and the Muslim Community Center. Skye pulled her hood over her head and started walking, not in any particular direction. There were houses in between the businesses. A body shop and a dry cleaner, then an apartment with cement steps. Skye sat down on the steps, under an overhang. More people were out on the streets: a man in a suit walking briskly, another man with two yippie dogs. Cars drove by. The clouds had become a lighter shade of gray. Skye stood up and kept walking; at Grove she turned left, past the radiator repair and the apartments with scrollwork and metal balconies. There was a park at the end of the street. She walked up the steps to the top of the hill and turned around; there was a view of the old Victorians and City Hall, and downtown San

Francisco in the background. It was a view seared in her memory.

She wiped the raindrops off the bench and sat down across from the dog park. Dogs were running around playing with each other; their owners huddled together with coffee cups and leashes and plastic poop bags. Her mother had taken her there, long ago, so she wouldn't be afraid of dogs.

She took out her sandwich. It was lettuce and cheese and sprouts and avocado on thick whole-wheat bread. Artisan bread. Something she hadn't heard about until her mother had brought it back from the farmers market. Normally, it would have tasted good, but now, when she took a bite, it didn't taste like anything beyond a soggy mass of dough.

She took out her phone and called Matt, who was surprisingly sympathetic.

"That sucks," he said. "But why don't you go back to her apartment? I'm sure she'd be happy to see you again."

But she couldn't do that, not with how she'd felt, not able to breathe, not able to trust her mother. Had it all been a lie? The time she'd spent imagining some blissful reunion with her mother. They'd start a new life together, and the past would become irrelevant. She'd been fooling herself all along. That was clear now.

Matt looked up hostels for her online and found one not too far away, on Mason Street. "It looks kinda fun," he said. "Just pretend you're traveling in Europe."

SHE ENDED UP ON the top bunk in a dorm room with three girls from Germany who didn't speak much English. They had assorted piercings and short-cropped hair in a variety of colors and chattered among themselves as if Skye wasn't there. At six that evening, she went out and picked up a burrito at the corner market and nuked it in the store microwave. It was getting dark, and she didn't feel comfortable wandering around in a strange neighborhood by herself, so she went back to the hostel and parked herself on a couch in the lounge. A couple of guys were watching football on TV, drinking beer and chomping on pretzels. She'd picked up a random paperback from the lending library, but it was impossible to concentrate. It was just one night, she told herself, but she was struggling to hold back the tears, feeling unfathomably lonely.

When she couldn't keep her eyes open any longer, Skye went back to her room, where she lay awake wondering what her mother was doing. Maybe Joanie had come back to the apartment and they'd gone out to eat. A neon sign was flickering, and there were loud voices on the street, midnight revelers. It surprised her how she missed Grace and Jackson.

At 2 in the morning, the overhead light went on and the German girls came in, drunk and talking loudly. "Oops, sorry," one of them said in a guttural accent, but she didn't turn off the light until they were finished in the bathroom and in bed. It was another hour before the room turned quiet.

The next morning, Matt called her, asking about her European experience.

"Very funny," Skye said. Her lips were quivering. She thought about all the nights her mother had probably spent sleeping on the street or in a strange bed, not knowing where her next meal would come from, maybe going to sleep hungry and strung out. It was obvious her mother was stronger than Skye, who no way could cope with that. It gave her a different perspective on how resourceful her mother must be. She was sorry she'd left the apartment without any explanation. (Of course, there had been an explanation, but it was a lie.) Her mother had finally opened up to her, something she'd wanted all along. Stupid, Skye thought. She wished she'd asked more questions, not felt so defensive and angry. It might have turned out differently.

For breakfast, the hostel served pancakes—without fresh blueberries—and runny eggs. Skye ate half of what was on her plate, then packed up and walked to the train station. She wouldn't be able to get into her room until noon, but she wanted to get out of the City, back to campus. It was foggy, with the sun struggling to come out. The streets were damp from the rain and the mist. There was a BART station on the corner, but she kept walking just to fill the time and ended up at Fisherman's Wharf. The station was nearly empty, and there weren't many trains that early on a Sunday. Skye leaned against a pillar, her duffel on the ground next to her, not feeling much of anything except maybe relieved she could go back to campus. Mostly there was just an empty feeling in her stomach, and her eyes were watery, her legs like rubber. She crouched down by her duffel bag, her body shriveled up into a ball. She wished there was at least one other person on the platform waiting, so maybe she wouldn't feel so alone.

When her train came into the station, she was the only one to get on.

By the time she got to her dorm, it was 11:30, and the RA let her in. "How was your break?" she asked.

"Good," Skye said, feigning a lack of enthusiasm, as if she'd rather be home than back at school. She unlocked her room, which still smelled of Evelyn's vanilla-bean candles, unpacked her clothes, and took out the notes she'd jotted down for the essay due the next afternoon.

Seated at her desk, she started writing the essay but fell asleep in the chair, her head propped up on her elbows.

When she woke up, it was 3 o'clock in the afternoon. She was hungry and groggy. She got out the pear her mother had given her, but it was smashed on one side. So instead of the pear, she nuked a bag of popcorn in Evelyn's microwave.

It was dark outside when Matt knocked on the door. The lights in her room were off except for the desk lamp that cast a small, crisp circle onto the keyboard of her laptop.

Matt sat down on her bed. "So? How was it?"

She didn't know what to tell him about the week she'd spent with her mother, and then she felt her lower lip tremble.

"That bad." He leaned over and wrapped his arms around her.

She relaxed into him, and the tears ran down her cheeks, onto his shirt.

She told him about going to the Museum of Modern Art, about the performance piece they'd seen and City Lights Bookstore. She got the book her mother had bought her out of the backpack and flipped through the pages. "It was fun," she said. "Really fun. She'd go to work and to her AA meetings, and I'd study and work on that paper I have due in philosophy; it felt easy. And then we'd go out to dinner. We walked all over." Then she told him about how her mother had suddenly seemed depressed and out of control and how she seemed to be blaming Mrs. McNulty and Social Services for everything that had happened. Skye wasn't ready to tell him about the photo of her father and the rape.

"I think she's been living in the City all this time," she said.

"Why would she hide that from you?" But then Matt seemed to understand how that might come about.

"She kept saying she wasn't ready to pick me up from Grace and Jackson's, like it was some epic burden to take care of me."

"That's not what she meant," Matt said.

Matt saying that made her mad because he didn't know—any better than Skye—what her mother had been thinking. But Matt was the only person she really trusted right now. She didn't want to say anything, risk having an argument with him.

Skye lay down on her bed, exhausted, and pulled the covers over her. Matt got up to leave. "No, stay," she said. "Tell me about your break. How was it being home?"

"Better, I guess. But I'm worried about my little brother. No one's paying attention."

Skye sat up in bed and reached out to hold his hand.

"I met my dad's girlfriend," Matt said.

He leaned over to kiss her. Skye put her arms around him, and they held each other without saying anything.

"What's she like?" Skye asked.

Matt frowned. "Nice, I guess. Really young. Like she could be my older sister."

"That must feel weird."

Before Matt could say anything else, Evelyn came in with a rolling suitcase and a backpack and two shopping bags of new clothes. She'd gone to Hawaii with her family and the new boyfriend, and they'd all gone windsurfing and horseback riding and biked down a volcano. After an exhaustive summary, she finally asked them, "How was your week?"

"Fine," Skye said. Matt nodded in agreement.

Chapter Eighteen

ALIX'S OFFICE DOOR WAS slightly ajar, and she could hear heavy footsteps coming down the hallway. The footsteps stopped, and there was a pause before Skye nudged the door open and came in. Skye sat across from her, looking down at her lap. That was almost always how their sessions started, Skye seeming to need some time to wind up or wind down, depending upon what had been going on with her since their last session. It wasn't that different for most of her clients. They all relied on pleasantries before they felt comfortable getting down to work. Some of her clients wanted to pry into Alix's own life, as if the session was about her and not them, and she'd have to gently explain why she wouldn't be sharing much at all about herself.

"Did you have a good break?" Skye asked.

Alix smiled. "Break? Yes," she said, thinking about the

hours she'd spent in the studio, pounding and kneading clay, centering it on the wheel, and ultimately smashing it against the wall. "Very nice. And you?"

Skye took off what looked like a new sweatshirt and crumpled it into a ball on her lap. She ran her fingers along the raised image of a cable car on the back of the sweatshirt. She told Alix about the week with her mother, going to museums and out to eat—she'd tried sushi for the first time. They'd browsed used bookstores, sat in the park listening to street musicians, gotten reacquainted with the City. Alix noticed that Skye's hair was not shorter but styled and brushed away from her face.

"She bought me some new clothes, too," Skye said. "But then the last morning, I don't know, I got really nauseous and I couldn't breathe. ... And the only thing I could think about was getting out of there. And the radiator, it was so hot ..."

Alix leaned forward, waiting for Skye to finish her sentence, wondering what had happened.

Skye's breathing was shallow, her cheeks flushed. Her hair was hanging down in front of her face, and there were beads of sweat on her upper lip.

"Back up and tell me what happened." Of course, Alix knew how to sound compassionate and reassuring, but the blank stare on Skye's face worried her. And the long pauses in between words that stumbled into each other, as if her words, too, were being suffocated.

Her mother was fun to be around, and it was easy spending time with her. Eva understood her in ways Grace and Jackson never did—maybe it had something to do with genes and their common past, or how close they'd been early on and everything they'd gone through together was like a bond. Even though she and her mother looked so different from each other, there were gestures they shared and foods they both liked—ethnic restaurants. They both sneezed when they walked outside into the sun and were antiwar and prochoice and believed gays should be allowed to marry, and they both thought organic tasted better than conventionally grown food.

"I haven't slept in three days. I'm exhausted, but when I put my head on the pillow, I can't fall asleep. Except I fell asleep in calculus yesterday. And I haven't eaten."

"Anything?"

"Yesterday I had a Power Bar and four cups of coffee."

When clients told her about sleepless nights and copious amounts of caffeine, Alix was never sure how much they exaggerated for dramatic effect. Except looking at Skye—the glassy haze in her eyes, her pale skin—Alix had little doubt she was telling the truth. Sitting across from her, not having slept in three days and having barely eaten, she looked broken, defeated.

Skye was pressing her hands against her stomach. "I don't feel good," she said.

Alix moved the garbage pail next to Skye. "It's okay. Just keep breathing."

Skye started to pack up her sweatshirt, shoving it into her backpack. "I need to go," she said.

"Skye," Alix said, "look at me."

But Skye didn't look up, though she sat back in the chair, the backpack half zipped on her lap. "I don't know, I don't know," she said, shaking her head. She was running her fingers across her hands as if she were remembering the night she'd burned them, inspecting her palms and the backs of her hands and her fingers for peeling skin. Her palms were sweaty, and she was staring at her fingers, the cuticles and nails, mesmerized. She reached into her pocket and pulled out an X-Acto knife. "Here," she said, handing it to Alix. "I heard once you have to slice the vein the long way," Skye said, "not across your wrist. To kill yourself." She demonstrated with the tip of her index finger, running her finger up and down her arm. Her face was expressionless, her tone flat. Skye had always looked young, but now she seemed about eight or ten, her body curled up in the chair, her voice tentative. "I probably shouldn't have it around."

Alix took the knife. "What happened?" she said, trying to maintain a neutral tone.

Skye tilted her head to the side. "It's not important. Not anymore. And anyway, I just gave you the knife, so it's not a problem."

Alix was relieved that Skye felt comfortable enough with her to bring in the knife, but still, she couldn't just let it go, not without being sure Skye was safe.

Skye took the photo of her mother out of the book and showed it to Alix. "My father," she said. She told Alix about finding the photographs and confronting her mother, and about the rape.

She was shivering and put her sweatshirt back on. "I shouldn't have left my mother's apartment. That was stupid."

Alix was watching her unravel. She was afraid to hear more, but she didn't have a choice. Skye taking the knife and thinking about how to use it, running it along her arm in anticipation, was generously called *practicing*. Only two steps away from attempting suicide. It would be easy enough for her to buy another X-Acto knife in the bookstore where she worked or the convenience store just off campus. She wanted to know if Skye had actually thought about using the knife, if she'd been suicidal.

"No," Skye said, "I didn't want to die. I just wanted the pain to go away. But in the hostel, I'd never felt so alone. Well, maybe one other time," she said. Alix assumed Skye was alluding to the night she'd spent in the shelter after the car accident.

Before leaving her mother's apartment, Skye had taken the knife off a shelf in the living room with other drafting supplies. She didn't know why she was drawn to the knife, but she slid the blade out and gently felt the edge, which was still sharp, then retracted the blade and put the knife in her backpack. Then at the hostel, it had been late, she'd tossed and turned, an angry rant in her head about Eva and Grace and Jackson. She'd taken the knife out and felt the blade, run her finger along the surface. It probably was too dull to cut into her skin, not without really pressing hard, but she'd cut into the tip of her finger just to see. Then the German girls had barged into the room, drunk, arguing. Of course, Skye had no idea about what, but it was heated, and they seemed not to notice that Skye was trying to sleep. The next morning, there was dried blood on the pillowcase, and that scared her even more. "I guess it was good those girls came in when they did. Why would I do that?" She was running her thumb over the tip of her finger.

"Is that where you cut yourself?"

Skye showed her the finger, which was still swollen, and there was a thin line of red. "It's sore."

It was obvious to Alix that Skye was emotionally overwhelmed, that she'd regressed—which was understandable given the circumstances. "I need you to promise me," Alix said, "that you won't harm yourself—at least until our next appointment. And I want to see you again this week, on Friday. You feel awful now, hopeless, but sometimes that's what needs to happen. And it's hard to imagine you'll feel any better. But you will. I promise."

Alix was consulting her calendar, and she wrote in Skye's name. "And how would you feel about telling Grace and Jackson? At least about what happened with your mother?"

Skye shook her head. "No way. Jackson, maybe, but then he'd tell Grace."

"I think it would be helpful." But Alix couldn't persuade her, and she had to let it go. At least for now.

Skye grabbed her backpack and headed for the door. She held on to the doorknob for what seemed like a long time, as if she might say something more. But then she opened the door and left.

Alix could hear Skye's footsteps slowly fading down the hallway, the rapping of her backpack against her body, a slight squeak in one of her shoes. She took a mint out of her desk drawer and chewed it quickly, and then she sucked on another. The peppermint oil stung her nostrils. She held a third mint on her tongue, letting the disc dissolve by itself.

Her phone rang, but she didn't pick it up, knowing it was Candy with her next appointment. Alix's chair faced her door, which was open. Across the hall, Betsy was talking on the phone, loud enough for her to hear. "I'm sorry," she said. "I know it's frustrating to you—and I'm a parent, too, so I understand, but we're bound by confidentiality. ..."

Alix checked her e-mail, looked at her appointment calendar, stood up and stared out the window. A line of students was getting on a bus that had just pulled up at the stop below. It was windy outside. The trees were swaying, and a tissue or a paper towel blew by. Skye was slowly walking across the lawn; her shoulders were slumped. Alix cringed, watching the effort it took her to trudge up the hill.

Twenty minutes later, Candy called again. Alix picked up the phone. "You can send up my next appointment," she said.

It was an intake. Sheila, a blonde, blue-eyed sorority girl from Utah, was flunking out of school for some undetermined reason. The dean of liberal arts had sent her to see Alix, hoping some form of magic might be applied—

something like a pressure bandage to stem the bleeding. "I don't drink any more than my friends," Sheila said.

I don't think I can help you, Alix wanted to say, but instead, she managed to take copious notes and nod sympathetically.

FRIDAY MORNING, ALIX STRUGGLED to sit through two meetings, distracted with worrying about Skye, wondering if she'd show up for her appointment. Financial Aid was rolling out new regulations on students' declaring independence. She snuck out halfway through, went back to her office, and stared out the window. The other meeting was her yearly evaluation with the clinic director. Nora was running late, and then she spent five minutes shuffling through the stack of papers on her desk, looking for the Form-120 she had to fill out. The lawsuit was heating up, and Nora spent the hour quizzing Alix on how she should handle the university attorney's demand for confidential records. "They could care less about my professional license," she said. "It's all CYA."

Her 11 o'clock appointment was a lesbian couple who'd argued most of the previous session. They insisted they'd done the communication exercise precisely as Alix had instructed, but halfway through, Sandy's ex-girlfriend had texted her and Jess had stormed out. "It's not my fault," Sandy said, and it was all Alix could do to keep them in their chairs. They left with even more detailed instructions, which included turning off their cell phones during the exercise.

At noon, she ate a cobb salad at her desk, answered a few e-mails, deleted the rest, and caught up on her notes from the previous week. Skye's appointment was at 2 o'clock, and at ten minutes after 2, Alix called down to Candy; she still hadn't checked in. I'll give her another five minutes, Alix thought, but then Skye knocked on the door and sat down.

"Sorry," she said. "I had to go to office hours."

There were dark circles under her eyes, and she was wearing the same jeans and T-shirt she'd worn on Wednesday. Of course, it was possible she'd worn something else in between or washed her clothes. But there was an acrid odor when she sat down, and her hair was greasy and even more disheveled than usual.

Alix asked how she was doing, but Skye wasn't very forthcoming, saying, "Fine." When Alix pressed her to elaborate, it turned out she'd gone downtown with some friends the previous night (not Matt or Sylvia or any of her other friends she'd met at the beginning of the school year) and gotten drunk, then slept it off most of the morning. It wasn't until noon that she'd managed to drag herself to class. "It was lame," she said, but in a way that implied she was proud of herself. "Besides, you told me to take it easy."

"I'm pretty sure that's not what I had in mind."

Skye flashed a smile, the kind of baring one's teeth that's more sarcasm than pleasantry.

She was being a brat, letting off steam, making it difficult for Alix to keep a neutral stance. Between Nora and her clients, she'd been playing referee all day long. "You're angry," she said, more as a place keeper than an intervention.

"No shit. They teach you to say that in graduate school?"

"But underneath all that bravado is a lot of hurt. And betrayal." Alix paused long enough to see if Skye had yet another quick comeback, but she was looking down at her fingernails, inspecting the cuticles. "And it doesn't do much good to take it out on yourself."

"What's your point?" Skye said. "I come in here and spill my guts, and that's all you have to say for yourself? 'You're *angry*'? I'm gonna fail two classes. My friends think I'm a flake, my roommate's annoying the crap out of me, my mother's an addict. ..." She zipped her backpack, threatening to leave. "Shit, I have two midterms this week, and I haven't done any of the reading."

It was a relief to Alix that she was concerned about her midterms; it meant Skye was thinking about the future. And anger was better than despair. But still, it was tricky how quickly the rage flipped into self-doubt and hopelessness. And she was isolated from her friends and family—however she defined family. "I know you want to solve everything right now. But you're going to have to be patient. With yourself."

"Patient? Really?"

Alix could feel her own patience dwindling. "What do you want me to say? That I have a magic wand?"

Skye's jaw tightened, her fist clenched. "You promised," she said.

"Yes, I did. And I'm still here." Alix took in a deep breath; she was irritated, worried, but trying not to let it show. "And what about you? What about your end of the bargain?"

Skye frowned. "What's that supposed to mean?"

"This isn't a one-way street."

"I'm doing the best I can," she said. "But I guess it's not good enough." Skye looked suddenly deflated; her cheeks were the color of dried-out sand, and she was breathing in heavy sighs.

Alix could see she needed to back off and let Skye be angry with her. After all, it was safer to be angry with Alix than with her mother, or even Grace and Jackson. "I'm sorry," Alix said. "I'm just worried about you."

Skye sat back in her chair, and there was a long pause as if both of them were trying to hit the reset button. Alix wondered if the girl had eaten anything that morning, so she took a packet of trail mix out of her desk drawer and gave it to Skye, who struggled to tear open the cellophane. It was painful to watch, and Alix had to stop herself from reaching out and opening the package herself. Skye ate slowly, one morsel at a time. Her hands were shaky, and it took a great deal of effort for her to chew and then swallow the nuts and raisins, a few at a time, her eyes out of focus, staring at nothing. Her body was limp, her face thin and drawn.

Alix opened the window. The chilly air partly camouflaged the smell of sweat and slept-in clothes, but the smell lingered, and Alix could taste it on her tongue like the moldy aftertaste of food neglected at the back of the refrigerator.

Then Skye started to cry—not aloud but silently. Her nose was running; mucus mixed with tears dampened her lap. Alix handed her the box of tissues, but Skye didn't reach out for the box, and it was awkward for a moment as the box hung in midair before Alix pulled back and left it on the floor in front of Skye. It was hard to watch her dissolving. She could see that Skye had no more illusions about what it might be like, if only … Everything Alix had feared was now sitting in her office. She wanted to call Betsy, but what would Betsy say? "It's a crapshoot. Use your best judgment."

"My mother called," Skye said. She'd left a long message apologizing—again. And then she'd launched into a rambling explanation about how she hadn't wanted to tell Skye everything at once, but Skye had pressured her and then she'd snooped in her bedroom. "She said she needs a break. Like we're dating."

Skye finished the trail mix, dropped the empty cellophane package on the table, and took a tissue out of the box. She wiped her eyes, blew her nose, and dragged another tissue out of the box. The scraping of the tissue against the cardboard box was loud and unsettling. Wadded-up damp tissues and pieces of lint were scattered in her lap and on the floor next to her. Alix had a bottle of water in her desk drawer; she opened it and handed the bottle to Skye, who took one sip, then another.

"So here we are. Back at the beginning," Skye said. "Like nothing's changed."

"That's not true," Alix said, shaking her head. "A lot's different now. Like finding out about a secret. And finally finding your mother after all these years. And your father. Knowing about your father."

Skye leaned back in the chair and closed her eyes; her head tilted to the side, and Alix wasn't sure if maybe she'd dozed off, but then she started to talk, her eyes still closed, a stream of words unleashed.

"I always figured my father for the good guy, the smart one who hadn't stuck around because ... because, I don't know, maybe he'd figured out how messed up she was. I mean, it never made sense. The drugs. It wasn't so bad; our life wasn't so bad. Why would she ... ? That's what never made sense to me. And now she dumps this crap on me. He raped her. I guess I wanted the truth, but ... I kept after her about the truth because I figured if I knew what happened, then I could piece everything together. I thought knowing would make a difference. But it doesn't make a difference, like families standing outside the prison gates, waiting to hear about some guy who murdered their daughter sizzling in the electric chair. And then they cheer, but it doesn't change anything. No one comes back to life, and she left me in some strangers' house in the mountains, and it doesn't matter why because here I am. Still. Without her."

Alix was watching Skye intently—her eyes squeezed shut, her face in a grimace, looking like a little girl betrayed by the only person she'd ever really loved. Despite months of Alix imagining Grace and Jackson as generous and kind parents,

Skye had been right all along: Who were they, really, except stand-ins, second-rate substitutes for her mother? Alix could feel her own defenses fall away after the months of hoping there was an adequate, simple solution for Skye—that eventually she'd overcome the loss, the devastation. Alix found *herself* crying, tears rolling down her cheeks, something that had never happened before with a client. She got up and reached for a tissue, gently pulling it out of the box, trying not to make any sound. It wasn't supposed to happen, except she couldn't help it. Alix daubed at her eyes and her nose; she closed her eyes for what felt like a brief moment, and when she opened them, Skye had stopped talking and was staring at her, puzzled. And then Skye broke apart and wept.

ON SATURDAY, ALIX DROVE to the beach. She walked most of the day along the surf's edge, sand caked between her toes. Families were flying kites, and there were surfers and boogie boarders wearing wet suits, flocks of pelicans and cormorants, and otters lounging on long strands of kelp, cracking open abalone shells. The fog didn't burn off until 3 o'clock in the afternoon, and then the marine layer wafted back in an hour later. The damp mist swaddled her. She collected driftwood and seashells at the deserted end of the beach, thinking how she might use bits of shell along with the broken coffee mugs, and then she sat on the sand and stared out at the horizon. With longer days, the sun set more gradually, and a peaceful quiet washed up onto the shore.

At their last session, Skye had sobbed well past the end of the hour. Alix had called Candy to let her know she was running late, and, having composed herself, she sat quietly watching while Skye's body convulsed in spasms. The air in the room seemed to grow thin, and Alix felt her body soften, and the complexion of the light turned crisp and unfiltered, as if the space between them had collapsed. Alix leaned forward in her chair. She could feel Skye's heart beating erratically in her own chest, and she kept breathing slowly and evenly—for both of them—until the sobbing shifted into soft tears. When Skye eventually looked up, her face had been washed clean, her eyes not so much red as shining, and she left the room without saying anything.

Thin places. It was Richard who'd first used the term. Sacred moments where the space between earth and heaven narrows. The stillness, the certainty of something much greater than herself: it was possible to be transformed. She'd experienced it a handful of times before, mostly with Richard, who'd thought of hang gliding that way. One time when they were sitting on the couch together drinking coffee and reading the newspaper. Occasionally when they made love. Another time with a client who'd had a sudden epiphany, realizing she'd been abused as a child and all those unclaimed feelings and thoughts made sense in a whole new way. It was impossible to capture those moments in her case notes, and she was reluctant to talk about them, even with Betsy, who, she realized, would surely have had similar experiences with clients—moments when the clock seemed to stop ticking and the noise and activity and motion all around turned still.

She wondered if Skye felt something similar, or was her leaving in silence out of embarrassment? The subject would be tricky to approach with her, especially since the experience was tied up with Alix crying, too. And she couldn't be at all certain what that meant to Skye. For Alix, it surprised her. She felt a great sense of relief. A huge burden had been lifted, and she was reluctant to attribute it to anything short of divine intervention.

But then it was Monday again, and Alix found herself increasingly distracted and worried about how Skye might have spent the weekend. She'd lain awake most of the night, picturing the girl ragged and torn, subsisting on handfuls of trail mix and coffee. Regardless of Skye having left the session with an aura of calm, Alix began to doubt herself and the entire experience. More than likely, Alix needed something positive to come out of the whole melodramatic mess. It was ludicrous to hope for some miraculous transformation.

On their way to the weekly case conference, Betsy casually asked about her weekend. Alix pulled her aside, rattling off whatever parts of the session were foremost in her mind. She'd cried in the session. Skye hadn't been eating or sleeping for weeks. Her mother had finally, inevitably abandoned her—again. Except now she knew something about her father. And there'd been a rape. It was devastating news.

"I'm sorry," Betsy said. "All along I was sure it would work itself out in the end—you know, trust the process and all. I suppose I've been quite cavalier."

Betsy's sudden lack of confidence was no help.

Chapter Nineteen

THE ART-SUPPLY STORE downtown was two stories, with every inch filled to capacity. Kits for the fourth grade California mission project; Mardi Gras masks, pink and green boas, and other assorted costume paraphernalia; easels and colored pencils, watercolors, acrylic paints, electric trains, sewing supplies, and paper and glue and picture frames. Alix was browsing up and down the aisles. She tossed a glass cutter into the cart, a ceramic file, a large tube of adhesive, a container of premixed unsanded grout, safety glasses, and rubber gloves. The how-to videos she'd watched on the web made it all seem pretty straightforward, like any idiot could glue colored glass onto a flat surface. In front of the checkout stand was a rack of do-it-yourself materials; she skimmed a Sunset book on tiling and mosaics. There were lots of glossy photos of birdbaths and tabletops and garden stepping stones and simple beginner projects like plaques and mirror frames. She added the book to her purchases.

The other day Betsy had noticed that Alix's hands were dry and cracked, and for the first time in years, she'd skipped her biweekly mani-pedi appointment. "I'm taking a pottery class," Alix told her.

"Glad to see you can make a mess. Like everyone else."

Alix drove home and laid her purchases out on the kitchen table—gently pushing aside the broken ceramic pieces. She'd already decided to decorate a wine bottle, thinking there was a certain elegance in drinking the contents and then appropriating the bottle for artistic purposes. And of course, there was no shortage of wine bottles in the recycling bin by the side of the house. She sorted the ceramic pieces by color, choosing the brightest colors—oranges and blues and reds—and then arranged them into swirling patterns. Then she scrubbed the label off the bottle and washed and carefully dried it. Safety glasses and rubber gloves on, she started at the bottom of the bottle—per the directions on the web—and put a daub of adhesive on the back of the shard of glass and held it in place. Some of the ceramic pieces she nipped in half. With others, she clipped off the corners with the glass cutters. She worked quickly, trying not to think too much, and an hour later, the bottle was covered with an attractive mishmash of erstwhile pottery. There were pieces she could identify—the first bowl she'd made in class. One of the fornicating rabbits. A chipped (and subsequently hurled) plate from her mother. The next day, she grouted the bottle. Even with a few cracks in the grout and the unevenness of the pieces, it was pretty good for a first attempt—something she hadn't counted on. She cradled the bottle against her chest, afraid she might launch it at the wall.

BUT SHE DIDN'T THROW the wine bottle against the wall. Instead, she placed it on the mantel above the fireplace. On the next trip to the art-supply store, she bought backing for a picture frame and a bag of assorted glass—flat, round gems in blue and gold and red. And cat's-eyes. And banded carnelian and blue chalcedony and red aventurine, all tumbled and smooth to the touch. She went through the house, haphazardly scrounging around in her jewelry box, an old dresser, a sewing box, Richard's tool chest, gathering glitter and reclaimed junk for the next project. Sunday morning, she laid the picture frame on the table and began arranging the broken ceramics free-form on top of the frame along with other odds and ends. A lone surviving earring—dangling pearls from a pair Richard had bought her on a hang-gliding trip to Patagonia. The cat's-eye and assorted multicolored gems. A peregrine falcon pin from the Audubon Society. Seashells. A piece of driftwood. Buttons. A carabiner Richard had used for hang gliding. A chunk of redwood burl she'd dug out from underneath the coffee table. More broken ceramics. She moved the earrings to the right side of the frame, the cat's-eye closer to the top. Then she started gluing them down with the adhesive, cutting the ceramic pieces to fit tightly against the earring and the chunk of redwood and the buttons.

By the time she finished, it was late afternoon. Alix had nipped the last shard of glass and placed it snugly between the falcon pin and a hexagonal bolt from Richard's tool chest. Sunlight through the front window glanced off the translucent pieces of glass, creating shifting prisms on the living room walls, and the leaves on the trees were translucent like liquid, and just as the sun set, everything was suddenly still, for just a moment the earth's revolution on pause. It was quiet, so quiet she could hear the rush of air beside her ears, and the light in the room shifted from yellow to deep gold to orange and purple. Just as she looked up, there was a flash of green beyond the trees. Like glare casting off the windows. It must be from all this glass or the wine bottle on the mantel, she thought and shook it off. But no, Richard had said it was a phenomenon caused by the refraction of light in the atmosphere; sometimes the flash was blue or red, but it never lasted more than a second or two. There was another flash, and Alix sensed Richard lingering behind her. A creak at the front door, his unmistakable scent of ocean and sand, flannel rubbing against denim, salt on the tip of her tongue. She closed her eyes and stood still, feeling his breath on her neck, the surge of energy running through her body. His considerable hands on her shoulders. When she turned around, his moist lips grazed hers, and he was cradling her in his arms.

That night, the moon set early and the sky was overcast, darkening into black. She lit a fire in the fireplace and poured herself a glass of wine. She ached to dream of him. Wasn't it possible to nurture a dream, asking Richard to stick around? She'd heard some people could even control their dreams. Lucid dreaming. The last six months, whenever she'd dreamed of Richard, it involved a car or a truck driving at top speed, careening down a mountain, and Richard, yelling out the side of the vehicle, "*Fly, baby. Fly.*" It seemed to Alix that over the course of the last six months, she'd had limited choices in those dreams: Either hang on tight, her hands clutching the steering wheel. Or crash. But this time was different. He hadn't come to say good-bye or to cajole her into moving on or to strong-arm her into flying off the side of a mountain.

The next morning, she woke to the smell of coffee brewing in the kitchen, and she knew he was still there.

WEDNESDAY AFTERNOON, THE WEATHER was warm. Skye must have run across campus to get to her appointment because she was sweating and out of breath by the time she got upstairs to Alix's office.

"I got a job on campus for the summer," Skye said before she even sat down. "I mean, I have to decide and tell my boss by Friday." She seemed upbeat, relieved.

"So you'd stay here."

Skye nodded. "Probably take a couple classes, get ahead."

"What about Grace and Jackson?"

"It's not up to them." Her tone abruptly shifted; her face tightened.

"That's not what I was asking." Alix tilted her head, wondering how to avoid stepping on any additional land mines. "Sounds like you've already made up your mind."

Skye was holding her body taut, biting her lip with that one slightly overlapping tooth, her eyes staring at the carpet near Alix's feet. Despite her attempts to appear disinterested, Alix could tell she was apprehensive, guarded.

"I care about you," Alix said. "What happens to you. If you and your mother work things out. Or Grace and Jackson." Then she hesitated, wondering if she was going too far. "I don't often cry, not with my patients. In fact, it's never happened before."

"It's no big deal," Skye said. "I just figured you had something going on."

"Going on? Like what?" Alix pulled back and took a deep breath, reaching for her cup of coffee. But she left it on the side table. "It's scary," she said. "You're so sure about Grace and Jackson; you've given up on talking to them. You haven't asked what I think—if you should stay here this summer. But I'll tell you anyway." Alix paused ever so briefly. "It doesn't matter."

Skye's eyes widened, and she blinked hard and rolled her head around, loosening up her neck. She was taking her time, as if to mask her curiosity. "What do you mean?"

"I mean, that's not the question you should be asking." Alix glanced down at her hands, weaving the fingers together. "What's holding you back? From talking to them? That's what matters."

Skye reached for a tissue, but instead of wiping her eyes, she folded and unfolded the tissue against her thigh, pressing a crease into the squares.

"I feel like I'm crawling back to them, like they were right all along."

"It doesn't have to be that way. Maybe you've misunderstood each other. Or you were simply protecting yourself."

ALIX HAD GOTTEN MORE selective with what she threw against the wall and what she kept, more often than not safeguarding the pieces she liked best. One was a straw-green glazed vase. She'd scratched a leafy design into the side and brought it to work, placed it at eye level on one of the shelves in her office. Every time she looked up, it made her smile. She liked the wave in the leaves, and the textured green glaze, and the generous curve of the body closing into a narrow, tall neck.

In preparation for summer, she'd cleaned out the back shed and given away Richard's tools—except for the hammers and a few wrenches and screwdrivers and a tile cutter he'd used for the upstairs shower. She had a work table installed for her mosaic pieces and the adhesives and different shades of grout. She purchased a massive tool chest secondhand to store the bits and pieces of her trade: the beads and jewelry and what she'd previously thought of as merely junk—nuts and bolts, and fishing lures, and seeds, and anything else she came across that she might embed into the side of a picture frame or birdbath or decorative plate. She got the plumber to dig a trench from the house and install a utility sink. Maybe sometime she'd buy a potter's wheel, except she liked going to class with Sally and the other women, who were spunky and creative.

The nights she went to the studio to throw pottery on the wheel, she couldn't really be thinking about anything else, not if she wanted the bowl or vase or plate to stay centered. She had to blot out her concern over whether Skye and her mother would ever reconnect. Or whether Jeremy would give up the delusion that his ex-girlfriend was ever coming back. Or whether Richard was going to show up again in a dream and then stick around the house to drink coffee with her in the morning.

"What about your book?" Betsy asked one day. They'd gone to a matinee, and then Alix invited her over to see the converted shed and her growing collection of dishes and mosaic wine bottles and picture frames.

"It's gathering dust," she said. In fact, she'd boxed up the manuscript and put it on a shelf at the back of her clothes closet—the summer closet that had been Richard's. *At least I don't have to loosen up that writer's block by throwing things against the wall*, she thought.

Of course, she missed strong-arming a plate or cup and hearing it crash against the brick patio. But the thwack of the clay against the rotating potter's wheel served a similar purpose. Only yesterday morning, stepping out of the shower, she'd admired the reflection of her burgeoning biceps in the mirror.

Chapter Twenty

WHEN HER PHONE VIBRATED on Sunday afternoon, Skye pulled it out of her pocket and stared at the display. In her last couple of conversations with Grace and Jackson, Grace had been unusually solicitous, asking about Eva in a way that suggested she thought maybe Eva really had changed. Grace's newfound acceptance made it even harder for Skye to tell them the latest about Eva. And about her father.

"I don't want you to get mad or anything," Skye said.

"Of course not, sweetie." Grace sounded all sugary, as if she never got rattled or angry with Skye.

"I wasn't at school over spring break."

She told them about having spent the week with her mother and how they'd gone to the museum and a couple of bookstores and Golden Gate Park. Grace kept saying, "That's nice." This gave Skye permission to continue, but she knew that eventually Grace was going to get pissed. She told them about walking all over the City and eating cannoli and about the Afghani food and staying in Joanie's apartment couch-surfing (although Skye wasn't sure it was Joanie's apartment). Grace said that was very generous of her mother's friend.

"What kind of food do they eat in Afghanistan?" Jackson asked.

"Well, I don't know what they eat in Afghanistan, but the restaurant served lamb and chicken and vegetables and garbanzo beans and rice and lots of neat spices like cardamom and cumin and mint and hot peppers." Skye rattled off items from the menu, picturing the place where they'd eaten, near the park. "And garlic bread and cookies with almonds and pistachios."

"No more Gino's for you," Jackson said. That was the Italian restaurant in Oakdale. The owner's name wasn't really Gino. It was Doug Pulaski, and he'd moved up to Oakdale from Fresno after retiring from the fire department. He figured anybody could cook up lasagna and spaghetti and calzones, and that was pretty much how the food tasted.

"But I thought you had to stay at school to study," Grace said. She sounded legitimately puzzled, as if she'd simply misunderstood Skye's reason for not coming home over spring break.

"I did have to study," Skye said. She could hear her own defensiveness.

"I wish you'd told us," Grace said. "There's nothing wrong with you wanting to spend time with your mother."

"I don't know, I just ..." Skye was afraid to tell them what was really on her mind. The conversation was going better than she'd expected. She didn't want them to know about the drugs or how her mother had lied to her. But she couldn't hold it in any longer and blurted it out. "He raped her."

And then she'd said it, aloud, without speculation. She'd thought about saying, *it* was rape, as if the assault hadn't happened to anyone in particular, certainly not to her mother.

"Who? What? Are you okay?" Jackson was stumbling over his words.

Then she realized the shorthand she'd used, without any context. "My father," Skye said. "She was drunk and passed out, and he raped her."

"Jesus."

"Oh, honey," Grace said.

Skye told the story in greater detail. About finding the photograph and pressing Eva, and how her mother had finally told her about her father and the other frat boys. She could picture Grace, her mouth open, the space between her eyebrows drawn tight, trying not to say what she really thought.

Jackson covered the mouthpiece, then came back long enough to say, "Just a second." There was a muffled silence on the end of the phone, and then whispering came through his hand cupped over the receiver.

"We're coming to see you," he said.

"You don't need to."

"Of course we don't need to," Jackson said, "but Grace wants to see the campus. You can show her around. And we'll take you out to dinner."

"I have a paper due next week," Skye said.

"No problem. It's just a quick visit."

"Really, I'm okay."

DESPITE SKYE'S PROTESTS, THEY insisted on visiting, and Thursday afternoon, Grace and Jackson showed up at her dorm room with a new blanket for her bed and a cherry pie to share with friends. Jackson joked about going I-talian for dinner. It turned out he'd gone online and found a couple of restaurants on Fourth Street in Berkeley, where there were yuppie shops; he figured it would be a fun outing. They squeezed into the front seat of Jackson's truck, Grace in the middle, Skye leaning against the passenger-side door. After getting off the highway, they drove parallel to the railroad tracks, alongside abandoned buildings and windblown refuse. The neighborhood didn't hold much promise for an upscale experience, but Jackson kept saying he knew where they were going. He'd found this place on Yelp, and it was rated four stars. Skye was impressed that he even knew about Yelp.

THE ROASTED ONION HAD a long, glossy bar and low-hung blown-glass lights, a patchwork of mismatched armchairs and antique tables, and Salvador Dalí–looking macabre prints on the walls. A newspaper review, framed in the front window, described the food as California fusion, "a mélange of Middle Eastern and nouveau California cuisine." Skye ordered a burger, sweet-potato fries, and a Diet Coke, Grace had the roasted-beet salad and Jackson a lamb kabob and asparagus. It was a side of them she hadn't seen before, a slightly hip side.

Skye played with her fork, furtively glancing over at Grace, who was oddly subdued. Even if Grace's menu choice was slightly hip, she was still wearing her outdated 1950s-style clothing: a baby-blue cardigan sweater buttoned at the top and a white blouse with a lacy collar. It looked like she'd put on some makeup—eyeliner and rouge and pink lipstick that she reapplied when they sat down. *Must be a special occasion,* Skye thought.

Jackson was smoothing the cloth napkin and straightening his utensils so they lined up. "Chester wanted to come along," he said. "Poor guy, standing at the door, watching our packed bags disappear from the house." He whined and moaned, but Mrs. Sloane down the street said she'd feed him and take him for a walk. And their new goat, Gabriella, was pregnant. "And did Gracie tell you? She's been asked to head up the local Meals on Wheels."

Grace offered a weak smile.

A row of thirty-somethings were drinking at the bar, popping pretzels and nuts into their mouths, laughing, and raising the noise level to a din. Jackson glanced over, then continued his monologue, only a bit louder. "I tilled the garden. I'm thinking about planting heirloom tomatoes this year. Joe Stanley got some organic plants into the nursery."

It was hard for Jackson to shoulder the whole conversation on his own, but he was somehow able to piece together enough random information about life in Oakdale to keep going, like a twenty-four-hour telethon. Grace's cousin Jenny was having a baby any day now; they already knew it was a boy. There'd been a mother bear and two cubs scrounging for food in the parking-lot Dumpster in front of the hardware store on Main Street. Jackson was already gearing up for that big remodel job this summer. It would keep him busy most of the summer.

It wasn't until they were halfway through dinner that Jackson asked her about spring break and the visit with her mother.

Skye shrugged. "I really wanted it to work out; I don't know what I expected, but I was sure it would be different this time."

"It must be hard," Grace said. "Dealing with it all on your own."

Skye had just bitten into a fry, but she stopped chewing. "I'm not alone," she said. "I've been seeing a therapist. At the counseling clinic on campus."

Grace put her fork down and wiped her mouth on the cloth napkin. Her eyes fell on the bartender, who was letting foam settle on a pint of beer.

"I'm glad you're getting help," Jackson said. "I wish I'd done that when I was your age—could have saved myself a lot of grief."

After dinner, they walked down Fourth Street, Jackson and Skye together and Grace strolling ahead of them. The street was lined with expensive shops—a place that sold handcrafted paper, a shoe store with three-hundred-dollar handbags from Italy, a clothing boutique that smelled of silk and scented candles. Grace wandered into an upscale kitchen store. Skye and Jackson followed, giving her a wide berth, scavenging through the bins and display tables filled with fancy gadgets like fish-bone tweezers and collapsible funnels, espresso makers, an herb mincer, tabletop grills, and other so-called labor-saving devices of questionable necessity.

Grace bought a new set of dish towels with little pictures of carrots and tomatoes and broccoli stamped on them.

Jackson and Skye sat down on a bench while Grace walked into a gift shop with rows of cards and earrings and beads. A woman weighted down with shopping bags passed by. Next door was a French restaurant; the trees out front were strung with lights. Grace was leaning over the glass counter, peering at the jewelry.

Jackson put his arm around Skye. "We're just worried about you," he said.

"You don't need to be."

Grace came out of the store with a pair of fused-glass earrings, yellow and red. Skye and Jackson got up, and they all walked slowly toward the truck. More streetlights were switching on. Skye could smell garlic and wine and French fries and waffle cones. All around them, people were smiling and relaxed with end-of-the-week liberation. Standing on the corner, about to cross, Skye saw that a sports car was waiting for them. Jackson waved him on.

"I wanted to tell you about spring break," Skye said. "I don't know, I was afraid …"

Skye figured Grace would launch into a discussion of why it was her own fault. Not wanting to hear her latest harangue, she walked on ahead, leaving Grace and Jackson standing on the street corner. Her head down, she walked quickly the last couple of blocks to their car.

But Grace caught up with her and was talking to her back. "I don't mean to push you away. …"

Jackson unlocked the truck door, and Grace slid into the front seat. Skye stood outside long enough to ponder whether she even wanted to get in. But then she got in next to Grace. Out of the corner of her eye, she could see Grace's face. The remainder of her pale pink lipstick had leaked into the creases above her lips. Her face was ashen and drawn. Her head turned to the side, she was staring past Skye, out the passenger-side window. "We were only supposed to take care of you for a couple of weeks. That was it. Hardly even any paperwork. But then we found out …" Her voice trailed off.

"At first, I wanted it to work out with your mother and see the two of you reunited. You were so sad, and I could hardly bear to hear you cry at night in your room. But then, I don't know, maybe a year later … it was as if one day you woke up and you'd forgotten about her. The phone calls had stopped, and the cards. Oh, sure, occasionally you wanted me to call Mrs. McNulty, and then you'd be miserable again. Weeks on end. Waiting for her. You'd sit by the front window, and whenever a car drove up, you'd jump off the couch and run out the front door to see who was coming up the driveway. When the phone rang, you'd insist on answering it. And then a couple of weeks later, we'd be back to normal. Like night and day. It was so painful, watching you want her back. We even tried to contact her a couple of times. You remember that time we were supposed to meet her at the park in Fresno? And one Christmas, I even bought you a card and signed her name."

Skye didn't know what to say. That she'd somehow been happier without her mother, it wasn't at all what she'd expected. "I don't believe you," she said.

Grace looked at Jackson for a way out, but Jackson had both hands on the steering wheel, staring through the front windshield. She bit her lip and continued, "You were so protective of her, making excuses, telling stories about all the things you two did together—trips you'd taken, all the friends she had, how she'd taught you to build little houses out of balsa wood."

"But all that was true," Skye said. "Well, most of it."

"I know, sweetheart, but ... Mrs. McNulty said you were making dinner and cleaning up after her by the time you were seven years old. All that puffing her up, making her larger than life. I couldn't figure out how it was ever going to work out with your mother. And you seemed so much happier without her."

Jackson started up the car and wound his way around the back streets, past the abandoned buildings and industrial trash bins, finally merging onto the highway. He needed Skye to help navigate them back to campus. About all she could manage to say was "Turn left at the corner" or "Right at the stop sign." Finally they reached the parking kiosk at the front gate, the stone archway just ahead. "I can walk from here," Skye said, opening the car door before he'd even come to a full stop. They wanted to come upstairs, talk about what Grace had said.

"Get a good night's rest, and then we'll take you out for breakfast tomorrow," Jackson said.

"I can't," Skye said, and started to walk down the path to her dorm.

Jackson got out of the truck and sprinted to catch up with her, leaving the motor still running. "You can't leave it like this," he said.

"Why not?"

Grace was leaning against the cab of the truck; she'd pulled the sweater around her thick middle and had her arms wrapped around her body.

Jackson grabbed Skye's shoulder, then quickly let go and put his hand in his jeans pocket. "I'm sorry," he said. Then he turned back toward Grace, nodding his head in her direction. "She only wanted what was best. We both did."

ON THE WAY BACK to her dorm room, Skye texted Matt. A half hour later, when he showed up in gym shorts, with his basketball in hand, she'd already eaten half of Jackson's cherry pie. Matt helped her finish off the rest. "Damn, this is good pie," he said. "So, they taking you out to breakfast in the morning?"

Skye shook her head. She was fighting back tears.

"What do you mean? They came all this way to see you," he said, shoveling in another forkful of pie.

He was right, but she was too mad to call them and say she was sorry. For what?

"You just gonna ditch them?"

It was Matt who suggested she call Alix to see if they could all meet together, Friday morning before Grace and Jackson headed back to Oakdale.

Early the next morning, Skye called the clinic.

"She's in meetings all morning," Candy said. "How about 2 o'clock?"

When she called Jackson, he was reluctant at first. "I don't understand," he said. "Why can't you just talk to us? I'm not sure how I feel about getting shrunk. And by a total stranger."

"It's not like that," she said.

But then he laughed and said he'd talk to Grace and they'd call her back. "I'm not promising anything."

SKYE TOOK THEM AROUND campus. She showed them the social sciences building and the math and science center where she had most of her classes, the performing arts pavilion, the rec center, with its Olympic-sized pool and volleyball court, and the student union, where students hovered over laptops checking e-mail and doing homework.

They happened to run into Dr. Morris, who had a stack of papers with him, essays he'd just graded.

"A real live professor," Grace said. "It's such a pleasure to meet you."

Grace had on a new mustard-yellow blouse with a wide bow that was attached to the collar. She readjusted the bow and smiled coyly, as if she'd just been introduced to a movie star or the governor of California. "It must be so gratifying working with all these terribly smart young people," she said, and reached out a limp hand for him to shake.

Skye cringed. At the moment, everything about Grace was annoying.

At quarter to 2, they walked over to the clinic for their appointment. Grace wanted to know what kind of credentials this

"Alicia" had. "Oh, I guess it doesn't really matter. As long as you like her."

"It's Alix, not Alicia," Skye said. "And I'm pretty sure she's a real doctor. There's a diploma hanging in her office, and besides ..." But then she decided not to get into it with Grace.

"I thought Alex was a man's name," Grace said, mostly to herself.

The path was narrow, and they were walking single file. "So how long have you been going to counseling?" Jackson asked.

"Since October."

Grace registered surprise. "I guess there's a lot we don't know."

Skye opened the front door of the clinic. Grace walked in but stood by the door, looking around. They went down the long hallway, Grace and Jackson lagging behind, and then Skye checked in with Candy, and they sat down, Skye on one side of the coffee table and Grace and Jackson on the other. They were early for their appointment; the waiting room was empty. Grace picked up a magazine and thumbed through it.

"So you come in every week?" Jackson asked.

"It depends," Skye said, trying to put as much distance as possible between them.

Jackson nodded, as if he knew what that meant.

Another client walked in, a nerdy-looking guy Skye had seen before in the waiting room. He stared at Grace and Jackson, then back at Skye, pushing his bent, metal-framed glasses back in place. Skye took out her phone and checked her e-mail and Facebook. Jackson was scanning the room, clasping and unclasping his hands. A couple more students checked in; Grace looked up, staring at a stick-thin girl wearing a bulky sweatshirt. It was Rachel, who lived down the hall from Skye. Grace stared, then slid closer to Jackson. Rachel and Skye ignored each other.

By the time Alix met them in the waiting room, everyone else had been summoned upstairs for their appointments. Alix introduced herself and shook their hands. "Nice to meet you," she said. And Jackson said thank you for seeing them. Especially on such short notice.

Alix showed them to a large room; Skye figured it was the one they used for groups. Alix had arranged the chairs in a circle. Skye moved her chair a little closer to Alix, with Grace and Jackson across from them.

Alix said hello again. They chatted about the drive from Oakdale and how beautiful it was in the mountains, how she'd been there a number of years ago with her … But then she stopped herself and finished the sentence "with a friend." Alix switched gears to talk about "ground rules." She wouldn't be sharing any confidential information about Skye. They could use the time to talk about what was on their minds. In a safe place.

Skye thought maybe Alix was on her best behavior, too, wanting to make a good impression on Grace and Jackson.

"Any questions?" she asked.

Jackson looked at Grace. "Just how we can help Skye, is all."

It wasn't supposed to be a competition for whom Alix liked the best, but even so, it put Skye on edge, wanting Alix to see what she'd been talking about all along.

Alix said, "I'm wondering what Skye has told you already."

Jackson looked at Grace, but it was obvious she wanted him to start. "She told us about spring break and spending the week with her mother," Jackson said. "We know it didn't go well—at least at the end. And Skye's been pretty angry at us lately, at Grace, mostly. We just want to help her, whatever way we can."

"Grace," Alix asked, "do you have anything to add?"

Grace was sitting up straight in the chair. "Not now," she said, pursing her lips. "I know last night. What I said. Well, she ran off, and I'm sorry. But it's the truth—everything I said was the truth."

Skye thought they were taking the easy way out, making it seem like they had no idea why she was upset with them, doing their best to give a good impression, maybe sway Alix's opinion. She looked at Alix, then out the window. A flock of crows was lined up on the telephone wire across the street. All the role-playing with Alix about what to say … she couldn't remember any of it.

There was a prolonged silence before she could gather the words together. "I just feel like, I mean, whenever I mention my mother, it's a big production, like she's some troublemaker, and I shouldn't want to see her. Like I'm some crazy person."

Grace scooted back on the chair and fanned out the bow on her blouse. "We never thought …"

Jackson was frowning the way he did when he was trying to figure something out. "How could we keep you from seeing her?" he asked. "Even if we wanted to." He had untied the leather hair clasp, pulled all the loose strands together, and was fastening it again.

Skye shrugged. "Like Mrs. McNulty when I was little."

Jackson said, "I'm not sure how Mrs. McNulty has anything—"

Grace interrupted, turning her chair to face Alix. "Her mother, in and out of drug rehab, it's a wonder she's still alive. But I guess you know that already. Besides, Skye, sweetheart, remember what we talked about last night? How miserable you were every time you heard from her?"

"That's just what I mean," Skye said. "My mother's not some misfit."

"That's not what I said."

Alix held up her hand like a traffic cop. "Let's stop for a moment."

"Sweetheart," Grace interrupted. "We're only trying to protect you. If that's a crime, then lock me up."

Alix reached out and touched Grace on the back of her wrist. "This must be very painful for you to watch. Here's Skye, desperately wanting a relationship with her mother, and yet, her mother's track record isn't what you'd call dependable."

"I just can't understand why, after all these years, she'd still hold out hope for that woman. With everything we've given her ..."

Alix was nodding in agreement. "It doesn't seem logical, does it?"

"She's always been so quiet, so independent. Like she never really needed us."

Alix turned to Skye. "What do you think about that?"

Skye shrugged, not wanting to make matters worse. She was already feeling ganged-up on.

Then Alix turned to Grace and Jackson. "Out of the blue, this little girl shows up on your doorstep, and you don't know when her mother's coming back, and at some point it seems obvious to you that she'll never come back. And you open your arms. But your heart ..."

"I wish we'd known from the start," Grace said. "How it would turn out. I could have ..." Her voice trailed off.

A motorcycle sped by, shaking the windows. A flock of birds darted away. But then the rattle and the high-pitched squeal of the motorcycle engine were out of earshot, and it seemed quieter than before, and they could hear air forced in through the vents. Skye looked up to see Grace struggling, her mouth half open, her upper lip moist and trembling.

She'd tucked a tissue into the pocket of her skirt, and she pulled it out and daubed at her lips and eyes. Jackson reached over and held her hand. "It's okay, sweetheart."

Skye hated it when Grace cried; it always seemed phony, like she was playing for sympathy.

Grace turned to Alix. "It wasn't fair," she said. "I was her mother. But then I wasn't, not really. Maybe if she hadn't kept looking for Eva ..."

Alix sat back in her chair. She had a look on her face Skye had seen before when she was mulling over what to say, trying to act like she didn't have an opinion, when really she did. Her head was tilted to the side, looking past Grace. She drew her teeth over her bottom lip. Skye thought she looked worried.

"Gracie," Jackson said, still holding her hand, "you can't blame Skye for wanting to find her mother."

"See? See what I mean?" Grace pulled away from Jackson and was pointing her finger at Skye. "We never should have ..."

Skye was focused on Grace's words, wondering how she'd finish the sentence. Except it was obvious.

"I didn't mean that. Skye knows we love her, don't you, Skye?" Grace was looking over at her, wide-eyed and teary. Expectant. "And then the other day, she calls and tells us about ... her father. I just, well, it breaks your heart." Grace was still daubing at her eyes with the damp tissue. Her chin was quivering.

Alix was staring at her hands, at the rough skin and colorless nails and dried cuticles. "When my husband died, I couldn't see beyond the next day." Her voice was soft, only slightly more than a whisper, as if she were talking to herself.

"Your husband?" Jackson asked. "What do you mean?"

The photo in her office of Clouds' Rest, with the back of Half Dome in the distance. Skye had figured the guy in the photo was her husband, but she'd assumed he was alive. That Alix was married. Skye had been there with Jackson one summer. They'd hiked close to fifteen miles, and afterward he'd told her, "Goes to show, now you can do just about anything."

Muffled voices were seeping in from the adjoining offices. Someone crying. Another voice, angry, and then someone yelling back: "*I hate you.*"

Alix shook her head and looked up. "The point is," she said, recovering her composure, "disasters and misfortune, devastating loss beyond our control, happen all the time. We all ache for a do-over. A chance to turn back the clock. Readjust the ending. I've interviewed hundreds of individuals who've overcome the most unexpected tragedies. And you want to know what I found out? Given a second chance—even knowing the outcome—you know who fares the best? Even in the most dire, tragic circumstances. Despite the fear and vulnerability, the anguish and risk. It's not the individuals who harden their hearts but the ones who keep their hearts open. *Those* are the ones who overcome tragedy. It takes courage to break ourselves open, turn our hearts inside out. And simply love. Again and again."

Out in the hallway, doors were opening. Their time was almost up. Skye wondered how it would all end and how it would feel to walk out of the building together. Jackson looked toward the door. "So we just have to believe, in the end, it'll all work out? For the best?"

"That's not good enough," Grace said. "I just don't believe … I've never believed it would turn out for the best. Maybe, like the doctor is saying, that's been my problem all along." She blew her nose and then slipped the used tissue into her purse and snapped the clasp shut.

Chapter Twenty-One

THE TRAIL BEHIND THEIR dorm was still damp from the spring rains, and there were tall stalks on the century plants and baby blue-eyes and black sage and red penstemon poking out of rocks and sandy crevices. The smell of rosemary and manzanita hovered in the afternoon air. Skye was jogging up the switchbacks, running on excess fumes. Matt was lagging behind, exhausted. He'd been up until 4 that morning studying and then had to take two midterms.

"Wait up," he called out.

Skye heard him, but she didn't slow down. In fact, she was quite pleased that he might be struggling up the hill behind her. At the top, she found a flat rock and sat down, and eventually she saw him trudging toward her. He stopped to catch his breath and then continued.

When he got to the top, he sat next to her, staring down

at the campus below. "I didn't realize it was a race," he said, panting. His face was flushed.

Skye broke off a sprig of sage and rubbed the grayish, soft leaves between her fingers, then held them to her nose. "It wasn't."

Matt frowned. He leaned over, pulling stickers off the bottom of his jeans; he retied his shoelaces. "Are you avoiding me?" he asked.

They hadn't spoken or texted or seen each other for a couple of days, and it was pretty clear Skye was distancing herself. Matt had just shown up at her room, where Skye was bent over her calculus book, struggling with a word problem. "You've done this one a million times," he'd said. But she'd slammed the book shut, put on her socks and sneakers, and run out the door.

Skye flicked the remnants of the sage leaves into the wind and watched them scatter. "All this crap going on," she said. "I'm just way behind." Off in the distance toward the City, the fog was creeping in through the river basin. The hills were mossy green. "I hate her," Skye said, her voice low. She could feel her jaw tighten; her eyelid was twitching. It occurred to her there was no way for Matt to know if she was talking about her mother or Grace, and the truth of it was, she was angry at both of them.

Matt shifted on the rock. The sun was low in the sky, and he looked up, squinting. A hawk flew overhead and then swooped down, catching a mouse in its talons. "Whoa," he said. "Did you see that?"

The hawk flew away clutching the mouse in its talons, flapping wings and a faint whimper carried in the wind.

Skye looked from the hawk, which had settled in a native oak with its prey, and then to Matt, who was looking at the hawk still perched in the tree, tearing at the mouse. His face was tanned from playing soccer, and he'd recently decided to try growing a mustache. Skye wasn't sure if she liked it or not, but she could see why she'd been attracted to him all those months ago with his lanky frame and easygoing manner. Of all her friends at college, it was Matt she most trusted. She'd figured out he never shared anything she told him with their friends—except maybe Casey. And even when she got mad at him, somehow Matt knew not to take it personally, that it had more to do with how confused and disappointed and angry she was at the misshapen twists in her life. And at the adults who hardly ever acted like adults. It was something she hadn't fully appreciated until just now.

"I *have* been avoiding you," she said. "I'm sorry. There's just been a lot going on."

"I figured," he said.

Another thing she appreciated about Matt: he knew not to press her, that she'd talk when she was ready. Skye could feel her body start to cool down; she wiped the sweat off her face with the sleeve of her T-shirt.

"My mother, I think she was using that whole time," Skye said. "At least toward the end. Over spring break."

Matt picked up a couple of rocks and lobbed them into the air, watching them drop into the bushes. There was a rustling of leaves, a dull thud, and then scurrying of birds and a small animal, like a squirrel or maybe a rabbit.

"You sure?" he asked.

Skye shrugged. "For a while, I thought it'd been worth it—the waiting. But now I just feel stupid." She'd been lured in by her mother, and now what did she have? It had been predictable, her mother disappearing all over again. And the rape. Knowing that she was alive because of a rape was too hard to talk about. Matt wasn't one to judge, but even Matt—if she told him—would see her differently. As damaged.

"So what happened with your parents and Alix?" Matt asked.

Skye decided not to correct him—that Grace and Jackson weren't her parents—because with everything that had happened with her mother, she was already feeling like an orphan.

"Grace keeps saying she wants me to come home for the summer, but she'll understand if I don't. Yesterday, I got this card in the mail from her, one of those gooey Hallmark cards. Said she'd been thinking about everything and she'd even gone to talk to the priest. She could see how her fears had gotten in the way. It's just hard to trust."

Matt pulled a half-eaten Power Bar out of his pocket and offered it to her. Skye broke off a piece.

"So you gonna go home for the summer?" he asked.

"Jackson said he has work for me with a new bid he just won. Grunt work, mostly, but that's what I'd be doing at the bookstore. And at least going back to Oakdale, I'll save on rent."

"You know they didn't go talk to Alix just to humor you." Matt leaned back on his elbows and stared up at the sky.

Still, it was hard for her to admit he was right. Grace and Jackson. If she had any family at all, they were it. Way more than her mother.

In a twist of proximity, she and Matt had fallen into a relationship that year, and she hoped they could stay friends—whatever else happened. Last week, he'd applied for a job in the bookstore for next year and was trying to figure out whether, with loans and working on campus, he could afford to come back in the fall. His parents were at each other, arguing over who would get the dining room set and the power tools and who was responsible for college tuition and how much child support was his mother going to get. His mother was calling Matt every other night, ragging on his dad, then breaking down, sobbing uncontrollably. She wanted Matt to take sides. Every sentence started with "Your *father*." "Like it's a four-letter word," he'd said. A couple of times, he'd laid the phone on his desk and let her rant, every minute or so picking it up to say, "Uh-huh, uh-huh."

Matt put his arm around her, and he was gently stroking her back. She hadn't intended to tell him the whole story about her mother, but she was lying in the crook of his arm, staring out over campus. They could hear skateboarders and high-pitched voices and the swimming coach yelling from the rec center pool. A plane rumbled overhead, too far above them to see, except for the fading contrails left behind.

"My father," she said. "I found out what really happened." She unfolded the story Eva had laid out about getting drunk the week before graduation and Skye's father and a couple other frat boys raping her.

"Wow," Matt said. "Really? I guess that explains a lot."

He sat up and peeled dried grass from his elbows. He was looking directly into her eyes. "You know it doesn't mean anything. About you."

"Of course it means something about me. Like your parents getting a divorce. It's not like you caused it, but still. It's not the same as having happily married parents."

Despite telling Matt it wasn't true, she was glad he'd said it. Maybe sometime in the future it could be true. It meant the past didn't have to define her forever.

"And then this weird thing happened with Alix."

With his eyes, Matt was following sounds caught in the breeze—a horn honking on the street, birdcalls warning of imminent danger. Two deer foraging in the field on the other side of the fence. But she could tell he was listening, waiting for her to go on, not interrupting with whatever else he might be thinking about.

"I don't know what happened, but all of a sudden I was crying, and I looked up and she was crying, too."

"No shit," he said. "About what?"

"It's so weird, but it felt like it was only us in the room, I mean it *was* only us in the room, but everything went quiet, and I didn't even say anything when I left."

"You gonna talk to her about it?"

Skye frowned. "She already thinks I'm crazy."

"I'll come visit you in the loony bin."

"That's not funny."

Matt sat up and stretched his back, with his long legs out in front of him on the rock. "Well, you know what I hate?" He picked up a stone from alongside the path and threw it down the hill. "I hate my parents. And my dad's empty-headed girlfriend."

Skye was digging around in the gravel with a stick. "I hate differential equations," she said, and lobbed a stone, hitting a nearby tree with a crack.

"And I hate stepping in dog shit."

"And broken shoelaces."

Matt stood up on the rock and strong-armed a stone all the way across the fence. He was towering over her, smiling. "And overripe bananas," he said, shouting now, each word strung out in a long, drawn-out phrase. At first, the two deer stared at him, paralyzed; then they quickly darted off. "And raanddom aaactts of kiindnessss." The breeze blew his voice across the pasture and down the hillside, where Skye could see there were students and faculty strolling by on the pavement, pausing to look in the direction of Matt's echoey call.

He sat down next to her, put his arm around her, and pulled her close. "That about covers it," he said. He was grinning, and he had that same smile she'd noticed the first day they'd met in Morris's class. Even then, she'd thought he was cute.

"You don't hate me?" she asked.

Matt pulled her closer. "Only a little bit. Lately."

"I guess I've been acting weird."

"No shit."

AND THEN IT WAS the last week of the semester. Skye had two finals and a paper due before going home for the summer. Walking down the clinic hallway, she was thinking about the first time she'd seen Alix. How she'd been afraid to talk about her mother and what had happened. It seemed like a lifetime ago. She hadn't thought counseling could help. Even recently, she'd wondered what was the point of all that talking?

Skye knocked on the door and went in. Alix was waiting for her.

Even after a year of seeing Alix, she felt shy starting the conversation. "I'm going home for the summer. Friday. Jasmine's got my whole social schedule set up. And Matt'll be home, too, so we can hang out."

Alix nodded. "And Grace and Jackson?"

It was obvious Alix was using shorthand to ask Skye how she felt about going home. Maybe Alix was a little shy, too. Or maybe she wanted their last session to go smoothly.

"I tried to call my mother the other day, but the number's been disconnected. It's probably better that way. I mean, I get what you were saying. She's probably never coming back, at least not the way I imagined."

"You never know. But still," Alix said, "I'm sorry."

Skye wanted to say "Thank you" to Alix for helping her with Grace and Jackson, and for sticking with her even after she'd run out of her office. And that lame phone message she'd left about their having had a *misunderstanding.* She hadn't appreciated it at the time, but now it seemed different. Now reaching out meant something. For some reason, she couldn't get the words out.

Skye took a pack of gum out of her backpack and offered a piece to Alix, who surprised her by accepting it. They sat quietly for a couple of minutes until she was ready to continue, the silence feeling less uncomfortable than before. Then she told Alix about having gone into the City with Matt and the rest of her friends, this time to a poetry reading at City Lights. Afterward, Skye had shown them her old apartment. The siding and scrollwork were painted the same colors, but Skye noticed the tree out front had grown enough to block the view from the second-floor window. The wobbly bannister had been repaired and the old wooden garage door replaced. While they were standing outside trying to figure out what to do next, a middle-aged man came out, dressed in a blue jogging outfit and running shoes. "Can I help you?" he asked. Skye thought he had a kind, trusting face. The sort of person a tourist might approach for directions.

"I used to live here. A long time ago," Skye told the man, looking up at the second-floor window. "With my mother."

"Really? Would you like to come in?"

Skye told Alix how she hesitated, but without thinking, Matt immediately answered for her. "Sure, that would be cool," he said. Suddenly they were all traipsing up the stairs. The man gave them a quick run-through of the apartment. Everything was smaller than she'd remembered, and the bulky, dark curtains in the living room had been taken down so sunlight streamed in, and it smelled of lemon furniture polish instead of fish sticks.

"It was weird," Skye said. "At first, I wasn't sure whether my bedroom was to the right or left of the living room." But then she remembered the window looking out on the alleyway and a view of brick walls and a church spire a couple of streets over. The room was used as an office now, so there wasn't even a bed in it, or a dresser. But hung on the wall was a wooden shelf she and Eva had made one summer afternoon. They'd painted it bright neon green, and it'd had ribbons with clothespins to hang toys. Skye took a closer look at the shelf; it was dusty, and the tacky sheen of the paint was dull. There were old paperback books, mostly mysteries, on the shelf, and the clothespins were gone. Her friends weren't interested in more than a cursory look around, and they congregated outside on the front steps, waiting for her. Only Matt stayed behind.

Skye looked up at Alix and saw the photograph of Alix's husband on the shelf, this time seeing it in a different way. Knowing now that he'd died. It made a lot of sense to her, realizing that Alix, too, had been going through a lot. She didn't know if it was okay to say anything.

"When did he die?" she asked.

"A little over a year ago," Alix said.

"I guess I wasn't the only one. Going through a hard time."

Alix nodded. Then they sat in silence for a minute. Skye was thinking about her old bedroom, and she figured Alix was thinking about her husband.

Finally, Skye said, "It was weird, but I didn't really feel much. Like that bedroom wasn't mine anymore. And the apartment and Golden Gate Park and the little Italian deli and Alamo Square: I'm hoping I can go to all those places, and I won't have to feel so tense and raw and shaken up."

"I imagine that'll all happen. In time."

As if their session were over, Alix stood up. But instead of opening the door, she reached above the bookshelf. Skye saw that she was cradling a small ceramic bowl.

"This is for you," she said, handing it to Skye.

Skye was surprised and she didn't know what to say. "Really?"

With the gift resting in her lap, Skye could see that in the inside curve of the bowl was a bird shaped from filed and clipped pieces of broken ceramic and glass, with a yellow beak and green-and-purple feathers and a large red eye. She ran her fingers over the wings and beak, the texture of the glaze and the intricate design. It seemed to her that this bird was staring at her, knowingly.

"It's a pelican, isn't it?" Skye said.

Alix nodded. "I had a dream once about a pelican," she said. "And this design. Well, I thought you should have it. You know, pelicans fly together in formation, surfing the edge of the waves, and they dive down. Deep. It's quite lovely to watch."

ACKNOWLEDGEMENTS

I first read about the notion of *thin places* in an article in the travel section of the *New York Times*, "Where Heaven and Earth Come Closer" by Eric Weiner (March 9, 2012). The term is most commonly used to refer to obviously sacred locales like the Tiger's Nest Monastery in Bhutan. Or Mount Kilimanjaro. Or the Great Pyramid at Giza. Equally in keeping with the concept of *thin places* is the experience of witnessing the aurora borealis or viewing a great work of art. I nearly wept when I saw Da Vinci's *The Last Supper* at Santa Maria delle Grazie in Milan.

But one need not travel to the other side of the globe to be touched by the sacred in our everyday lives. Such is the work of psychotherapy, where everyday, uninspired conversations can reveal deep connections and moments of transformation. I am grateful to the many clients over the years of my practice who allowed their pain and vulnerability to reveal the *thin places* in our lives. The work—not always easy—was most certainly a privilege.

I am blessed with a substantial group of supportive, loving friends and family, many of whom have read drafts of this book, or asked about the book, or waited expectantly for the fruits of my labor. They have no idea how much their enthusiasm fueled my efforts. I am also grateful to Evelyn Somers Rogers, for her editorial acumen. She taught me that a good story is not the same as a good life. Her expertise and clarity were indispensible to the creation of what I believe is a novel worthy of reading. To my children, Ben and Sarah, with whom I have shared many thin moments. And to Maxine, who teaches me every day about the thin veil between heaven and earth.